THE LYING GAME

Book 1 of the Love Games Duet

MICKEY MILLER

Edited by
BECCA HENSLEY MYSOOR

Edited by
DELANCY STEWART

PREFACE

For a free book, sign up for Mickey's Email list here:
https://landing.mailerlite.com/webforms/landing/y8s9b0

𝕊 I 𝕊

CARTER

It's natural to think hate and love are opposites.

They're not.

Actually, indifference is the opposite of love, not hate.

And indifference is precisely what I'm feeling right now as I stare at the tall blonde I met last night, who is still in my apartment. She's been lingering this morning, sticking around and watching TV in my penthouse.

The time has come for me to kick her out.

"I have practice soon, so it's time for you to go," I say, nicely but without room for discussion.

She blinks a few times, and leans over on the kitchen island, letting out a slow breath. Trying to be cute. "I can just hang out here while you're gone. And be waiting for you when you come back." She lifts her eyebrows and tilts her head as she tries to tempt me.

Clenching my jaw, I stare her down.

Last night, we were enjoying ourselves.

But this afternoon, I don't feel a shred of desire for her.

All I feel is the distinct sensation of wanting this awkwardness to be over, and for her to leave.

Am I an asshole?

Yes. And I'm fine with that.

I was very upfront last night with Natasha about my 'no strings attached' policy when it comes to pleasure.

I don't do relationships. They're not for me. Maybe I'm paranoid, but when you're worth millions of dollars you never know how a woman might deceive you. Maybe she'll play the part of a perfect girlfriend up front, then after a year you'll find out she has a giant secret she's been keeping from you, lying to your face every day.

And yes, that's happened to me.

Natasha stares at me, squinting and giving me this 'Blue Steel' type of look where she wants to seem like she's not trying too hard, but I see right through it.

My eyes drift over to my bookshelf. I notice my copy of *The Great Gatsby* put on top of the shelf. Natasha must have been reading it.

My muscles quiver, seeing the tattered copy of the book that I read junior year of high school. My then girlfriend Lacy and I would read the passages to each other after school. I was so into her, I thought I wanted to spend the rest of my life with her. She asked me why I didn't press for sex, like the other guys were all doing with their girlfriends. I had this zen calmness back then. I just knew we'd be together forever, so what was the hurry?

It's funny the things you think you 'know' when you're seventeen.

I 'knew' I'd be with Lacy.

I 'knew' I was a relationship guy. Not a fuckboy.

Then Lacy broke my heart with a lie.

Little did I know back then, I would become the king of

one night stands. And I thank Lacy for breaking my heart to show me that.

Like James Gatz himself, if I reached for a relationship, I'd only be a boat beat back against the current, in search of a green light that doesn't exist.

Shaking my gaze off from the book, I refocus on Natasha, my smirk returning.

I love my life these days.

I'm twenty-seven years old, just signed my first multi-million dollar contract with the Chicago Wolverines.

I enjoy my lack of responsibility when I'm doing anything besides playing professional basketball.

Noticing me drifting off, Natasha steps around my marble kitchen island and runs her hand along my shoulder.

"You look pensive. Everything alright?"

I swallow, suddenly thinking that maybe my slapstick version of Natasha isn't appropriate. At least she reads. Maybe I've underestimated her, maybe she is relationship material.

"I can be waiting for you . . . when you get back," she adds, her voice full of sultry suggestion. She runs her tongue over her upper lip.

I tense when her finger grazes me. "Look, Natasha. I think you're great. Last night—and this morning—was a lot of fun. But you don't want me, believe me. I have a lot of issues."

She furrows her brow, and a curious smile spreads across her face. "I like issues."

I run my thumb and forefinger across my forehead.

"You've never seen issues like mine, believe me."

"Doesn't seem to affect your, ahem, prowess." She lets her eyes drift below my belt.

I let out a slow exhale. This is probably most guys' dream

come true. A hot blonde begging to be nothing but a friend with benefits.

Taking a moment to assess, I search inside myself for feelings. After all, she's smart. Attractive.

But I feel absolutely nothing for her.

Just then, my phone buzzes with a text. Picking it up, I play like someone's calling me.

"Hey Chandler, what's up?" I say to no one on the line.

"Oh we have a team dinner after practice tonight . . . oh totally forgot about that . . ."

She sighs, and I smile as I nod into my phone like Chandler is continuing to talk to me.

It's not that I mind being more forceful with her and simply telling her we are done. It's more that I enjoy the thrill of the lie.

Just then, my phone rings. For real.

Natasha shoots me a funny look.

"Were you just . . . faking a conversation?"

"Call coming on the other line," I say, waving her off. "Hi Mom."

Rolling her eyes, Natasha walks away.

"How's the best son in the world?" my mom drawls sweetly.

"Hey, Mama. What's up?"

"Well, the reason I called is, you obviously know Mrs. Benson."

My heart does a tumble at the name 'Benson.' I hold the phone away from my face, clutching it hard.

"No, Mom, I completely forgot that you two went to wine night together every Saturday in high school after my games. Why do you ask about her?"

"Well Carter, I have a favor to ask. Lacy is moving to Chicago for a modern dance tryout."

My heart skips a beat. I can already feel my blood pressure rising.

"Lacy's going to be in Chicago?"

"You didn't know? I figured she might have called you or you would have seen her Facebook updates."

My jaw tightens, and I try not to bite down too hard on my lip. My mom has no idea Lacy and I aren't exactly on speaking terms, and haven't been for years. "She must have forgotten to let me know."

"So, do you think she could crash at your place while she's there? Tryouts are an unpaid thing. Mrs. Benson is worried about Lacy having to pay rent. We were casually chatting at dinner last night, and I mentioned your new place and how you have that extra room. Apparently Lacy's living arrangements fell through at the last second. And Lacy is too shy to ask for favors, you know how she is. So that's why I'm calling."

I move my mouth to start talking, but nothing comes out.

It's just past the first of June. It's the tail end of spring, and we're headed into summer in Chicago, after putting up with one hell of a winter. This is the first summer I'll be living all by myself, in a place that I officially own.

I've already declared the theme of this summer to be freedom.

The freedom I've earned with a lifetime of dedication to my sport, which culminated just a few weeks ago when I signed that monster contract.

Freedom doesn't mean spending a summer with my ex-girlfriend.

My mom can sense my silent resistance.

"And you two always get along so well, anyway. It's only eight weeks and then she'll be out of your hair."

I grind my teeth.

Only eight weeks.

She's got me between a rock and a hard place.

Lacy Benson always knew how to fuck with me.

Still does, after all these years.

As big of an asshole as I am, I can't say 'no' to my own mother.

"Just eight weeks?" I bite out.

"Just eight weeks, and she'll be out of your hair. I talked with Mrs. Benson. She says her audition is at the end of July."

My cat Smokey brushes my leg.

She licks her paw.

I can feel the tension on the other side of the line.

"Of course she can stay with me, Mom," I finally bite out.

"I thought you'd be fine with it. I mean, you two get along so well."

"Of course we do."

"She'll be arriving on the train tonight around seven-thirty. I'm sure she'll be tired. She left yesterday morning."

"That's great. Just great. I can't wait to see her," I lie.

My mom and I say some more pleasantries, then we hang up.

"Smokey," I growl. "Come here. I'm done playing games."

I stare her down.

Finally, she rolls her neck and jumps into my arms. Maybe she senses the anger emanating from me just thinking about Lacy's name.

Well, if Lacy's going to be here, maybe I can finally get some revenge.

Maybe it would be fun to make this summer a living hell for her.

Natasha walks back into the room in heels. She shakes her head, and puts her hands on her hip.

"How was your chat with 'your mom'?" she says, making air quotes.

I smirk.

"You're an asshole," she says, shaking her head.

I nod. "I know."

"I can handle asshole. But I can't handle a blatant liar. I'm leaving."

As the door slams, I feel nothing in my heart.

Not desire. Not hate or ill will. Just indifference.

The way my heart feels about Lacy Benson, however, is another matter entirely.

I'm not indifferent to her. I hate Lacy with every bone in my body for how she lied to me.

❦ 2 ❧

CARTER

My mom doesn't know that I hate Lacy Benson.

I'm good at keeping secrets. Especially from my mother.

From watching us interact over the years, she thinks Lacy and I are best friends.

Probably because whenever our moms see us, the two of us see which one of us can craft a bigger fable about why we like each other so much--and were 'still friends' after our big breakup.

After we broke up, we would play the lying game. Whenever we met in front of our moms, I would make like I was a puppy seeing their owner after she'd gotten back from a long day's work. I'd spread my arms wide. "Lacy, it is *so* good to see you!"

"Oh please!" she'd say, her smile even more exaggerated than mine. "It's so good to see *you!* The pleasure is all on this side! How have you *been?*"

She'd usually pat me on the nose or make some other patronizing move to show how much she liked me--which made our parents think we had the most cordial breakup ever. As soon as our moms were satisfied, we'd stick our tongues out at each other like we were in second grade.

So in public, we pretend to like each other. Our moms were best friends in high school, and still are best friends, and we didn't want to make every single time our moms hung out about how badly Lacy and I hated each other.

Because we're nice people, who want our moms to be happy.

And I hate Lacy even more right now, because I have to rush out of practice to make sure I'm home when she gets to my apartment. My hair isn't even fully dried from my shower.

I fume in the car on the way home, turning my Drake playlist up to eleven.

The guys from the team are going out to dinner tonight, and I've got to head home to let a frigging girl into my apartment.

I don't even give women I'm *sleeping with* the key to my apartment.

Taking a deep breath, I think of my mother and her kind heart.

This will make her happy, I remind myself.

I navigate through Chicago's crowded downtown streets.

Chicago only has two seasons: winter and construction. And June sure isn't winter.

Google maps takes me on an alternate route today to avoid construction, but all the same I end up trapped on the highway where four lanes are merging down to one for no apparent reason. Par for the course during construction season.

This is why I never drive during busy hours. And I wouldn't be doing it tonight, except of course that Lacy needs me to let her into my apartment.

And now I'm stuck in traffic. I glance down and see a message from a new number.

Where are you?

I don't have Lacy saved. But I recognize our shared area code from Blackwell. It's surely her. I also don't text and drive. So I'll get there when I get there. I drop the phone back to the seat next to me.

Smiling to myself, I bob my head and sing along with *Energy* while I think about today's practice and make a mental list of all my workouts for the week. No sense in letting the traffic you can't control put you in a bad mood.

A traffic jam, a near accident, and about thirty minutes later, I walk into the lobby of my building.

She doesn't even notice me walk through the revolving doors at first.

I take a moment to look her over. She wears ridiculously big sunglasses. Her long black locks cascade around her shoulders.

She looks the same as she always did in high school, when I'd sometimes cross paths with her during indoor sports practice. I'd be heading back from the court, and see her just starting out dance practice in the multipurpose room.

Same gorgeous alabaster skin. Same freckles on her cheeks as always, and a little birthmark near her right ear.

She wears blue jeans and high heeled black boots with a black short-sleeved T-shirt that says 'lovers.' Lacy's a little bit punk, a little bit dancer, and a whole lot of attitude.

Probably feeling my presence as I look down at her, she finally looks up, clutching a coffee drink.

"Oh my gosh, Carter! It's so good to see you!" My entire body tingles at the sound of her voice. It's gotten sweeter and smoother since I last saw her, years ago.

She flashes me her best fake smile—the one I've come to know so well.

"No, it's so good to see *you*!" I parrot, playing along. "I just love when my mom invites people over to my brand new luxury apartment," I grit out, my voice low. "It's just like when we were six years old and we'd have playdates together." I offer her a cocky smirk.

She stands up, her smile defiant.

Excitement rushes under my skin.

She bites her lower lip while she runs her eyes over me.

Despite my deep-seeded vitriol for this woman, there's no denying the carnal reaction I'm having to her right now.

What I'm feeling for Lacy isn't love. But it also definitely isn't indifference.

Any red-blooded man would be attracted to her, though. She's utterly gorgeous.

She lets down her sunglasses so I can note her ice cold stone face. We squint at each other, narrowing our eyes for a classic staredown.

Twisting my tongue, I push it out the side of my lips.

"I think you've got something right here," I say, staring at her cheek.

Putting her glasses back on, she crosses her arms. "Bullshit."

"Ah, finally you let the claws out. I thought we could at least keep our bullshit pleasantries going while I walk you upstairs. I'm doing you a huge favor, you know."

"Did you get my text?" she asks, grabbing the handle of her giant suitcase.

"I did," I nod. She jerks her head to the side. "So no text back? You can't let me know you're going to be . . . " she looks at her phone. "Forty-five minutes late?"

A giant, sarcastic smirk covers my face. "This is going to be a great eight weeks. I can't wait to see more of this little move."

I imitate her head jerking motion, and exaggerate it, moving my head up and around in a slight circle, sort of like a turkey. "I mean I do love seeing you all worked up. Maybe it's the late night caffeine from the soy latte?" I eye her drink.

She puts a hand on her hip. "It's a cappuccino, thank you very much. And so no answer to my question? Great. Good to know we're still on the same page."

"You mean the page of hating each other?" I push her hand off her suitcase handle and grab it. "Here, let me take this for you."

"Don't act like you're a gentleman all of a sudden. I can take my bag up."

"Please. Allow me. I'm a gracious host. And I don't text and drive. Texting can wait." I wink.

She rolls her eyes. "Ever heard of hands free? And it's a *roller* suitcase. This building has an elevator."

"It's broken, actually. And I live on the forty-fourth floor."

"Bullshit." Her tone is seething.

And we're off to a fantastic start.

I signal the security guard behind the desk.

"Hey Raymond, is elevator four still broken?"

"Yep. Rats short circuited it. So sorry, Mr. Flynn."

She glares at me angrily.

"Fine." She grits out, slipping her hand off the suitcase. "You can take it. But it doesn't mean I'm going to like it."

I lean in closer to her ear. She's five-foot nine or so, but I still tower over her easily.

"Hey. You know what else?" I say with a bemused smile.

"What else, Carter?" she does the turkey-moving-its-neck-motion again.

"You're fucking welcome."

It's just like her to refuse my offer, then when it requires actual effort on her part—she takes me up on it.

I roll her suitcase into the elevator bank, and she follows me.

"Guess we'll have to take elevator three," I wink.

She rolls her eyes, smacking her lips. "I should have known you were lying."

We head upstairs to my apartment.

At the very least, Lacy's going to provide some entertainment for me while she's here.

3

LACY

Five minutes in, and Carter's already toying with me for his own amusement.

Sure, the little game about the elevator was just to mess with me. To prove a point that I wouldn't want to carry my giant suitcase up forty-four flights of stairs.

We ride up the elevator, and I peer at Carter from beneath my giant sunglasses.

How is it possible that after five minutes of being in his presence, my temperature feels like it's risen already?

He's got that same smug, phased-by-nothing smile.

Same laissez-faire, does not give two shits about anyone other than himself attitude.

Same chiseled jaw and built frame that I absolutely refuse to be attracted to.

"So you've really never heard of voice to text?"

Carter shrugs as the elevator dings when we hit floor forty-four. "You're welcome for being able to crash here, by the way. On such short notice."

My chest tightens as he rolls my suitcase out of the elevator, leading the way down a hallway that screams expensive, ritzy apartment. As if I didn't notice from the outside how this giant building is pure glass. Oh, except for the gold-plated windows on the first floor.

It's the exact opposite of the way we both grew up in Blackwell. The biggest parts of both of our houses were our yards.

Carter jingles his keys, and I take a deep, silent breath, trying not to let my frustration show. I feel like I'm six years old again, a little kid with no keys to her own house, dependent on a parent to unlock the door.

As the door swings open, I try not to dwell on the fact that he's right. This was unacceptably short notice, and Carter is doing me a huge favor. But is it my fault my current boyfriend—well, ex-boyfriend, as of yesterday—decided to break up with me suddenly while I was on the first leg of my overnight Amtrak ride from Blackwell to Chicago?

My stomach knots as Carter hangs his key up on a ring just inside the door.

I was crying when I called my mom, and she was the one who suggested I could stay with Carter.

I resisted, but with no other options, I convinced myself Carter and I could get over the feud stemming from our misunderstanding years ago. I convinced myself it was teenage stuff, and that now, in our twenties, we could move on. So I sucked up my pride and let my mom ask Carter's mom for me.

Moving to Chicago for dance was supposed to be a giant personal win for me—a win I badly needed.

Instead, I feel like giant failure, all alone in a big city.

He turns to face me.

To say he's grinning would be an exaggeration. A trouble-maker's smirk tugs at the corners of his expression, as if he's the keeper of some secret I'll never know, but one that holds the key to my existence.

To make matters worse, as much as I wish I could deny it, the years have been extremely kind to Carter. His boyish good looks have been replaced by bigger muscles and a harder expression.

I scour him for a flaw. Even the big birthmark on his right forearm seems to round him out and give him character. My heart pounds. Yes, he's extremely good looking.

I clench and unclench my fists at my sides.

"Welcome to my humble abode. It's baller, I know."

My stomach turns. He really has made a one-hundred eighty degree turn from the boy I used to know. "Yes, so humble," I seethe sarcastically. "I'm glad to see you haven't forgotten your roots."

"Ouch. I'll let you save your compliments for now."

"I've got plenty more where that came from."

"Glad to hear it. Just know, I'm not happy about this arrangement."

I glance around. 'Baller' is a severe understatement. I've never in my life seen an apartment this loaded. It's a corner unit, so two of the big windows point out to Lake Michigan and to the city, both with breathtaking views. The kitchen is huge, featuring a giant marble island countertop. A few steps lead down to the main living area where he's got a big, L-shaped sofa, a flat screen TV as big as most movie screens, and a dining room table with a few chairs. There's also a clear glass door leading out to a big balcony.

"You'll be in the guest room. This way."

He leads me down an off-white hallway and stops at a wooden door, flipping a light switch inside the room. He rolls my bag in.

"What do you have in here anyways? Bricks?"

I step into the room.

"Changes of clothes. It's mostly for dance."

"I'm surprised you're giving that another shot. I thought you gave up on that life already," he bites out.

I grind my teeth, face him, and take a step toward him. I pull off my sunglasses so he can see my eyes. If this stay is anything like these first ten minutes have been, I'm not going to be able to let my guard down for a single moment.

"You don't want to start the passive aggression game with me," I seethe. "You know I'm here for dance, no need to rub it in that I haven't landed a professional spot yet. Besides, you know I can beat you at this game."

He furrows his brow. "A little good natured ribbing won't hurt you. It'll toughen you up. You've always taken yourself too seriously. That's your problem."

"Oh! I've been here for ten minutes and you're already diagnosing my issues? Thanks, Freud. I'll take a pass."

"Believe whatever you want. The fact you're getting your panties in a bunch tells me all I need to know."

"I'm not going to be spoken down to while I'm living here. You're doing me a favor, yes. Because my stupid—" I stutter, and clear my throat. "My ex broke up with me twelve hours ago. Consider your small gesture of letting me use this room as a way to make up for shitty men everywhere."

"Ohhh, so that's why you needed a place to crash on such short notice." Carter nods slowly, letting out a little chuckle. "Don't blame me that you can't find a loyal man."

My blood boils. "Don't do this. Can we please just be civil while I'm here?"

His jaw twitches. "You really need to learn how to take a joke, Laces."

I cross my arms, refusing to acknowledge his use of my childhood nickname.

"Why don't you give me the tour, and I'll be going to bed soon."

"Bed? Already? It's not even nine o'clock."

"I have dance early tomorrow. And would you please give me an extra key?"

His nostrils flare, and his eyes widen. "Did I just get a 'please?' Let me take your temperature." He places the back of his hand against my forehead.

I snatch his hand off my head by the wrist. "Just give me the damn key."

I follow him as he heads out of the room, a little upset with myself because I feel like I've let Carter win a small battle. I showed him that he was getting to me.

Note to self: brainstorm how to put Carter back in his place.

The man thinks he's God's gift to humanity. His attitude is evident in everything, from the way he walks, talks, struts, and plays basketball.

"We've got the kitchen here. Couch and living area over there. TV," he says, pointing out the ridiculous television.

"Used for gaming, films, and watching the Sports Channel highlights."

I hear a low purring, and a grey cat approaches me, rubs my legs. "Aww," I say, reaching down to pet the cat.

"And you've met Smokey," he says. "She keeps an eye on everything around here." he winks.

"And what's this?" I ask, pointing to a corner with some wires and a speaker.

"This," he says, is where you plug in—or I should say—where I plug in my tunes when I need some musical therapy. Or at the end of a date."

I freeze up, picturing how many girls must throw themselves at him.

And I'm sure when he gets them back to this apartment, it's not hard to seal the deal, if that's what he's looking for.

"Let's agree to keep each others' romantic situations out of each others' minds," I say.

Shuddering, it crosses my mind that Carter is probably dating a lot while he's in the city.

"Oh? I mean, you're the one who brought up that you just broke up with your ex."

I swallow and say the painful truth. "He dumped me."

"Oh. My mom didn't mention that." Carter's eyes flit from my bags back to me, and for a split second I think he might actually show a shred of empathy.

There's an awkward beat, and then he keeps on. "Anyway, this leads to the outside." He continues, sliding a door open to the balcony. "This is where I like to overlook my kingdom."

"Kingdom? This overlooks the city of Chicago."

"Exactly," he smirks.

I grind my teeth and shake my head. I walked right into that one.

"And this is the hot tub," he continues. "With the weather getting nice, I'll be out here a lot."

"Yeah? With the guys?"

"Ha. Yeah, I'll have the occasional steaks and cigars meet up out here with 'the guys.' But usually this is where I bring girls to let them know they've won the prize."

"Prize? What prize?" I look around the balcony. Other than the hot tub and an empty table and chairs, there doesn't seem to be anything.

He smirks, and turns his head away from the gorgeous view of the city overlooking the lake. "I mean me, Baby-cakes," he says with a wink.

I roll my eyes.

It's hard for me to believe this is the same Carter I used to ride bikes around with when we were in middle school. The same Carter whose basketball games I used to dance the halftime shows for junior year, then go to Wendy's and get hamburgers, have pickle races, and then make out in his car, sitting in my driveway and hoping my mom or dad wouldn't peel open the window shade and see us.

I wonder if he still has shades of that nice person deep down. But the old Carter seems mostly gone, replaced by this combative version of Carter. My stomach lurches a little, and I wonder if maybe I'm partly to blame for this changed version of him.

For the lie I never told him about his father.

But even as I try to feel empathy for him, it's clear from his crossed arms--and needless bragging--that he plans on being extra mean, while I'm here.

"Please. Stop trying to prove that women actually like you. It's not working," I bite out.

Although with his looks—and ability to be charming when he wants—I feel as though my insult ricochets right off him.

He takes a step toward me. My heartbeat quickens, and I take a sharp, deep breath. His shadow blocks the last rays of sunlight as it sets over the horizon.

"You can joke all you want. But if you think I'm going to start diluting myself because I've got a lady in the house, you've got another think coming. I don't mind doing my mom this favor, but Lacy Benson, I swear to God, you will not affect how I live this summer. Is that clear?"

The wind hits my cheeks as I stand against the railing of the balcony. I look down, and the people look like little tiny ants.

"I think living on the forty-fourth floor so high up is getting to your head," I quip as I slide around his arm to the other side of the balcony. "Do I appreciate you doing me this favor? Sure. Am I going to let my summer be ruined by you? No. I'm here for eight weeks to crush my dance tryout. This is everything to me. You think I'm a distraction for you? I'm as upset about this as you are."

"Just a little kid's summer camp, eh?" he teases.

I take a deep breath. The way he says it makes me feel small, like a little kid.

"At the end of the eight weeks, I have an audition for the The Blue Illusion team in New York," I explain. "If I make it, I'll move to New York. So for God's sake, why don't we just let bygones be bygones and get along?"

He looks me up and down, as if thinking over the answer to my question.

"Hell no. Let me make this crystal clear. You're on my turf. And we're doing things my way."

"Screw you, asshole," I mutter.

"Yes! I finally did it."

"Did what?" I scrunch up my face.

"Got you to call me an asshole. I'm going to keep a running tab."

I stifle a growl.

"Anyway, I'm going out for a little bit. You must be starving after all that travel. There's some crackers and cheese in the fridge if you're hungry."

Fucking. Asshole.

I bite my lip as he smirks, walking away.

I follow him back inside the living room, and I pause as my eyes zoom in on his bookshelf.

A tattered paperback of *The Great Gatsby* sits on top of it.

My heart skips a beat. My memory rushes back to those afternoons we used to spend reading excerpts from the story out loud like a couple of nerds. The spring after basketball season ended--and he knew he was going to Kansas for ball-- he took a supreme interest in my English class. He mostly became interested, he said, because I was so interested.

I'd lay my head on his stomach, close my eyes, and feel the vibrations of the story as he would read to me. Every once in a while, he'd land a kiss on my forehead, just to surprise me.

Heat flushes my body, centering in my throat at the memory.

In a trance, I open up the book to the first page, and sure enough, there's my signature with a heart.

"What are you looking at?" he asks, his voice booming from the kitchen.

Whirling around, I put the book behind my back so he can't see. "Just remarking that you don't have a single book about dance on this shelf."

"Well, it's not really my thing."

"Right," I say, then take off to my room, waltzing past him so he doesn't see I've taken his book.

Heading to my room, I hear the shower turn on. Heavy metal cranks on the stereo system, flooding the bathroom and the hallway with music.

Tossing the book on the desk in my room, I put in my earbuds and try to listen to my music—Tchaikovsky's Nutcracker—but it's impossible. Whatever horrible music he's listening to creeps through into my ears. It's overpowering.

I try my best to focus on the task at hand, which is Google-mapping the location of the studio so that I arrive on time—no, early—tomorrow for the first day of practice.

And then I hear Carter shouting at the top of his lungs, belting out the lyrics to the song.

Sighing, I lay on my side on my pillow, looking out at the skyscrapers in the night.

Shaking my head, I frown at my luck. Norton broke up with me this morning. And now, here I am with Carter fucking Flynn, again. It's deja vu of the worst kind. I thought I'd never have to see him again. Thought I was done with him and his asshole ways forever. I thought wrong, obviously. Eight weeks of this torture. He seems intent on making every moment of our stay together a living hell. Why, though? Is there a way out of this?

I pull out my computer and do a quick Craigslist search for cheap places in Chicago. I find one nearby.

One-thousand dollars. And it comes with three roommates.

My heart sinks. That might not be a lot of money to some people, but it sure is to me.

Another, in a neighborhood on the south side goes for just five hundred dollars. But it's far away from the studio. I do a Google search on the area, and a few muggings come up in the local news.

Two months' rent at a grand each month. That's two thousand dollars I didn't budget for.

I pull out my phone and the credit card app. I stare at the number on the screen.

Rage wells up inside me. I try not to let it consume me.

I'm still in disbelief that I've ended up with five figures in credit card debt. Most of it's from my dad's emergency room visit that I paid for, so as not to stress his heart condition even further. I never told my mom.

I take a deep breath and there's a knock on the door.

"Yes?" I answer.

Carter opens the door, and he's soaking wet. In only a towel.

I pause for a moment, doing a double take.

He's always had the most chiseled frame of any man I've met. Even when we were in high school. But now, he's sculpted like a Greek god. It's almost unfair how good he looks. Abs carved out of rock. The widest shoulders I've seen in my life.

"Your key," he says in a gravelly, low voice. He steps inside, holding it up, and sets it on top of my dresser.

Smirking, he turns around and is about to close the door.

With a herculean effort, I manage not to stare at his ass as he leaves.

Until he turns around and looks over his shoulder.

"Do you like it, Lacy?"

"Like . . . what?" I choke out, using my full brain power to keep my eyes focused on his gaze.

"Do you like the place?" Snorting, he furrows his brow. "What else would you . . . ohh. Okay."

"Screw you, Carter. You're so damn full of yourself, I'm surprised you don't have pictures of yourself everywhere in here."

"I do, actually."

He tips his chin toward a framed picture of him slamming a basketball over someone. It hangs on the wall above the bed, right behind me.

I drop my face into my hands. "You've got to be kidding me."

"Have a good night," he winks, and starts to walk out, but pauses, his eyes fixed on my desk.

"Did you take my book?" he asks, the smug tone drained from his voice.

"That's my book," I bark out, instinctually.

Squinting at me, he flips through the pages.

Carter looks up, and our eyes lock. For the first time since I've laid eyes on him today, I sense a hint of vulnerability coming from him. He blinks a few times, his gaze softening slightly.

After almost six months of dating in high school, we broke up. The book was the only artifact I never got back from him.

I'm surprised he still has it.

Tossing it back onto my desk, he turns and walks out.

Letting a breath out, I look back at my credit card app, in disbelief.

My phone buzzes with a text from my baby sister, Eliza.

ELIZA: MAKE IT IN OKAY AND EVERYTHING?
    Lacy: Yeah, I did! Staying with Carter. This should be interesting.
    Eliza: Ew, I'm sorry! Did you try looking for new places?

I SHUDDER. MY SISTER'S GOING TO BE A SENIOR IN HIGH school. Along with the full story of Carter and I, she also doesn't need to know the perils of credit card debt.

LACY: NO, IT'S FINE. I'LL BE AT DANCE EVERY DAY, ANYWAYS. This is just a place to crash.
    Eliza: Oh Well, my summer ballet camp starts next week!
    Lacy: SO proud of you for doing that. I'm super tired right now. Love you. Proud of you <3
    Eliza: Okay! Chat soon?
    Lacy: Definitely

MY HEART WARMS AT HER LAST TEXT. SHE'S A BALLERINA, while I'm a modern dancer. She's on pins and needles to know if I make it through the eight weeks and get the spot with Blue Illusion.

Eight more weeks of torture by Carter.

I can make it. I vow to myself I will.

I will not let Carter Flynn get the best of me.

❧ 4 ❧

LACY

I somehow manage to sleep incredibly well Sunday night. Something about a day of traveling knocks me out. I feel a sort of warm tumbling inside my stomach when my alarm goes off at six A.M. Carter's words ring in my ear.

Just a little kids' summer camp, eh?

I'm not sure if he's just messing with me, or if he truly doesn't think I can dance any more.

Here's the thing about dancing professionally. If you're twenty-five like me and you haven't made it yet, most people will write you off. Especially when you failed your last audition two years ago, and you've been out of practice for the same amount of time.

I was lucky I got this spot for the summer camp. They called me last Friday, when one of the forty dancers who was supposed to take part in Georgina's tryout had to drop out. My name was first on the waitlist, so I took the spot.

As a result of the last second opportunity, I thought I could stay with my boyfriend for the duration of the tryout since he was conveniently located in Chicago.

And hence, he broke up with me, leaving me in this

desperate situation, forced to stay with Carter. I guess I am lucky in a way that our moms are such good friends. If I couldn't stay with him, I have no idea where I would have ended up. I probably would have had to hole up in a low-grade hotel and run up more credit card bills.

I walk to the the theatre on State Street in downtown Chicago, where we'll be practicing.

I smile at the marquee lights as I walk by. Some day, I will perform in a big theatre like that.

Hopefully in New York. My dream city. Something about the place calls out to me.

Morning coffee in hand, I head into the the practice studio, where I'm greeted by a host of dancers sprawled over the floor, stretching before class.

I notice that in between the women, there's a man with long, brown hair, in black tights and a tight white T-shirt, who could give Carter a run for his money as most sculpted man of Chicago.

Carter. Why do I still think of him like that? Why does my roommate have to ooze as much sex appeal as two men normally have? I shake my head.

And then I realize I've been staring unthinkingly into the mirror right at this other man.

Apparently, I have a problem.

"Hi Honey," the man says with a giant smile. "You can't just stare like that and not introduce your sexy ass to me."

My jaw drops, and I raise my voice. "Excuse me?!"

He rolls his eyes and his neck, then circles the gaze of his blue-grey eyes back to me. "Please don't get all uppity on me for commenting on how beautiful your form is."

Smiling, he reaches out a hand. Oh. I should have been able to figure this out. But my gay-dar isn't as good as it was in college. I suppose being isolated in a small town will take you a little off your game.

"I'm Lance," he says as I awkwardly stare at him.

"Lacy. Pretty early to be commenting on our form, isn't it?"

I take a sip of my coffee.

"That's where you're wrong, honey. It's *never* too early . . . at least for me. And I'm sorry if you don't like me commenting about your body. It's just that," he looks around and leans in. We're out of earshot of everyone else. "You have a magnetic energy. And yes, I am only into guys." He winks. "Just thought we could get that one out of the way."

I smile, and relief pours through me. "That's good to know. I'll be honest, I haven't had the best luck with men lately."

He shakes his head vigorously. "You and me both, sister! Tell me, have you ever figured out why most men are such assholes? I can't, for the life of me."

I laugh. "Lance, I think we are going to be friends."

The room quiets down when a woman in her forties enters. She's got a mix of black and grey hair, and is in fantastically good shape.

"That's Ms. Georgina Fleming," Lance whispers.

My eyes widen. "She's the one who makes the decisions about the final cut, right?"

Lance nods. "She's ruthless."

Georgina clears her throat, and you could hear a pin drop. This is going to be an interesting day.

◈

CLASS IS INTENSE. I GET TO KNOW SOME OF THE GIRLS AS well as Lance.

"Want to grab a drink?" he asks me as we leave the studio at the end of the day. "I'm parched."

I shrug. "One glass. I guess."

I intend to stay focused while I'm here. But something tells me I'd do well to make a new friend on my first day.

Lance and I head to a nearby happy hour, and I learn some things about him. He's from southern Illinois, came out when he was twenty-four, when he moved to Boystown in Chicago. At age twenty-nine, he's in a similar situation to me. In dancer years, we're on the older side. He needs to win the spot with the Blue Illusion or, he says, he'll probably never make it.

He asks who I'm living with.

"An old friend. Kind of."

Lance narrows his eyes. "Kind of? What's that mean?"

"Well, we're from the same small town. Our moms are friends. But we don't get along, to put it lightly."

"Why don't you get along if your moms are friends?" he asks after taking a swig of my drink.

I hesitate, and he senses it.

"Personal?" he asks.

"I don't feel much like getting into it right now. Anyways, we've got another early class tomorrow, and I've got to pick up some things from the grocery store tonight. Lance, so great to meet you though. I feel like I have my first city friend."

"Anything you need, you sexy bitch," he winks, and I chuckle loudly.

It feels nice to know there's at least one man out there who is in my corner.

I get a bag of groceries, and I'm shocked as I check my watch riding up the elevator. It's almost nine o'clock.

Time to go to bed already. I'm actually a little relieved I won't have to spend time lounging around Carter's apartment, since I'm trying my best to avoid him while I'm here.

I turn the key in the lock, and I notice a faint noise

coming from inside the apartment. A faint tune of some kind. Is Carter singing, possibly?

When I open the door, I recognize the noise, and it's all I can do not to drop my bag of groceries.

The noise is clearly coming from Carter's room.

It is not singing.

Well, not how most people define 'singing.'

It is a woman screaming.

Not even moaning.

Screaming.

With every ounce of her being.

I hear a few, slightly inaudible words said as I stand frozen next to the refrigerator.

"Oh that's good," she says. And then, "I'm coming again," and some others.

I put the the groceries away angrily, dumbfounded.

I slam the refrigerator door.

I grind my teeth and just stand there a moment. Listening.

I'm as much in awe as I am curious.

Who needs to scream that much during sex, anyway? What is she, putting on a show?

My nails bite into my palms, heat flushing through my body.

I try not to picture them, but Carter's body pops back into my mind's eye.

I don't even have to imagine how good he looks with his shirt off.

But the thing that gets to me the most isn't even that he's with this other girl right now. Or how pretty she probably is. I bet she's one of those air-headed brunettes like the other ones at class today.

No, the thought that really consumes me is that no

matter how hard I try to deny it, my stomach is hardening right now. My breath is shortening.

Heat concentrates between my legs.

The fucking asshole.

My skin tightens, and I get the sensation that my flesh is crawling.

I pick up the phone and dial Lance's number. "Hey you sexy thang," he says. "You looking for a booty call already? I told you, I can't help you."

I smile. "No, it's just, ah, can I come crash at your place tonight? I have a bit of an, ahem, situation in my apartment."

"Sure thing Sugartits," he says, and I love the fact that he doesn't even ask me why. Just says yes.

The corner of my mouth turns up in a smirk at his little nickname for me. He texts me his address. I grab a few of my things and call an Uber.

❁❁❁

LANCE'S JAW MIGHT AS WELL BE ON THE GROUND. "NO SHE was not!! Who actually screams like that?! That's like, porno bullshit screaming."

"I know. Ridiculous, right?"

"That's like, beyond ridiculous. Here's the sphere of what actually happens."

He draws an imaginary circle in the air with his finger, then points outside the circle. "And here is a girl screaming like that for twenty minutes non-stop. 'Oh your cock is so big.' Please. I've seen plenty of cocks. And most guys are all talk."

I sink further into his couch, feeling a little better.

Lance wrinkles his nose. "Tell me more about this guy, aside from the fact that you went to high school with him, your moms are best friends, and you hate each other for reasons unmentioned. What does he look like? What does he do?"

I purse my lips, slightly agitated that Carter is still the topic of conversation. "Uh. His name is Carter."

"Carter . . . who? Maybe I know him."

"Carter Flynn."

Lance spews out the water he's been drinking, and his eyes go wide.

"Carter. Flynn. The basketball player?"

I nod. He gets up and starts dancing around his room. I roll my eyes a little, but I can't help but smile.

"No! You. Are. Living. With. The city's sexiest man. Like literally, he was voted Gentleman of the year last year in Boys' Magazine's 'guys we wish played for our team.'"

I frown. "He is—objectively—attractive, yes. And unfortunately I think that may have given him a huge ego boost yesterday in addition to his huge . . . never mind."

Lance practically goes cross-eyed as he walks back to me on the couch.

"Uhm what?! You can't just 'never mind' me like that. Have you actually seen it? How big is it? Spare me no details, Lacy. I can take it."

I sigh. "I don't know. I saw him in a towel yesterday. But who knows. I'm trying to block him out of my mind. Sorry, but do you mind if we talk about something else?"

Lance crosses his arms, and nods somberly. "I would think living with the world's sexiest man would be amazing. I guess the grass is always greener. Well, you're welcome to crash on my couch as often as you want."

"Thanks."

He narrows his gaze. "Even if it's his house, super loud sex past nine P.M. is a dick move. So what are you going to do to get back at him?"

"I'll think of something," I say.

"I have an idea, if you're up to it. It might be a little crazy for you though."

I arch an eyebrow. "I can do a little crazy."

He waves me closer to him and cups my ear.

"Are you seriously whispering? Isn't this your apartment?"

"Shhh," he says, and whispers his idea into my ear.

"Ho-ly shit," I say. "That *would* teach him a lesson."

He winks. "I've had enough of these stupid cocky assholes, too. Let's get him back and see how he likes it."

My heart races at the thought of Lance's plan.

"It's Monday. You're thinking . . . tomorrow already we can do that?"

He nods, and puts his fingers together like he's Mr. Burns from the Simpsons.

It's not the sort of thing I would have ever come up with. It's absolutely diabolical.

And it's definitely going to help me teach Carter a lesson he'll never forget.

❦ 5 ❦

CARTER

Sometimes people accuse me of exaggerating about my special talents.

I think that's because most guys don't really deliver. They talk a big game, and then when it's time to come through, they can't get the job done.

Just so I'm being clear, I'm talking about sex. Fucking. Coming. Orgasming. You know, the stuff everyone loves doing but most people are scared to talk honestly about.

Like last night.

Look, there's no reason to beat around the bush. Lacy hates my guts.

So why would I change up my attitude and behaviors to suit her? If I'm with a girl, I'm not going to hold back. That would be a shame for all parties involved.

I'm still lounging on the couch when Lacy gets home.

She says nothing, then comes and plops down on the couch, all smiles.

"Hi," she says.

"Hey yourself," I retort back, still staring at the screen.

"So I've got a friend coming over tonight," she says. "We've got to work on some moves."

"Oh?" I smirk, turning to face her. "Couple of hot dancers coming over? Sure thing. Maybe you can put on a show for me."

"I'll ask," she answers coyly. "Thanks so much, Carter," she pauses. "You're actually sometimes a good guy, you know."

I laugh a little, but then narrow my gaze.

"'Good guy' and 'Carter' are two words that don't belong in the same sentence. I'm willing to admit that. 'God' and 'Carter,' however. Those two shall hereafter always be said together."

"Will you just shut up and let me give you one compliment?"

I sigh, and look at Lacy, all cute as she twirls a few locks of her long black hair. It's suspicious, but maybe she's realizing this isn't a war she's going to win.

I ignore the question and ask her something I've been wondering. "How's your mom doing anyway?"

"You're . . . asking a real question?" She jerks her head back.

I put my hand on her shoulder, and give her my best fake sincere face.

"Every time you say 'God' and 'Carter' in the same sentence, I ask something thoughtful. That's how this works."

She rolls her eyes, normalcy returning to her expression. "She's doing fine. I called her last night to tell her how I've settled in. And she wants to know the name of your new girlfriend?"

"Girlfriend? What on earth are you—?"

"The girl you were with last night."

"Oh. Her? She was no one."

"No one sure is loud. So she doesn't have a name?"

I shrug. "That's just kind of how it goes with me, Lacy."

She arches an eyebrow. "So I'll be listening to the 'Carter's women' playlist all summer long?"

I shake my head at her. "I'm twenty-seven. I don't know where you got off being so stuck up, but some people do like to have fun. Have sex. It's what adults do. Maybe you should try it some time."

"Oh I like to have fun, too."

"Do you now?"

"Yes." She looks down at her phone. "Oh, looks like he's here."

My stomach burns unexpectedly as I process one of the words she says. "What do you mean, *he?*"

Okay, I know there are guy dancers. But when I initially said she could dance with a friend in the living room, I was definitely picturing two girls.

Her blue eyes meet mine, her gaze hard. "What do *you* mean 'he?' My friend Lance. He's one of the dancers."

As she gets up off the couch and calls on her cell phone down to the front desk, for some odd reason I have to stifle a rush of adrenaline that comes over me. She stands there in a white tank top and pink booty shorts that say 'dancer' on one cheek and 'pink,' on the other, and I feel my jaw twitch.

First of all, why the hell do they keep making those booty shorts that just say the color? It has never made any sense to me. But I'm not one to make a cause out of protesting girls in hot short-shorts.

Second of all, and more importantly—just two minutes ago I was picturing some sort of double hot girl dance session taking place as I watch TV.

My dreams are tarnished when Lacy opens the door to my penthouse and—very clearly—a man appears.

"Hey Lance!" she says. She hugs and kisses him.

On the lips.

What. The. Actual. *Fuck.*

One day in, and she's bringing a . . . a date to my place?

"Hey there," the guy says as he comes on in.

He's probably six foot two. He's got long brown hair, and, shit—I'm man enough to admit the guy looks a lot like that Fabio guy from the old romance novels. His hand rests on the small of Lacy's back.

"Thanks so much for letting us use your place to practice our routine. I'm Lance, by the way."

He sticks a hand out, and I try to mask how begrudgingly I'm shaking his hand.

"Nice to meet you Lance." I can't avoid the vitriol that comes out as I say his name.

What kind of fucking name is Lance anyway? Sounds like a kid I played t-ball with who could never hit the fucking ball. Larry would even be a better name. Larry, the name of a guy who loves to wear leotards.

I clench and unclench my fists as I watch them. Why am I letting these two get in my head??

"I think we should stretch it out, first," she says in a sultry voice, taking Lance by the hand to the living room, just to the right of the television.

I plop back on the couch and try to focus again on the classic game I'm watching, the Michael Jordan versus Charles Barkley matchup of 1993. But Lance is bending Lacy's legs behind her back—literally.

And I can't help where my mind goes.

Lacy has definitely come into her figure over the last few years. I give her that.

Have I thought about her romantically?

Sure, a few times, maybe.

Is it anything serious? No.

My coveting gaze drifts to Lance as he presses her legs wide apart, helping her stretch.

And pangs of jealousy flare through me.

I'm not about to watch her get worked out by some other guy.

I consider my plays here. I could kick them out. I could continue watching this sideshow.

Instead, I call up my teammate Chandler and arrange to meet up in my building's gym for a night-time workout.

Chandler is as big of a gym rat as I am, so it works out.

"I'm gonna jet out of here for a little. You guys do your thing," I say, and head out.

❧ 6 ❧

CARTER

While I'm waiting for Chandler to arrive, I crank the treadmill up to six-minute mile pace and run.

I put my headphones in and listen to Rage Against the Machine *Killing in the Name* as I pump my arms and legs. Rage fills my heart—the real kind. I sadistically enjoy the pain I get from running so fast. I learned a long time ago not to fight pain.

Seeing Lacy with that long-haired dancer made me feel cut down in a way I can't explain.

I growl and crank the speed up another notch on the treadmill.

I'm pouring sweat, about to start growling just to freak out the guy on the treadmill next to me when I hear yelling and take off my headphones.

My teammate Chandler is standing next to me, off the treadmill, yelling at me.

"Jesus, buddy!" he yells as I slip one of my headphones off. He glances down at the stats from my run, and shoots me a weird look. "Are you training for a fucking eight-hundred meter dash? Why the fuck are you running a five minute, forty-five second mile?"

I shrug as I press the button to turn off the treadmill.

"I was in the mood to run fast."

He shakes his head at me.

"You've got issues, dude. Fucking masochist."

"Don't we all? At least my issues will help me come basketball season when it's time to channel this energy sprint up and down the court for forty-eight minutes."

"Right." He nods. "Shoot around first?"

"Absolutely," I agree, stepping off the treadmill.

We head to the basketball gym to get a few practice shots in. I turn on the stereo system—some delta notch techno this time—and pass to Chandler while he shoots three pointers.

"Seriously. What are your issues?"

I snort as I pass him the ball. "Long fucking story."

"I got time."

"They're personal. "

"Hey, I've got issues too," he says and takes a shot.

"Yeah. Not like mine."

"Try me."

"My new roommate—who I hate—is dancing around my living room with some fucking Fabio-looking douchebag."

Chandler shoots—and drains—another three pointer. The guy is good.

"I don't get it. Why in God's name do you have a roommate? I thought you were pumped about this being the 'summer of Carter?'"

I heave a sigh as I pass him another. "Basically our mothers are best friends. They went to high school together. So ipso facto, Lacy's a family friend. I've never had the heart to inform my mom how much I hate her. Neither has she. So we've kept up this little game of liking each other over the years. When my mom called me to beg to let her crash here —I couldn't say no. It's my *mom*, dude."

"I get it." He shoots and follows the ball as it swishes into the basket again. "Your turn."

He points to me, and I run behind the three point line so he can pass to me.

"So this begs the question," Chandler says as he sends me a perfect pass, "Why do you hate her so much? You're twenty-seven years old. You're crushing life. Why would you want to keep holding a grudge?"

"There's some things in life you just don't forget."

Gripping the ball to shoot, I eye the rim, but my balance feels off. My stomach clenches up like I'm carrying a brick. In a flash, I remember what good friends Lacy and I were in our early years. Those golden years, when we were just two silly kids whose moms were friends. She was the dancer, I was the basketball player.

A memory comes to mind of us playing on the court in the park halfway between our houses in Blackwell the summer I was thirteen, and she was twelve. I was heading into eighth grade, I think, and she was going into seventh.

Ever since I was ten years old, I'd looked forward to going to play basketball at the park in the summer and after school.

The truth of the matter, though, was that I didn't start out wanting to go to the park to play ball, as much as I went because I knew Lacy would be there, one of only a couple girls playing with the guys.

I'd always pick her to be on my team when I could. On the court, she moved with this smooth grace. We made a great team.

I shudder, wobbling a little as my gaze unfocuses. Lacy was so bright and cheery-eyed every time I saw her. I'd catch glimpses of her dancing in the park when she thought no one was watching.

Growing up without a father—I'd felt bitter to an extent, like I was gypped of something all the other kids had. But Lacy's dad had went downhill, too, and she still had a sparkle and a smile in her eye every time I saw her. Her optimism gave me the fuel I needed at that time to be hopeful. She showed me what it meant to disregard obstacles and ram right through them.

The truth, something I'd long kept hidden from even myself, was that she was the one who inspired me to treat basketball with finesse—like a dance with a ball on the court.

Until she lied to me with a straight face for an entire year and changed everything.

The hair stands up on the back of my neck as I remember what she kept from me, even when we were dating for half that year.

"Bro. You gonna shoot?" Chandler quips with his hands on his hips.

Refocusing my gaze on the hoop, I launch the ball.

The shot clanks on the rim, missing badly. Chandler grabs the rebound and holds onto the ball. "You never answered my question. What could be so bad that you can't be civil with each other?"

"She fucked my best friend."

His mouth drops open. "Oh."

I smirk as he tosses me another pass. "Just kidding. She kept a secret from me."

"What secret?"

I shake my head. "Doesn't matter. I'm over it—there's no point in digging up those old skeletons." I shoot and miss badly again.

"Yeah. You are totally over it," Chandler says, passing me the ball. "You're the second best three-point shooter in the league and you just bricked two. I'm sure this has nothing to do with you focusing on something you're completely, totally over."

I shoot again, and I can practically feel my blood coursing with the anger. The shot is too strong, and I miss long.

"Forget this," I quip. "Let's go inside and hit some weights."

"Whatever, man." Chandler shrugs. "I'm not asking for your life story. It's just a question."

I clam up, not wanting to go on about this.

Once we're in the weight room, I throw plates on the bench press and get ready to lift.

Chandler helps me with a lift-off, and I pump out eleven repetitions with ease. On the last one, I can't get it off my chest.

Chandler, spotting me, goes to grab the weights. "No help!" I yell. "Don't touch."

He backs off.

I scream as I try to push the weights up.

Even Chandler gets a worried look on his face as I let out my gorilla yell. And he is used to my antics from practice.

I can't lift the weight.

He leans down and helps me get the bar off my chest. "What the hell has gotten into you, man?" he shakes his head.

Breathing hard as I sit up, I say nothing. I let the painful burn in my chest muscles throb through my body as I stand up. I'm not in the mood to talk about Lacy and I right now.

"Not gonna talk? Okay. The stoic masculine, that's you. I used to be like you before I met Amy. So no comment?" Chandler continues. "My turn, then." I stand up and he sits on the bench. "Thanks for the late night lift session, anyway, bro. I love getting pumped up late. I hope Amy is ready for a session later though. I always have to blow off extra steam after these."

"A session?"

"Yeah. A session. With my fiancée." He wiggles his eyebrows, and I get the innuendo.

Whipping out his phone, he fires off a text. A few moments later, I see a selfie in lingerie show up on his phone and I lean in to see close up.

"Nah ah ah!" Chandler says, closing out his messenger before I can get a good look. "My eyes only."

🐾

WE LIFT FOR ABOUT ANOTHER HOUR, AND THEN I HEAD back to my apartment, hoping Fabio and Lacy are done with their godforsaken dance session by about now.

I shut the door, and I don't see or hear anything. Thank God.

Then, I do a double take when I see a half-full bottle of wine on the coffee table, along with two empty wine glasses.

My nostrils flare, that same rage surging through my heart. But this feeling is nothing compared to a few seconds later, when I hear screaming.

Lacy's voice. "Oh God, yes, just like that!" she yells.

What. The. Actual. FUCK.

My heart pounds as I hear an assortment of noises coming from her room.

I pour myself a glass of water, but I can barely drink it my mouth is so wide open in disbelief.

It's like listening to a bad porno *en vivo*.

Lacy's voice. "Fuck me just like that!"

Slap slap slap. The sound of *skin on skin.*

Leotard's voice. "Yeah, oh God, yeah, you're so tight!"

Slap slap slap.

"Oh my gosh you're so big!"

My blood bakes. I poke my tongue lightly into my cheek and inhale a long breath.

In my. Fucking. House.

If I were a tea kettle right now, I'd be boiling over and spewing steam everywhere. I chug my water, lift up my glass, and consider chucking it against the ground.

My breath heavy, and my hands shaking, I slip my noise-blocking headphones over my head, and crank up a song by *Disturbed*.

I switch to my messenger, and run down the list of girls who have sent me messages today. Somehow, I know calling a girl over isn't going to fix the hole in my heart. It's something I've felt for many years, though I can't put my finger on its origin.

The summer I found out about my father, is the summer my bitterness took hold.

My cat follows me as I walk out onto the balcony and the hot summer night air hits my face.

When the song hits the chorus, I scream loud enough for the whole damn city to hear.

❧ 7 ❧

CARTER

The next morning, I wake up in a cold sweat from a dream I've had.

In the dream, I'm sleeping when Lacy walks into my room.

"HEY," SHE SAYS. "I'M SCARED IN MY BED BY MYSELF. CAN I get into bed with you?"

"Sure," I say in my dream, like it's the most normal thing in the world.

"I don't understand why we can't just be friends," she says as she slips under the covers with me. "I'll forgive you for what you did if you forgive me."

My stomach clenches up. "I'm still not over that."

Her face puffs up, and she starts to cry. "I don't understand you insist on carrying on this grudge."

I clench my jaw, and even in my dream I feel my chest vibrate with raw anger.

"It's your fault. You should never keep things from me."

"I can make it up to you," she says, licking her lips.

She's never looked as sexy as she does in my dream. Her big, baby blue eyes look up at me like a puppy dog who just got caught on the couch, but will do anything it takes to get back in my good graces.

I'm so damn aroused as she slips her hand down my abs, and farther, until she's inches—no, millimeters from gripping my cock, her gaze fully focused on mine.

I'm rock hard, at full attention. But before she can lower her hand, the door swings open, and a monster of a man stands in the archway.

IN THE WAY ONLY A DREAM CAN MANIFEST, THE MAN IS A hybrid mixture of my father and Leotard Larry.

Hence the cold sweat when I wake up.

My cock is as hard as I am confused by this dream.

Extremely.

My erection points straight up at the ceiling mirror, standing at attention.

I rub my eyes, put two feet on the floor, then get down to do some pushups to get this hard-on to disappear. In just my basketball shorts, I head to the dining room to start some coffee.

But as I approach the dining room, I smell something odd.

The place already smells of coffee, eggs, bacon, and hashbrowns.

To my goddamn surprise, Leotard Larry is already up, smiling as he cooks up a storm in my kitchen.

I clench my fists for a moment, then let the tension drop.

Because he's got a big, warm smile on his face. And it appears to be genuine.

"Good morning!" he sings.

I blink a few times. He's got on shorts that are way too short even if this man is a dancer, a lime green tank top, and he's wearing my 'kiss the cook here' apron, with a down arrow pointing to the crotch.

He's got bacon frying up in one pan, eggs in another, and the oven is preheating, probably so he can throw in the hash-browns which are resting atop the stove.

Jesus. This guy certainly knows his way around the kitchen.

"Morning," I growl back. I've always been suspicious of nice people. What kind of guy makes eggs in the morning for his one-night-stand?

"Oh my. Did you sleep okay?" he asks, leaning in. "I've got some coffee here for you. Cream or no? Well, you know the way around your own kitchen. Silly me. I hope it's okay I'm making breakfast for everyone."

I'm still groggy, and in a haze of disbelief that Leotard is making breakfast.

Lacy really knows how to pick them.

I pour myself a cup of black coffee and take a seat on a stool next to the island counter, watching him work the pan. He seems like a damn expert.

"So. Good night last night?" I arch an eyebrow at him, panning for information.

He turns and winks, still with that same sly smile that still leaves me wondering what the hell is going on with him.

"How about you, how was your workout last night, big guy?"

Big guy? The last time I got called that was by my mom. When I was seven.

"Fine," I say gruffly.

"It really shows. You probably eat a lot of protein, though. How many eggs for you?"

"Four," I say.

"Oh wow," he says. "I'll have to throw in another one on for you. Is scrambled okay?"

I nod slowly as I take a sip of my coffee. Footsteps pitter patter down the hallway, and Lacy comes toward the kitchen. Her shoulder length hair is all messed up.

Sex hair.

I've seen it too many times not to recognize it. I open my mouth to make a comment, but then think better of it.

Might as well not show my cards. I don't want her having the tiniest inkling that I actually give a shit what she does. I attempt to pry my eyes away from her, but it's impossible. She's got on tiny short shorts and a tank top that shows off her belly button. And slippers.

The only proper way to describe her right now is 'casual sexy.' Does she even have a bra on? Fuck, those are some perky breasts.

Breasts. I hate Lacy.

Clearing my throat, I plaster a casual smirk onto my face and pretend I'm looking out the window as she gets to the kitchen.

She sets an empty bowl of popcorn in the sink, then kisses Leotard on the face.

"Morning. Mmm it smells delicious. Thanks for cooking, honey."

"My pleasure," he says, and she strokes his arm.

And the way he says pleasure while locking eyes with her makes me want to vomit.

"Coffee?" he asks.

Lacy nods, then comes to my side of the island to sit next to me. I flinch when she puts her hand on the side of my abs as she reaches across for the cup he pours her.

"Whoa. Are you okay?" she smiles at me, a devil's grin.

"Fine. Just had some weird dreams."

"Oh, you did?" she rests her hand on my forearm. "Want to tell me about them? I've been reading a few books on dream interpretation, actually."

I pause and look down, staring at her hand on my arm. I bring my eyes back up to her, my gaze steely. "Hands off the merchandise," I growl.

She looks down, and then reacts as if surprised. "Oh. I didn't even think about it. Sorry." Getting up from her chair, she brushes my shoulder with her boob. And her hand lingers for just a moment too long on my arm.

What the fuck is going on?

Am I imagining this? Why is she touching me right in front of her one-night stand? I decide to call her out on it.

Right after this delicious, amazing-smelling meal compliments of Leotard Larry, the modern Fabio.

⚜

AFTER BREAKFAST, LEOTARD LARRY LEAVES. LACY AND I are sitting across from each other at the island. She scrolls through Instagram on her phone.

"What. The hell. Was that?" I spew, feeling my muscles tense. I hope she's ready for a morning battle.

Actually, I hope she's not.

"*That* was a man who knows how to cook." She pats her belly, smiling, and picks her fork up off her plate, stares at it, and then cleans it with her mouth. "Good thing dance class is in the afternoon today. I'm going to have to invite him over more often."

I stand up and walk around to her side of the island, taking a seat next to her. Even sitting at the high bar stool, she's got to twist her head up to look at me.

"That's not what I'm referring to."

"Oh?" she says casually, not looking up from her phone. "You're going to have to stop speaking in code. I'm not a mind reader, you know." Finally, she brings her eyes up to meet mine. They glow with defiance.

"Don't you dare play dumb. You know exactly what I'm talking about."

She shakes her head and glances back at her phone. "I'm just not sure, Carter. You're going to have to be more specific."

"Oh? You need me to be specific? Here you go." I muster my best girl-imitation voice. "Oh my God. You're so big! Fuck me just like that!"

She furrows her brow.

I return to my normal voice. "Were you making a fuckin' porno last night? What the fuck?"

She shrugs. "You were the one who told me adults have fun relationships. So I took your advice to heart. Thank you." She winks.

I rake a hand through my hair. I consider calling her out on what felt like obvious flirting during breakfast—her hand on my forearm, her boob brushing my arm, but I'm sure she'll just deny it.

I'm smart enough to know that's on purpose. She's a dancer. Dancers are taught to move through every space with purpose. Lacy Benson is trying to fuck with me. Unluckily for her, she's dealing with the best.

"What are you trying to do, Lacy?" I squint. "Drive me up a fucking wall?"

"Why would you care who I sleep with? And as far as the porno, comment, do you ever listen to yourself? The other night was disgusting. You think I want to listen to that all summer? You're such a hypocrite."

I scoff. "I let you crash here, and this is the thanks I get. You buffing some guy the first week."

She puts down her phone and leans toward me. "Why are you such. An asshole."

"Born that way. It's in my genes, obviously. You should know that better than anyone."

She bites her lip. "You want to go there?"

"Not really. But you know why I am the way I am more than most. I'm just stating the facts."

Her eyes get a little foggy. She swallows. "I am really sorry about how that all happened. You know. I never meant to hurt you. I—"

"We're not fucking talking about this at nine thirty in the morning on a Wednesday."

"Oh really?" She stands up, and starts heading down the hallway toward her room. I follow a few steps behind her. "And when exactly are you planning on talking about it? It was like nine fucking years ago, at least! Get a fucking grip, Carter! It's time to grow up. Not sure if you noticed this, but everyone had their problems growing up in Blackwell. You act like you're this special case! Newsflash: you're not."

"Wow, thanks for the breaking story," I say sarcastically. "In other news, I'm not having this discussion."

Her eyes gloss over, and I resist the emotions coming over me. She's playing a game. Trying to get me to feel sorry for her. I won't let her affect my emotions. "You were pretty shitty to me too, you know. And I'm trying to forgive you. Maybe you could learn something from that."

She slams the door to the bathroom in my face.

I clench my jaw, and a fist. I want to pound on the door.

And I especially don't want to talk to her about it now that she's boinking some guy in my apartment. Even if he does make one hell of a breakfast.

"No more sex in the house," I blurt out.

She opens the door a crack. "Really? You can agree to that?"

"I will. If you will."

"Done."

She shuts the door again.

The fact of the matter is, Lacy and I will never be friends again. I've accepted that. She, apparently, hasn't.

I go to my room to get ready for basketball practice later, my heart as hard as a diamond.

Smokey must sense I'm feeling angry. Purring her way into the room, she jumps up on my bed, asking to be pet.

"Well alright, Smokey. If you insist."

❦ 8 ❦

LACY

When my first Saturday night in Chicago rolls around, I hang out with Lance again. This time, I go to his house. It's a welcome night of relief after a week full of dance rehearsals.

"Oh yes, Lacy! Oh God, yes!" Lance cries.

"Mmmm that's the spot!" I yell, unable to contain my laughter. "So big! So deep!"

I shovel popcorn into my mouth on Lance's couch as we recount the story of our acting shenanigans to his boyfriend, Joseph. He is doubled over in laughter.

"No. You did not say that!"

Lance smiles deviously. "We did. And all the while—" he claps his hand against his bicep, which makes a loud skin slapping sound. "*Romancing the Stone* is such a good movie, isn't it?"

I nod, but my smile dissipates when I think about the way my conversation with Carter went after breakfast this past week. Since then we'd both been purposefully avoiding each other.

Maybe trying to bring up Carter's father the night after

I'd faked having sex with my new gay best friend was not the best way to go about things. I see that in retrospect.

"Lacy! You're not saying anything," Joseph says.

"Oh, sorry," I say, zoning back in.

"I asked, do you think he suspects anything?" Joseph says.

I shrug. "I don't see why he would."

"So he has no idea we were just sitting in your room watching *Romancing the Stone* while making excessive sex noises. And he has no clue that Lance is gay?"

I shrug, looking away from them and not answering the question.

"What's the matter?" Lance asks, sensing my slight melancholy. "I thought you hated Carter."

"I do hate Carter," I confirm, but my face gives away that I can't help but feel weird about the fact that I've thrown yet another lie on our complicated past.

"Why do you hate him so much?" Joseph interjects. "He's too hot to hate."

Lance looks over at me. "I hope you don't mind. While I was making breakfast, I snapped a few shirtless pics of Carter sipping his coffee while he wasn't looking."

My jaw drops. "You did what?"

Smiling, he pulls out his phone and shows me the pictures he took of Carter, looking ridiculously attractive as always as he sits on the kitchen island, steam radiating up from his coffee cup.

"You tell Carter I can come over and make breakfast for him any time he wants," Lance winks.

"Ohh! I can help, too," Joseph adds.

I sigh, frowning. "I'll let him know."

"What's got you down, Lacy?"

I hunch my shoulders. "I just remembered my birthday is next week," wanting to steer the conversation away from Carter.

"Seriously? Which day?" Lance asks.

"Friday."

Joseph raises his eyebrows. "Friday? I have off next Friday."

Lance frowns. "Where would we have a party anyway?" His eyes suddenly light up like a little kid at Christmas. "Oh! We should have it at your place!"

"My place? You mean Carter's place."

"Yes! There's no denying how absolutely amazing your apartment is, Lacy. You've got a hot tub, a balcony, a big TV, a sound system . . . we can definitely fit forty people in there. No way we are all cramming into my tiny apartment."

"Whoa." I hold up my hands. "Where are we getting forty people?"

Lance rolls his eyes. "From dance camp, duh."

"I'm not inviting all forty people. I don't even know most of the dancers."

"So what better way to get to know them than to invite them over to your seriously luxurious place!"

"Carter's place, you mean."

"Look, you want to win this audition at the end of the eight weeks, right?"

I nod. "Of course. But what does that have to do with having a party?"

Joseph puts his hand over Lance's thigh, and they make eye contact, both shaking their heads.

"If you want to win the audition, there's more than just skill required. You need to play the social game, too. Invite everyone over. Even that—what's the girl who thinks she's hot shit?"

"Davina."

"Yes! Davina."

Davina is Italian-Russian, born in New York, who walks

around the dance floor like she craps rose petals. Lance has obviously noticed my vitriol for her already.

"I don't know if Carter will let me have so many people over."

"He will," Joseph says. "I'm sure of it."

"How are you so sure?"

"Come on. Forty hot dancers—all girls aside from me—in his house? I don't think he'll mind."

I nod, but feel my chest tighten a little. "Good point."

⌘

SUNDAY MORNING, I WAKE UP FEELING FRESH AND READY to enjoy the city.

After rolling out of bed, I walk into my bathroom to shower off, and my eyes practically bulge out of my head when I see Carter standing in the bathroom, facing the sink mirror.

My bathroom.

And he's one hundred percent naked.

My stomach coils with confusion, my lips parting slightly as I blink a few times and try to find words to say.

Carter just smirks, facing the mirror. I see him watching my gaze as I take in the profile of his carved frame from the side as he stands facing the sink.

"Uh . . ." I stutter, forcing myself to say something, anything. "I wasn't expecting to see you here. Don't you have your own shower?"

My heart hammers like a bass drum.

"Master shower is broken," he says simply in a low voice, twisting his head to meet my eyes.

Carter turns his body toward me, a towel draped over his shoulder.

Why the hell is his towel over his shoulder and not around his waist?

Butterflies flap in my stomach as I blink several times, my mind a little foggy from the wine I had with Lance last night.

What is with Carter and I accidentally running into each other in towels?

My eyes travel down Carter's perfect V of a body, and his crotch is like a magnet.

Dear God.

I pull my eyes back up to his smirk as he stares.

He takes a step toward me, hands on his hips.

I want to leave. I want to get out of there and hide my head back under my pillow.

But my legs feel like heavy as tree trunks when I try to move.

And somehow I feel like he's challenging me, just seeing how much he can fuck with me.

Is his shower really broken? What kind of a millionaire can't just call a handyman in two seconds to fix that? I swallow as Carter hovers inches from me. I can hear his breath. Smell his fresh, woodsy scent.

"W-What body wash is that?" I ask, clearing my throat. "Smells good."

He has to look down so his eyes can meet mine.

"Body wash?" he asks, offering me a half-smile. "Is that what you're thinking about?"

I can hear his own audible breath. Or is that my own breath getting heavy? I can't tell. I'm losing myself in the space between Carter and me.

"Yeah," I breathe. "I'm curious about your body wash."

"Oh." The smile leaving his face, he leans down, and his towel brushes me as he whispers against my ear. "Because I could have sworn I just saw you stare at my cock for a good two seconds."

I shake my head. "It was just kind of there. It's not a big deal."

I try to move again, but I stumble as I try to twist my feet in place, and have to grab Carter's arm for balance.

A slight grin returns to his face, and he clutches the side of my neck in return. His grip is surprisingly soft. His thumb grazes my ear, sending shivers through my entire body.

"Pretty clumsy for a dancer sometimes, aren't you?"

I open my mouth to speak, but the words don't come out.

"Carter," I whisper. "What are you doing?"

My tongue runs along my lips.

In a panic, I take my hand off his arm but he's so close to me it grazes his lower abs. And comes dangerously close to his dick.

I'm suddenly fearful.

Of Carter, in a way.

How strong he is. How he could overpower me. How uncontrollable he's been known to be.

I heard him scream the other night when I was faking sex with Lance to get back at him.

So as our eyes lock, I feel like he's the hunter with precision focus, and I'm his doe-eyed prey.

But that's not why I'm scared.

I'm scared because I find myself wishing he would do those things to me.

I imagine what his abs would feel like, pressed up against my body.

How his impressive package would feel buried deep inside me. As much as we messed around in high school, we never made it to sex. I never even saw him naked.

Over the years, I've occasionally found myself wondering what he would be like in bed. Rough? Gentle? Some combination of the two?

I can't see Carter being gentle.

Not anymore, at least. I have a sinking feeling that the soft kisses Carter graced me with in high school were the last time he was gentle with anyone.

These are the thoughts that run through my mind as Carter's massive hand grips just under my ear. He runs his thumb along my cheek, our eyes locked together.

I feel like he's hypnotizing me.

"I would appreciate it if you wore a towel," I manage to say.

"And I'd appreciate if you didn't parade around here in your booty shorts all day."

I push his hand off me, narrowing my eyes. Taking a step back, I spin around when a realization hits me. Does Carter . . .? Holy shit. Is Carter checking me out, too?

My heart practically beats through my tank top.

I turn around and look at him over my shoulder. "Oh, you mean these shorts?" I say, arching my back and poking my ass out even more, gauging his reaction.

This time it's Carter who freezes up, staring as I slowly draw a hand up one side of my shorts.

I flinch, my eyes bulging when I see his cock literally twitch.

He looks up at me and smirks again. "You have a sexy ass, Laces. What do you want me to do about it? Not look, even though you're shaking it right in front of me? Any man who says otherwise is lying. And you know I wouldn't lie to you. Not any more, after all we've been through."

I swallow, and turn back around, hands on my hips. "Fuck you Carter. Get your shower fixed. And by the way, it's common courtesy to wear a towel around your waist, not drape it over your shoulder."

He shrugs. "Like you mind. Besides, my house, my rules."

I huff and head back to my room, slamming the door behind me. I collapse on my bed in a pool of sweat.

Entitled. Cocky. Asshole.

None of those words do Carter justice. He's worse than all of those combined.

I run my hands through my hair and over my neck, letting out a loud exhale. One week down, I remind myself.

Seven to go. And then no more putting up with Carter.

I tremble as I lay on the bed, my legs quivering. I dart my tongue around my lips and take inventory of my body.

My pulse is still quick. I try to deny the impulse coming over me, but that only makes the shiver of pleasure more powerful.

I think about Carter's hand on my neck. The vibrations of his low voice as he growled against my skin.

I can't stop myself. I slip a hand under my shorts and down to my opening.

Circling a finger around my already wet clit, I put a hand over my mouth to stifle a moan. A light-headed dizziness comes on, but the pleasure is mixed with tension. I bring my hand away from my mouth and run it over my neck, where Carter touched me. My heart pounds and my eyes flutter.

Heat flashes through my body, and I can't tell if it's pent-up desire, or just plain ire. What does it say about me that I'm soaking wet for a man as cocky and dickish as Carter?

My eyes hood, and my thoughts melt away, muddling as I press my fingers down harder. I'm more turned on right now than I ever remember being.

I bet he's right on the other side of that door.

I fight against this attraction. Somehow I feel as though if I touch myself after he gets me riled up, I'm letting him win.

I can't help it.

In a fury of madness, I slip my shorts off, spread my legs, and rub my clit harder, arching my hips into my hand and letting go as warmth floods through me. It's been too long since I've done this.

Maybe I just need to do it once, and I'll get this ridiculous fantasy out of my system after I explore it. Then, I can go back to hating Carter for the asshole he is.

I slip two fingers inside and curl my abdomen.

"Oh yes," I whisper, and cover my mouth. I put a pillow over my face so he can't hear my moans.

The feeling crescendos as I let my mind drift off.

I desperately picture Carter on top of me. I can feel the weight of his body as he pushes inside me, as he overtakes me, needing me as badly as I need him.

The thought of Carter coming inside me is what does it.

I cry out into my pillow, my hips quivering as I come harder than I ever have before.

When it's over, I'm still turned on, breathing hard.

The relief I thought would come over me never comes.

I hate him.

And I want him.

I wish I were lying.

But the truth is exposed as heat rushes through me, no matter how hard I try to pretend otherwise.

❧ 9 ❧

CARTER

Well.

That cat is out of the bag.

So to speak.

And I'm not talking about Smokey. She's always out of the bag.

Back to the serious stuff. I'm not going to lie, when it comes to showing my junk, I'm not on the insecure side. I do enjoy the speechlessness it can imbue in the lucky lady who is graced with my presence.

I wish I could frame the mental picture I took of Lacy's shocked look when she saw me naked—and couldn't stop staring.

This whole 'no sex' at my apartment thing is bugging me, though.

I know it's barely been a day. Patience hasn't been one of my virtues in years.

Sure, I could rent a hotel. Or go to someone else's place. But why would I have bought a multi-million dollar penthouse just so I could tell girls, "sorry, can we actually go back to your place?"

It's the principle of the matter. But I'm getting worked up, having Lacy around here. She fills the apartment with her fresh, feminine scent. It's like cherries and citrus and fancy shampoo.

She has become even more attractive compared with the high school version of Lacy I remember. Wider hips, fuller lips.

But it's more than that. I'm not used to living with women —I have a twenty-four hour rule, normally. I don't spend more than twenty-four hours in the same building as a woman I am screwing.

Even though Lacy is hidden away in her room right now, her essence seems to have penetrated my entire penthouse.

I can't even sit on the couch without smelling her. I flip through my phone lazily, glancing at the messages girls have sent me today. All booty call requests.

Hey Carter - you doing anything special today?

Special?

Oh yes honey, I've got some very special activities planned.

Or here's a good one. A snapchat selfie with the words 'miss u!' written across her tits so I can't see her nipples. I sigh, looking at myself in the mirror. With just basketball shorts on right now, I could easily snap a selfie back to them, and give them a little boost of that dopamine they want. But I'm not in the mood for putting up with bullshit today.

However, I am quite tense.

I stand up and roll my hips a little bit, a motion my physical trainer taught me. Yeah. I definitely feel tight. Probably from the heavy leg weights and plyometrics workout I did at practice yesterday. In addition to me and Chandler's late night lift session.

I frown looking into the mirror.

Or, you know, it could be from the fact that I want to fuck my roommate.

There. I said it. I admit it.

The half-chubby I've been walking around with is her fault.

And no, that doesn't mean I *like* her.

What, you've never wanted to fuck someone you hate?

I crinkle my nose.

Lacy is in her room alone. And Lance hasn't been over since Wednesday.

She went back into her room awful fast after our little encounter. And she's quiet. A little *too* quiet if you ask me. Maybe she's awake.

My jaw drops a little at a possibility.

I picture Lacy in her room. On her back. Legs spread out as she pleasures herself.

Thinking of me, of course, I smirk.

She'd better be.

Heat surges through me and blood rushes to my cock.

Fuck a chubby. I've gone full mast. I'm pitching a tent standing up right now thinking about Lacy. How she'd feel. I bet she's tight. Oh God yeah, she's tight for sure.

Maybe that tension I was talking about isn't all in my hips.

I need to get rid of this tension. I could rub one out on the couch? No, Lacy could come out of her room at any moment. That would be awkward.

Or...maybe she'll catch me whacking it, and we'll have some porno-like hook-up.

No. I push that possibility out of my mind. Even if I want Lacy, no way am I allowing myself to be with her. She doesn't deserve how well I'll be able to fuck her.

Lacy has no idea the things I could do to her body.

Although I'm sure after she saw me getting out of the shower, she's got a few notions.

I'm about to head to my room and take care of business when I hear footsteps creeping down the hallway. She's coming.

I glance down. Mother of hell, I still have an erection the size of a small arm sticking straight out at a right angle.

Without thinking, I drop down to the ground and start cranking out pushups in the living room on the carpet.

Hot tip, ladies: If you ever walk into a room and your roommate is randomly doing pushups, it might be because he was just thinking about rubbing one out to the thought of you.

I hear her laugh. "Do you ever stop working out? You're so vain."

"If you really want to help me out, you should sit on top of me and make this a little harder."

"Really? Okay."

My stomach tightens as Lacy takes a few steps toward me.

I didn't anticipate her taking me up on my offer. And dear Mother of God, my erection is not going away.

"You know, you're not going down all the way to the floor. Maybe that's why it's so easy."

I grunt as I slowly try to go a little bit lower without jamming my penis into the floor.

Maybe I can't go all the way down because my horse cock is blocking me. Ever thought of that?

"But if you insist, I'll make this a little harder for you."

I try to glance at her to gauge her expression. I can't tell if she even knows what pun she just made, or if she is being totally innocent.

She's got on yoga pants and a tight tank top, and she sits her ass right on my back.

I keep cranking out pushups. Slowly, so I don't jam my cock into the floor.

"This is awkward," she says. "It's like I'm on a merry-go-round ride going up and down. Here, I have another idea."

I hold my arms straight, in plank position for a moment as she gets off. Then she does something that sends chills down my entire body.

She lays down on her stomach on me. Her boobs press right into my bare back.

Holy fuck. I can feel her nipples.

My heart hammers hard and my entire chest is flooded with warmth.

Her legs press against the tops of my legs. She wraps her delicate hands around my abs.

"Okay. I have better balance now. Try again."

She slips her hands a few inches lower, from my upper abs to my hips.

Suddenly, a surge of anger hits me, and I guess at what she's doing.

"Come on, Cartwheel. Take me for a ride. Let's see what you got."

My nostrils flare like an angry bull as she throws my childhood nickname out there.

For a brief moment, I remember when I picked up the name. I was a carefree kid once, that kid who did cartwheels and backflips at recess just for the hell of it.

I've come a long way since then, though. I press up and down and do a fury of pushups like Lacy weighs nothing.

She wiggles her hips into my ass every rep I do. Presses her boobs into me the same way. And lets out a soft little moan in my ear every time I push her up.

The hypocrisy is maddening.

She's the one toying with me.

Trying to pretend it's my fault we hate each other.

"Ohh. Oh boy! I better hang on tight," she says as I hit

my tenth pushup, and her hand slips even lower from my hips.

One odd finger swats my cock over the mesh of my shorts.

An accident?

"Lacy," I growl, stopping at the top of my pushup, out of breath. "What. The fuck. Was that?"

"My bad," she says, and she bites my ear a little bit.

That's. Fucking. It.

I let myself down, and roll her off me so she lands on the rug, on her back. She lets out a yelp.

Once she's on the ground, I straddle her waist, pinning her to the ground. She tries to sit up, but I grab her hands with mine.

My voice comes out, a low, gravelly growl. "What the fuck do you think you're doing?"

Both of us are breathing hard.

She swallows. "You wanted me to help weigh you down for pushups. So I helped you."

"Don't bullshit me, Laces. I know your lying face when I see it."

She tries to hold eye contact with me, but she can't. Classic Lying Lacy tell.

"Let me go, Carter," she seethes, although her tone is less than convincing.

I lick my lips, staring at her, and I feel her wiggle her hips up into me again.

"Carter . . ." she breathes.

"Tell me," I growl, "What the fuck you think you were doing? Grabbing my cock like that."

"I didn't grab it. I barely touched it. And you made a weird, jerky motion. Your cock touched my hand!"

I scoff, and even almost crack a smile at the sheer ludicrousness of her claim.

"My cock slapped your hand. Wow. I don't think I've ever heard that one before. You were holding onto my hips three inches from my dick."

She grips my hands hard as she twists her hips left and then right trying to jockey for some kind of position. I'm not sure where she thinks she's going, seeing as I'm double her weight.

"Fuck you," she breathes, her chest heaving. "I fucking hate you, Carter. You made everyone in high school hate me over a stupid little lie that wasn't my fault. And for some stupid reason you're the only person I know in this city right now. I hate the fact that I actually have to be dependent on you. And sure, I was having a little fun running my hands over your body. Like you haven't had a million girls do that. I know I'm not special. But I'm different. You know why?"

I press her hands down into the rug, still straddling her.

My voice is hoarse, like something is caught in it as I try to speak. "Why?" I growl through gritted teeth.

"Because I know you, Carter Flynn I know where you came from. I know how fucked up you had it growing up. But I also know that there were plenty of kids who had it harder than you. But did you forgive me for something stupid I should have told you when I was sixteen years old? No. That's why your heart is black. And that's why you'll never, ever, have a girl like me. Who knows you? I mean who knows the real Carter? I'll just answer that for you: no one. You and your revolving door policy with women aren't because you're some big shot. It's because you—"

"Shut up!" I yell, closing my eyes, my voice quaking. When I reopen my eyes, Lacy's lips are parted, her breath bursting in and out as she keeps silent. I can feel her hands shaking slighty as I pin them down to the rug.

"Stop. Just fucking stop," I say, gnashing my teeth. "We're done here. Done talking about this."

"Good," she spews. "I'm glad. One more thing though."

"What's that?"

"Your cock is resting on my stomach, and it's hard. Looks like you have some tension. You better do something about that. Maybe call one of the insta-whores in your rolodex to give you a happy ending."

I bite my lower lip, loosening my grip so Lacy can slide out from beneath me.

When she stands up, she grabs her keys off the landing. "I'm going out to take a tour of the city with Lance. So you've got enough time to call over one of your whores. See you later, Douchebag."

She shuts the door with a thud.

I turn to my cat. She saw the whole thing. Smokey's really been a witness to a lot.

Standing up, I rub my face with my hands.

I want to call Lacy out for shitty behavior. For what shitty behavior, though?

Flirting with me a little?

Fucking with me and rubbing her body into me?

I heave heavy breaths as a realization sets in.

I text Chandler.

CARTER: DUDE I AM TENSE AS FUCK TODAY MAN. ANY remedies?

Chandler: Yeah, stop having so much pent-up rage. Therapy?

Carter: Good one

Chandler: Also, yoga. I'm going tomorrow night after practice. Amy's taking me.

Carter: Yoga's for pussies."

Chandler: Yeah? Well Amy looks hot as fuck while she's doing it. So it's basically partial foreplay with stretching. Also, I swear to God those hip openers do wonders. You want to be playing ball when you're forty, don't you?

   Carter: I'll go.

   Chandler: Amy says feel free to bring your roommate if you want. See you tomorrow

❧ 10 ❧

LACY

"**S**o I'm insane, right?"

As we head out of dance, I finish giving Lance the rundown about what happened yesterday with Carter, and how ridiculous pushup dialogue turned into me writhing on top of him.

Lance puts his hands on my shoulder, stops me, and blinks a few times.

"Did you . . . ya know? While you were wiggling your hips on top of him?"

"Ya know? What do you mean?" I narrow my eyes.

Leaning in, he looks around to see if anyone else is within earshot before speaking. "Did you have an orgasm?" he whispers.

I roll my eyes and scoff like it's the most ridiculous thing in the world.

"No. Of course not."

"Well, you were tempted. I bet you at least got a little turned on."

I bite my lip and look down. As down to Earth as Lance is, I think I'll just not mention the little solo session I had after I saw Carter naked.

Which was, ironically, before the pushup incident.

When he baited me to weigh him down for pushups I couldn't help but call his bluff. And if I was going to call it, why not have a little fun with him and mess with him, since he'd been doing the same with me?

He raises an eyebrow. "Lacy. Don't lie to me. You looked down. You can tell me if you're getting turned on by Carter. Even if you do hate him, love is not the opposite of hate."

"You don't think it is?"

"Oh God no. Joseph and I have the best sex when we hate each other. Indifference is the opposite of love. Not hate. Hate is a different shade of the same emotion."

I cross my arms. "Not with Carter, it's not."

"I don't understand what he could have done that was so bad."

I sigh, and look around to make sure no one else from dance is in the lobby. Davina hustles toward us, her long blond hair bouncing with every stride.

She flashes a smile as she passes us in the lobby, and I can't tell if it's fake or not. She's grew up in New York City with parents from a mom from Italy and a dad from Russia, and she's got this high falootin' 'I'm a little bit better than everyone else' attitude about her.

"Hey guys!" she says in a super bubbly voice.

Maybe I'm also a little jealous of her because she's the number one. She's two years younger than me, and she's a lock to be selected to Blue Illusion.

Me, on the other hand? I feel like it's an uphill battle to get a spot. And a long shot.

"Hey you," Lance says with a wink, and I'm not going to lie. My heart warms that apparently the 'sexy bitch' part of that phrase is reserved just for me.

"Hey," I say, trying to be good-natured. "You nailed that opening routine today."

She waves my compliment away. "It was nothing. I just need to thank this guy for being such a big strong man." She grabs Lance's bare bicep.

A wash of jealousy comes over me, and suddenly I have a stark realization. I am a little jealous of the attention another girl is giving my very gay, sometimes-fake-boyfriend. This is not a good sign for my personal mental health.

"Anyways, I've gotta run. See you," she says.

Lance bites his lip. "Adios."

She throws her head back in laughter as she continues out the revolving door.

Lance and I follow, then pause on the sidewalk. It's rush hour, and the hustle and bustle of the city is palpable. Cars are at a standstill in rush hour traffic. Lance lives up on the north side of the city, and I'm lucky because I live close by.

When I glance at him, I notice that Lance is just staring at me.

"Honey, you look tense."

"I am tense," I admit.

He sighs. "You need to get laid, don't you? It's all that tension you've been building up with Carter. It's just begging for a release."

"Maybe," I respond. "But I'll find an outlet for it."

His phone buzzes and he checks it. "Well, speaking of tension release. There's this new thing at the yoga studio Joseph and I belong to. It's called Vino and Vinyasa."

I giggle. "That's a catchy name."

Lance puts his hand on my shoulder and massages my neck. "It's the ultimate stress reliever. It's been getting really popular. If you want to go, let me know. It starts in a half hour and I'd have to sign you up right now through the website."

"I'm in."

"Yes! You're going to love it. And with those hot pink tights you have on, you might even attract a guy."

"These are quite obnoxious," I admit.

My stomach coils, just thinking about 'attracting a guy,' though. It's not something that's remotely on my radar right now. Especially after the way things went downhill with Norton.

Except for my attraction for Carter, which is rapidly building in spite of—maybe even *because of*—my dislike for him.

"I'll call us a Lyft. Oh, and after yoga, you can tell me all about why you hate Carter. I have a feeling this isn't a quick 'on the sidewalk' conversation."

"How do you know?"

"Because you keep avoiding telling me."

"Oh."

"Lyft is almost here. Are you ready for some downward dogs?"

I blow out a loud exhale. How is it possible that I both wish I never have to see Carter again, and at the same time want him in my bed tonight?

I hate decisions.

"Can we just skip the dogs and just go to the wine bottles?

"Where's your leotard, man?" Chandler ribs me as we sit on our mats.

"Dude, screw you. You said this was going to release the tension. Not piss me off more."

"It will. Fuck, I'm about to release some tension right now if I'm not careful."

I follow Chandler's gaze as his fiancée Amy walks into the room. The guy is so damn in love, and it's completely disgusting.

Amy enters the room wearing hot pink yoga pants and a white top. She's on the shorter side, maybe just a hair over five feet tall. When Chandler sees her, his face lights up and his entire demeanor changes.

"Hey Squirt," he growls, ignoring the other people who are trying to come in as he blocks the entryway to give Amy a long kiss. He walks back over to me, and Amy sets up her mat directly in front of Chandler.

"Hi Carter," she smiles. "I heard you have some tension you need to get worked out."

I scoff and say jokingly, "You told her? That was confidential."

Amy, on all fours, is making a very suggestive pose as she aims her ass right at Chandler, who is sitting cross-legged on his mat.

He winks at me, leans over, and whispers. "We're going to work out some tension later tonight. I can't wait."

I roll my eyes again, half at how pathetic Chandler seems, and half jealous that he's so into Amy.

"Fuck you, dude, you're disgusting," I whisper.

Chandler just smirks. "She's wearing the pink pants. That means she's extra randy," he says as though he's a scientist who has made this painstaking discovery over years of experimentation.

I scrunch up my face. "Did you seriously just use the word 'randy?' And how the hell do you know that?"

He scrubs a hand across his jaw, and glances back and forth to make sure no one is within earshot.

"Pink is the same color as the pussy."

"So because she's wearing pink, she subconsciously is hornier. Got it. What did you get your degree in, again?"

"Psychology."

"Oh." I shrug. I don't know. Maybe he has a point.

Space is tight in the studio, and Chandler and I are easily the tallest, biggest guys there. We barely fit on our mats. Chandler doesn't seem to mind, as this means he gets an up close and personal view of Amy in her pink pants.

I get up to fix my mat, and when I sit back down I have to blink a few times when I notice who—also in pink pants—is directly in front of me.

"What the . . . Laces?"

Lacy is right in front of me. And Leotard Larry is to her left. "Oh my God. You do yoga?"

Before I can say anything, the instructor dims the lights

and calls out. "Okay, class, let's bring our hands to center." Her voice is quite soothing.

Lacy turns toward the front of the class. I swear I see her sneak a glance at me by looking at the walled mirror in front of us. "Let's examine our intentions for the class," the teacher continues. "And also take a look at the baggage we're bringing today. Are we angry, sad, or tense? Let those negative emotions fall away."

I close my eyes and do my best to let the world fall by the wayside.

I open my eyes for just a moment, and I see her.

My heart starts to hammer.

This is bullshit. She was all worked up after she saw me in the shower yesterday. She was moaning in my goddamn ear while I was doing pushups, for goodness sake. And now she's got pink pants on, and she's hanging out with Larry again?

Just who does this Fabio motherfucker think he is?

My mind flashes back to straddling Lacy, my hard cock resting on her stomach. She could feel it. She knows what she does to me. But even more, she knows what I do to her.

So she wants to take that energy out with Leotard Boy? This is bullshit.

"Downward dog. Sir?" I feel a tap on the shoulder. It's the instructor. I notice everyone else is already out of the sitting position and into a downward dog.

"My bad," I say.

"You look tense. Let everything fall away. Your body will thank you."

She walks away, and as I get into position I do a double take, because Lacy is in downward dog three feet from my face.

Shaking her pink ass right in front of me.

I bite my lip, and my heart rate speeds as I get into downward dog.

Anger surges through me. "You've gotta be kidding me," I mutter to myself.

I glance over at Chandler, and he's sneaking a look at Amy, who is blowing kisses back to him. She even rolls her eyes back in her head like she's having an orgasm, and Chandler cracks up.

"Absolutely disgusting," I whisper.

He winks. "Just remember what I said about pink."

After sun salutations, we do a few warrior poses and then someone requests hip openers. "Of course," the instructor says. "Let's get into puppy pose, then."

She models the pose in the front of the class. I rub my left eye, because there is no other way to describe what she is doing—in my dirty mind—other than doggie-style sex practice pose.

Puppy pose.

Lacy breathes out in front of me, and the noise sounds starkly similar to how she moaned in my ear yesterday. Except this time, she's on her knees, sticking her ass straight up in the air, and putting her head low to the ground, arms out in front.

I feel my dick twitch, and that's when I realize this class is a total loss if what I wanted was to get the tension out. My balls will be aching even more after this.

I close my eyes and zone out, doing my absolute best to concentrate on the poses, and not the fact that Lacy is almost right on top of me in the crammed yoga studio.

Taking a deep breath, I try to lend my attention to the actual yoga exercises and be 'mindful.'

Or something.

But when I open eyes for a brief moment, she's staring back at me.

As soon as my gaze finds her, she turns back toward the front.

WHEN CLASS ENDS, AMY INSISTS THAT WE STAY FOR THE wine portion of the happy hour. I resist, but she insists, and next thing I know I have a glass of pinot noir in my hand and I'm introducing Amy to Lacy.

"Oh my gosh!" Amy says. "You have pink pants too." Amy glares at Chandler. "I told you pink was in."

Chandler chuckles. "You only wear pink when you are . . . in the mood."

"In the mood for what?" Lacy asks.

Amy sighs. "It's just Chandler's stupid theory. That I wear pink when I'm horny. It's a bunch of bull, though."

There's an awkward pause as everyone considers the implications of the pink. I nod, admiring that Amy doesn't hold anything back. I met her a few times over the past season, and even though I don't approve of my guy friends taking the plunge and getting married, Amy is so damn smiley and bubbly all the time that I can't help but like her.

"Anyways, how rude of me," I add. "Lacy, you should introduce your boyfriend. You guys, this is Leo."

"It's Lance, actually," he says, shaking hands with the group. He gestures to another guy standing next to him with black hair and eyes, also wearing full-on yoga pants. "And this is my—my friend, Joseph."

Joseph does a weird eye-roll, and shakes hands with the group too.

I notice an odd energy in the air, but I can't quite put my finger on it.

"So, Carter," Leo says. "It's Lacy's birthday this Friday."

"Oh. And?" I arch an eyebrow.

Joseph lets out a loud sigh, which is weird. What does he care that I don't give a shit about Lacy's birthday?

"And," Leotard continues, "we want to have a party for her with the rest of the dance crew."

"Great. It's a free country, so you can definitely do that," I inform him.

"Well," he pauses, clearing his throat. "We want to use your penthouse. We figure it's the best spot."

"Oh my gosh!" Amy smiles, her eyes wide. "That would be so fun! You're new to the city, right?"

Lacy nods.

"Wait," Amy pokes Chandler. "What about the yacht you and Carter rented for the summer?"

"Um, you have a yacht?" Leotard echoes, jerking his head back.

I clench my fists. At the beginning of the summer, Chandler and I both got big contracts, and we decided to celebrate by going halfsies on a party yacht that we can use on Lake Michigan.

"We're not using Empire for a silly little birthday party," I say, using the proper name of the yacht. "It's more for team events. You know, bonding and stuff."

Lacy shoots me a look of death when I shut her down.

Amy gasps, putting her hand over her mouth. "That's a great idea! We can invite the team! And Lance, how many dancers would be coming?"

"Well, we'd invite the whole summer camp. There are forty of us, although not all forty would come, probably."

"Wait a minute," I say, holding up a finger as my wheels start to turn. "Forty dancers—I'm guessing mostly women— on one boat?"

Lance nods. "Yes, I'm the only guy this summer."

I slap my hand on the bar table. "You know what? That sounds fucking great, actually. I'll invite the team, and maybe some other guys." I slam my wine, and my mind races with possibilities all of the sudden.

"Lacy's birthday is on June twenty-first. It's the longest night of the summer. Fuck it, have everyone pack an overnight bag! I'll hire a captain and crew for the night, and we'll bring this motherfucker out on the lake! It'll be a night to remember!"

"Oh my gosh, really? You'd pay for all that?" Amy asks.

I wave her off. "Of course I will. You know, you're right. I've been a scrooge lately. Like you said, Lacy's new to the city. We should give her a proper welcome." A huge grin spreads across my face.

Lacy's face turns to a look of terror.

I wonder if she realizes what I just realized.

Amy leans on Chandler's shoulder, then speaks as though she's just read my mind. "Forty dancers. A dozen or so professional basketball players. Free drinks on a yacht all night. That sounds like paradise. What could go wrong?"

LACY

On Friday morning, my mom and my sister call me at the same time and sing a duet of happy birthday to me. After the song, my sister gets on the phone. "Hey! How is camp going? Tell me everything!"

"I'll fill you in as much as I can. I'm actually in the lobby on a ten-minute break right now."

"Oh. Wow. Well thanks for picking up for me."

"Stop it! Of course I'd pick up."

"No seriously. It's amazing what you're doing. By the way, did I tell you I'm visiting NYU this summer with Mom? I'm applying to their dance program. If I get in, I'd be there for four years! And you'll be there too!"

"I'll be there if I get the spot," I say, tempering her excitement a little.

"Why wouldn't you get it? You're amazing."

"Of course I am. But so is everyone here. I have to show them something special to get a spot."

"So . . . what's stopping you?" I beam listening to my sister's unabashed optimism. Oh to be eighteen again.

"Nothing," I respond. "Absolutely nothing. And let me

know how the visit to New York goes. Send me some pictures."

"Absolutely. So what are you doing today, to celebrate turning twenty-six?"

"Well. A friend is throwing me a party . . . on a boat."

I hear a loud squeal on the other end of the line. "A boat!? I'm so jealous."

My hometown, Blackwell, is totally landlocked. So when we were little, my sister and I used to fantasize about traveling on a boat around the world. And now, that fantasy was coming true. Kinda.

I give Eliza the run-down.

"This Amy girl sounds cool. I think you should hang out with her. And she's engaged to Chandler Spiros, right? What's her secret?"

I sigh. "I have no idea. She seems . . . just really nice. I'm not sure. Apparently she's inviting some baseball guys, too, because one of her girlfriends is married to Jake Napleton."

I hear a gasp on the other end. "Oh. My. Gosh. I wish I could fly up for today! That's like, amazing. Are you super excited?!"

I lie and say that I am, apparently not very convincingly though.

"Are you okay?"

"Yeah. Totally fine."

"I don't believe you. What's going on?"

"I'm just stressed out about making it onto Blue Illusion. And a little homesick. And I'm turning twenty-six, you know? It's the wrong side of twenty-five."

I strategically leave out my worries about credit card bills. And the fact that since our Sunday push-up romp, I've been doing everything in my power to avoid running into Carter, while obsessing over what Lance said: love is not the opposite of hate.

"It's only six more weeks, right?"

"Right."

"You got this," she says.

Suddenly, I realize how immature I'm being. Here my baby sister is, telling me how I'll be fine while I throw my adult problems on her.

"I know! I am excited for tonight." I say the words, and all of the sudden, I truly am feeling good about tonight. I've avoided Carter all week while living in the same house. "It's my birthday, dammit. And I'm gonna have a good time tonight."

"Say hi to the water for me."

"For sure."

Davina comes into the green room and waves to me.

"There you are! You're on. We've been looking for you."

I hang up, and as I walk out to the practice stage I'm left with a silly smile on my face.

Tonight will be fun.

You only live once, right? If Carter hates me so much that he's willing to throw a party just to shove his money in my face, I might as well enjoy it.

Friday night could not be more perfect.

To my surprise, Carter, Amy, and Chandler decide to turn my birthday into a huge black tie affair.

I put on a bright, strappy, floral dress that Amy loans me. It turns out we are both around the same size, which is handy.

Lance, Joseph, and I are the first ones to arrive, aside from Carter and the captain.

My jaw drops as we approach the boat. It's huge, and

making me rethink the old adage of 'it's not the size of the boat that matters.'

We climb on board, and already I see a hive of servers busying themselves on the deck.

Inside, we find candles lit, a stocked bar, and a buffet dinner being prepared.

Joseph fixes Lance's tux. I adjust the back of my dress.

Carter appears on the other side of the dining hall, directing one of the servers about what to do with a box of beers. He notices us across the room and glances our way, unsmiling. He flexes his jaw.

Maybe it's the lighting. Maybe it's the tux. Maybe it's the fact that I now know exactly what's underneath that tux. Whatever the cause, a hot tingle spreads over my face, limbs, and core. I actually shiver in place.

"Holy shit. That is one sexy man," Joseph nods. "I see why you made him breakfast."

Carter approaches with a cocky smirk and long, confident strides.

I poke Lance's side. "Remember. Fake boyfriend mode."

"Right," Lance shoots a glare at Joseph. "And Joseph— you're here for the girls."

His shoulders sag. "Right. The girls."

"You can still talk to the basketball players," Lance adds.

"Did I mention how much I love you two?" I add.

"Louie and Jake, good to see you again," Carter's voice booms and he shakes hands with Lance and Joseph.

Joseph smiles. "It's actually Joseph."

"Right," Carter says, nodding slowly before he turns to me. "Happy birthday, Laces," he winks. "Thank you for giving me an excuse to have a solstice party and invite a crew of hot dancers to hang with my buddies. I'm going to get a shit ton of bro-credit for this."

"Well I'm getting a lot of girl credit. So I guess it's a win-win," I snap back.

But why does it feel like Carter is definitely coming out on top with this arrangement?

Lance wraps his hand around my waist. Carter's eyes fall to his hand.

"Anyways . . . Oh, hello. Who's this?"

Davina walks into the room, wearing a red dress. Carter's gaze flashes to her.

That same shiver I just felt when I saw Carter across the room comes back. Except ten times worse this time.

Lance must feel my body shake.

Carter says hello to Davina and a minute later, they are heading to the bar together, big smiles on their faces.

"You okay?" Lance asks. "You're shaking."

"I'm fine," I growl.

"Really?" Joseph asks. "Because the way you're looking at that blonde right now, I think you might start spewing venom from your eyes."

I shake my head. "It's just . . ." I let out a frustrated sigh. "Davina is a lock for New York. And the minute she walks in, Carter is all over her. Why do some girls have all the luck?"

"I think we need to get ourselves a round of drinks," Joseph says, then hesitates. "Drinks are free, right?"

I nod. "Open bar!"

"Well thank you, Carter," Joseph adds.

We head over to the bar on the opposite side from Carter and Davina. A few more dancers and ballplayers start to file in.

"Get me a rum and coke with a lime. I'm going to the bathroom. Be right back."

When I come out of the stall, Davina is standing in front of the mirror fixing her hair.

"Hey," she says with a bubbly smile. "Happy birthday! And

wow, your friend Carter is really nice."

I scoff. "He's not nice. That's just a front. He's a total cocky asshole."

To my surprise, Davina isn't deterred. Instead, she actually raises her eyebrows. "Really? I love assholes."

"You do?"

"Yeah. I get bored with nice guys. They're too . . . nice."

"Oh," I say, backpedaling as I wash my hands. "Well he's not that much of an asshole, actually. But he's known for being a womanizer. He has a twenty-four hour rule."

"What's a twenty-four hour rule?"

"He doesn't let girls stay at his place for more than twenty-four consecutive hours."

Her eyes widen. "Oh my gosh. Really?"

"Oh yeah."

Her shoulders drop, and she looks relaxed. She grabs my arm. "That is so refreshing to hear. You know, I have a problem where guys get attached to me. And we're only here for six more weeks, right? So what's the point in getting attached? You guys are just friends, right?"

My stomach hardens.

Why does everything I say seem to have the opposite effect of what I intend?

"Yeah," I swallow. "Just friends."

"Oh, wow. Thank you so much, Lacy. I wouldn't want to step on your toes."

"Oh, and Davina," I add. "I hate to say it, but he doesn't like blondes. Prefers brunettes."

"Well I guess I'll have to see if I can change his mind then." With a smile on her face, she walks out of the bathroom.

I facepalm and puff my lips out, exhaling.

"What is the matter with you, Lacy?" I say, staring into the mirror.

✤ 13 ✤

CARTER

I think every single one of my teammates comes up to me and thanks me at some point in the night.

And not like a flaccid shrug of a thank you. Like a 'holy shit Carter you are the fucking man how did you get all these gorgeous dancers in one place' hard cock thank you.

And the weather is beautiful. The captain takes us far out onto Lake Michigan, and we all watch the sunset from the deck as it sets over the beautiful empty lake. We get far enough away from the city that we can even see some stars.

All in all, it's a gorgeous night, except for the fact that I have to watch Lacy parade around with her boyfriend—what was his name again, Luke?—all night. It's infuriating. And now that we're out on the lake it doesn't matter, but I did not give Leotard Man permission to bring a plus one, so I don't know what this Joseph guy is doing here.

Every time I see Lacy, she shoots me a look of death.

This past week, she constantly avoided me. And I'm not going to lie, I do enjoy watching her parade around my apartment. Whatever she's wearing is hot, because it's her.

Whether it's yoga pants, pink booty shorts, or her dance clothes.

But tonight, she's got this floral dress on that is absolutely stunning.

Davina, her friend, keeps talking to me, and I'm nodding at whatever the fuck she's saying as I look out into the water, picturing Lacy naked.

Fucking A, how long has it been since I've had sex now? A full week? I haven't even rubbed one out.

"So?"

"So . . .?"

"I was saying, I heard a rumor you're a player. Is that true?"

"Define 'player,'" I say.

"A guy who hates women."

I squint. "Well in that case, yes, I'm a player. I absolutely hate women, except when they're saying 'Oh God, oh God, Carter," I say, imitating a girl's voice.

"Wow. You really are an asshole," Davina scoffs. "She was right."

"Who was right?"

"Your roommate. She warned me about you."

I grin, always interested to hear what Lacy might be saying about me behind my back. "Well it's all true. You should probably stay away from me. Glad you got the warning up front," I wink.

She leans in.

I swirl my vodka soda around. Amy and Chandler approach, breaking up our one-on-one.

Thankfully.

"Carter!" Amy says, running up to me and giving me the best hug I've had in some time. After she releases me, she says, "This party is amazing. Everyone is having so much fun. And that's so cool that Lance brought his boyfriend and they're chilling with Lacy."

I cock my head. "Um, excuse me?"

Amy rolls her eyes. "Uh, yeah! Lance and his boyfriend Joseph. I just saw them making out downstairs. Was that not . . . okay?"

Everyone turns to me, probably wondering if I'm some sort of homophobe.

Which is not true at all, by the way. My cousin is gay, and I once literally beat the shit out of a guy who tried to make fun of him.

My mind runs over a montage of the past couple of weeks where Lacy was hanging out with that guy. The screams coming from her room. How his hand was wrapped around her tonight, right in front of Joseph.

I glance at Amy. "Larry—I mean Lance—is gay?"

"Oh yeah," she says. "One hundred percent."

"And that's his boyfriend he's with? The same guy we saw at yoga?"

Amy nods, seeming confused by my question. "I don't understand what's so confusing about this."

I rake a hand through my hair, fumbling with my thoughts. Maybe he's bi? That's the only explanation that comes to my mind. "I need another drink," I finally say. "I'm heading downstairs."

I walk quickly, and don't invite Davina as I stride down the steps, two at a time.

Downstairs, the dance floor is popping off. It's actually a hilarious scene: a bunch of lanky basketball players and a few others.

I even catch Jake Napleton—one of the few baseball players from Chicago who got the invite—grinding with his wife. Not only does that guy like to play dirty—he also likes dirty dancing, apparently. Good man.

I rub my eyes, then scan the crowd until my eyes land on

Lacy.

Boom.

She's off to the side of the dance floor.

Taking off, I make a beeline for her.

Her eyes widen a little bit when she sees me. "Hey," she mumbles.

I don't think I've ever felt such an intense focus on her. "Where's your boyfriend?" I growl.

She swallows, and her voice shakes. "I-I'm not sure."

I give her an up-and-down. "Come with me."

A look of fear spreads across her face. "No."

I take her arm, and whisper in her ear, my voice gravelly. "That wasn't a fucking question."

I swear I can feel goosebumps rise up on her bare arm.

"Okay," she gulps. She follows me, and I don't think she has a fucking clue what's about to go down.

But neither do I.

All I know is, this girl has the ability to make me lose control, and we're reaching a boiling point.

❧ 14 ❧
LACY

My heart swirls as I follow behind Carter as he leads me to God knows where, down some hall in the giant labyrinth of the yacht.

"Where are you taking me?" I demand.

"Somewhere we can talk," he says.

"Why? We have nothing to talk about," I seethe.

He stops at a door, and pulls out a set of keys from his tux pocket. "You know, you have a funny way of showing your gratitude for this amazing birthday party."

I snort. "Fuck you. You only had this party so you could hook your friends up with the dancers. This had nothing to do with being there for me."

He opens the door and we head inside to a suite. He's got a full bar, a huge bed, and a balcony overlooking the water at a lower level.

"Holy shit. How'd you get this room?" I gawk.

He smirks, pressing his tongue against the inside of his cheek. "It's my fucking yacht. Remember?"

"Oh."

He heads to the bar in the room. "Would you like a shot of whiskey?"

"Please."

Standing behind the bar, he pours the shots.

"Your boyfriend isn't going to be jealous that you're doing shots alone with me, is he?"

"No, why would he be?"

He shrugs and hands me a full shot glass. "Just a thought. Cheers. Happy birthday, Laces."

I shake my head as I take down the shot, the heat of the liquor coating my throat. I let the discomfort throb through me. I'm not sure why Carter has brought me here, but I might as well stop holding back around him. And with how tongue-tied he's had me lately, the whiskey definitely helps.

"Only you could sound like an asshole while you're giving me a birthday shot."

"Is that what I am to you? Just an asshole?"

I nod. "You've never given me reason to think you're anything else."

He cocks his head, his gaze locked on me. His eyes look smokey in the dim light of the room. "Laces. Do you remember when you were in second grade, and I was in third?"

Liquid heat rushes into every corner of my body, and I already know what he's going to say. "Why are you bringing this up?"

Coming around the bar, he stands in my personal space. I want so badly to reach out and touch him. But something holds me back. I don't want to make the first move. If I do, he wins, somehow.

"I taught you how to tie your shoe laces. You were a late learner. All you wanted to do was take off your shoes and dance around at recess. Do you remember that?"

I swallow the knot in my throat, holding back a teary rush

of emotion. "Don't bring that up with me. We were kids. It doesn't matter anymore."

"I always admired your free spirit," he continues. "Yet with an aura of discipline. I never told you this. But the way you danced constantly—at recess, on the way home, at lunch, sometimes, you didn't even need music—inspired me to put everything I had into basketball. Looking back, you were the reason I became so obsessed with the sport. You made it okay."

Blowing out a loud breath, I run my hand down Carter's ear and cheek. "So why can't you forgive me for the silly mistake I made?" My heart palpitates as I await his response.

For a split second I see the flash of another man inside Carter's dark pupils. A man who might have a conscience. Turning his head down, his nostrils flare.

"You lied to me for so long. A full year. How could you look me in the eye every day we saw each other, and not tell me what you knew?"

My whole body tightens. "How can you never forgive me for something I did in high school? My mom told me not to tell you. I was respecting the relationship between you and your mother!" I fire back.

"Don't bring my mother into this because you can't admit to yourself how badly you hurt me."

Tears pool in my eyes. "We both—"

He cuts me off. "You knew my mom had been lying to me. You betrayed the trust of an entire childhood. I considered you one of my best friends. Not to mention the fact that we were fucking dating."

I wipe away the tears, and feel a calm resolve coming over me. "That was high school, Carter. That's teenager shit. You want to hold twenty-six year old me responsible for something I did way back then? Get a grip."

He slides his hand onto my hip and up my side, spurring

goosebumps over my whole body. "Get a grip. For as sensitive as you can be, you're cold-hearted when it comes to me. Do you want to know what the worst part is?"

"What?" I exhale, my voice shaking as he brings his hand to my cheek.

He flexes his jaw, and glares at me. Involuntarily, I reach my hand out and touch his forearm. Goosebumps roll through me all over, desire filling every inch of my body. His eyes lock onto me like lasers. "The worst part is that as bad as I hate you, I can't stop being incredibly attracted to you. Every fucking second I see you, Laces, I want to rip your clothes off and do terrible, unspeakable things to you. It makes no goddamn sense."

My heart beats like a bass drum.

"You want to punish me?"

Carter lets out a deep breath, but doesn't say a word.

"So why don't you?" I breathe, inching my face closer to him.

"Fuck you," he growls, his focused eyes searing into me like lasers. "Don't tempt me. You don't want to push me over the edge."

"Fuck you, Carter," I murmur.

Undeterred, he interlocks his hands with mine and presses me against the wall, squaring his hips and legs against mine.

The boat rocks a little, and Carter rocks into me with his hips with it to keep his balance.

Warmth surges through my body and pools in my core. I try to stifle it, but a quick moan escapes my mouth.

My eyes widen, and I cover my mouth.

"Fuck you," he repeats, saying the words slowly, with a slight grin. His low voice lingers over each sound of the phrase so that it sounds more like an invite than an insult.

My skin tingles, and my cheeks redden as he touches me, his long fingers dwarfing mine as he presses into my palms. I can feel the hardness of his cock riding up my legs and abdomen. I clench up, trying with my whole body to deny the ravenous lust I'm feeling for him.

This must stop.

As turned on as I am, I can't just let Carter ravish me just because he looks so damn sexy in a tux.

Even if I want him more than anything.

Closing my eyes, I remember how hard I've worked to get to into this summer dance competition. And a romance with a man as unpredictable as Carter will throw everything into flux.

"Carter," I swallow, pulling on the lie that Carter still believes. "I can't do this. My boyfriend's upstairs."

He smirks. "Fuck your boyfriend."

"Please, Carter . . ."

His hand slides onto my hips, and down the side of my thigh.

"Just admit it," he whispers against my ear. "We've both got some tension we need to get rid of."

Part of me wants to push him away, but another part of me wants this so fucking bad. I hesitate, saying nothing.

"Hell, I admit it. There's no use in denying it. I want you, Lacy Benson. No matter how much I might hate you."

I can feel my defenses breaking down. The part that wants Carter is in control of my body.

"I hate you, Carter," I manage to mutter, a meek protest.

"I hate you too," he growls. "But I'm also done resisting you."

"Holy fuck," I mutter, and he slides his huge hand up my thighs, slipping my dress over the curve of my ass.

He handles my ass roughly as his lips pound into mine.

This isn't just a kiss though.

I feel like I'm being manhandled.

And damn, does it feel good.

Like I'm a toy he's been thinking about playing with with for years, and only now did he finally make the decision to pull me from my box and see what I can do. And I've been sitting on the shelf, dreaming about this day.

I moan and arch my hips up into him, running my hand over the outline of his thick, hard cock still trapped in his tux pants.

Slipping his hand to my thong, he pushes its front to the side, sliding a finger over my pulsing clit. He pulls his face back from our kiss and smirks, cupping my cheek to make sure I look him in the eye.

His touch is rough and strong, but I swear I see traces of the old Carter I used to know, before I messed him up with my year-long lie.

The good Carter.

"Wow. You are wetter than the lake. Tell me, Laces. Is this for your boyfriend, or for me?"

Goosebumps form all over my skin. Running his nose up my neck, he whispers in my ear. "And no more lies."

The way he says 'lies' sends a shiver through my entire body.

"It's you," I answer honestly, though my voice shakes.

He smirks wider. It's not even a happy expression. It's the expression of someone who has just been victorious in battle.

My anger returns, and I realize just what I'm doing. And with who.

And that I can't stop.

He cups my face, and I let my hand drop down his waist and onto the outline of his cock. I wrap my hand around it--still with the cloth of his pants separating me--and bolts of desire engulf me.

"If you hate me, you have a funny way of showing it," I murmur.

I rub my cheek on his shoulder as we grind our bodies together in clumsy, passionate heat.

The heat of hate.

My chest aches with a swirl of desire, anger, and relief that this man is taking what he wants. It's not lost on me that Carter does not give a shit I'm here with a boyfriend.

I arch my head back as he circles his finger over my clit. My toes curl, my calves tighten. Pleasure ratchets through me.

"Are you on the pill?" he asks as I grind myself on his fingers.

"Yes."

"Come here," he says, taking my hand.

He leads me to the deck that overlooks the water.

The sun has long since gone down. A summer breeze brushes my face.

"You have the nicest ass I've ever seen," Carter growls as he runs his hand along my flesh. "But that's not even what does it for me."

"What does it for you?"

"That it's you."

My stomach tumbles as I consider his words. Can he really be serious? That he's thought about me like this before?

"Stick it out farther. I like how it looks."

I swallow and arch my back more. I feel like I'm on display for him. But like I'm in a trance, I obey.

"How long have you wanted this, Lacy?"

A chilly breeze hits my face, strands of my hair swaying in front of my face and I hesitate.

"Don't lie to me, either. No more games," he adds.

"I-I don't want you," I lie, a gut reaction. The words are out before I can consider them.

He slips a hand between my inner thighs, and runs it up my skin until it grazes my slit. "Right. You don't want me."

I moan and bite my lower lip to stifle the noise.

"Is that why you're so wet right now? Because you don't want me?"

The bass of the yacht's dance floor vibrates the walls of the room. The whiskey shot and the other drinks course through me. I don't want to admit to him how long I've thought about this. I can't.

Maybe I don't even want to admit it to myself.

"I . . . don't want you Carter. Even if I did, I don't do one-night stands . . . oh God. Carter." The words flow out of me, reflexive lies as I try in vain to stave off his advances.

He presses his fingers inside my pussy again. I want more. I want deeper.

I want so badly to heal the chasm between us.

I can't let him know. I refuse to give in, even as my legs quiver.

He fists my hair into a knot and pulls on it, spinning my head around to look at him.

"Well, I guess I should go then." He looks calm. Collected. Undeterred. He slips his hand from between my legs.

"No," I gasp, reaching between my legs and grabbing hold of his hand. "Keep going. Please."

I raise my eyes until they meet his, and he knows I want everything he can do to me.

"You want me to keep going? You sure?" he teases.

"I like it when you touch me Carter," I admit.

"And I like the way you moan when I touch you."

"At least we agree on something," I mewl.

Butterflies flutter inside me as he wraps his arms around my chest and pulls me up from my bent over position against the wall of the deck. His hands rub all over my body. I grind my bare ass against his cock through the tux pants, vaguely gyrating to the vibration of distant music. Cupping my breasts, he arches my back into him and kisses my neck so hard it hurts.

I let out an angry moan and slip my hand behind me to unzip him.

"Turn around," he says.

I turn and face him. He cocks his head a little bit to the side. Taking a drink in his hand from the bar in his room, he eats me alive with his eyes. "Good. I want you to take off your clothes. Leave the shoes."

Nervously, I slip my dress over my head, then look at him. He nods in approval.

"And the bra and thong too."

I freeze. He looks menacing, and absolutely powerful.

I unhook my bra, leaving me totally naked except for my shoes.

"Hands behind your back," he says.

I do it.

My eyes fall away from his face.

He tips my chin up toward him.

"How close did you get to coming when I was touching you just now?" he asks.

"Very close."

One side of his mouth turns ever so slightly up in a half-smile. "If you want that with me, you're going to have to earn it. Do you understand?"

I swallow hard and nod. "What do you want me to do?"

He lets go of my chin, and my gaze turns downward again. His hands run over my shoulders, down my skin to my tits. He presses my nipples delicately between his thumb and fore-finger, squeezing harder until I groan.

"Fuck yeah, Lacy. I love when you make those noises. So incredibly sexy."

He unbuckles his belt, takes down his pants, and brings his cock out of his briefs so it dangles inches from my face.

I bring my hands around from behind my back.

"No," he says.

"No?"

"Like I said, you need to earn it. Open your mouth."

I open it, and lean forward to try to take him in my mouth.

His hand caresses my head, and he turns my gaze back to him.

"You're going to have to open a little wider than that, Laces."

Laces. Using my childhood nickname at a time like this.

For some reason I feel competitive all of the sudden.

Or maybe it's the heat pooling between my legs. I want him to fuck me so bad. If I don't get my release from him, I might go insane.

I open my mouth as wide as I can and take him.

I want to tell him, fuck you and your cocky attitude, your ability to turn me on, and your big cock.

He knots up my hair and guides me back and forth on his cock. Starting slowly, he gives me a few inches at a time. In and out. In and out.

"Good girl," he says, pulling out. "Bring your eyes up to me. I want to see them."

I take a few desperate breaths before he thrusts his hard cock inside my mouth again, deep this time.

I try not to gag, but he's so damn powerful as he fucks my face.

But I'm in awe of the power I have over him as I hear a low, gravelly moan from his lips.

"Holy fuck that's good." He wraps his hand through my hair as he continues to fuck my face.

When he pulls my hair away this time, I'm gasping for air. He tugs on my hair and I stand up.

We share a lucid moment, examining each other's faces as

if we're both unsure if this is real. Maybe this is all a dream, and when it's over we'll go back to reality.

He grins—which worries me. I'm always worried his next devious idea will be my undoing.

But to my surprise he kisses me on the lips. "Your turn," he says. I squeal as he picks me up by the hips.

We kiss as he walks me to the bed and lays me down on my back.

"I'm naked. Why do you still have clothes on?" I protest.

"Shut the fuck up and spread your legs," he growls.

Seconds later, his tongue is on my clit and I'm leaning my pussy up and into his mouth as he licks me with all the same vigor with which he fucked my face.

As I watch him and feel him with my knees pressed back against my shoulders, it's an odd turn-on that he still has his tux on.

I tremble and grasp behind me, trying to hold on to anything that will make sense of this moment.

The thoughts come in fleeting bolts between charges of pleasure.

The hottest man I've ever known has his mouth on my cunt.

But I hate him.

This asshole is just using me for his own pleasure.

But his tongue feels so damn good right now.

He just face-fucked me with almost zero regard for the fact that I could barely breathe.

Not his fault he has a huge, airway-blocking cock.

The battle in my mind melts away as I feel the cusp of an orgasm coming.

I grab onto his head—the closest thing to an anchor in the vicinity—with both hands and twist my pelvis into him damn near violently.

Heat rolls through me and I know I'm on the brink of coming.

And he lifts his mouth off of me.

"You're close, aren't you?" he smirks, my juices still on his lips.

"Get your tux off," I beg.

He frowns. "I give the orders here. I need you to turn around now."

My eyes go wide. "Turn around?"

He doesn't say anything, just raises his eyebrows a little and stares at me.

I do as I'm told, turning around and getting on all fours.

I hear his footsteps on the ground as I face forward on the bed.

"You're a stubborn girl, Lacy," he says. "And I like that about you. But if we're going to do this, we're going to do it my way. Do you understand?"

I nod.

"Say, 'yes, I understand,'" he says.

"Yes, I understand."

"Good."

I feel a hard slap on my asscheek and a jolt of adrenaline runs through me. I moan, and then turn to him as he rubs the area of my skin he just smacked. "That all you got?" I smirk.

His jaw drops a little and he spanks me again. I breath hard as his palm hits me.

"Harder," I whisper. I close my eyes.

Thwack. Rub.

Thwack. Rub.

Thwack. Rub.

Why the fuck do I like this so much?

I hear Carter breathing hard, and the shuffling of shoes.

Buttons coming undone.

His belt buckle hits the floor.

And then I feel him, his warmth, behind me.

He runs the head of his cock over my pussy slowly. Back and forth.

I start to speak, to tell him 'just put it in already.'

But I stop myself.

That will only make him wait longer.

So I keep my mouth shut, my eyes closed, and focus on the feel of Carter's hard flesh as he presses inside me, inch by tight inch. The pressure builds in my core.

Carter's broken me.

I'm utterly and totally at his mercy.

"Please, Carter," I beg. "Fuck me, baby. Fuck me."

He slips his cock all the way in, then grabs my hair and pulls hard as he fucks me. He guides my head behind me, allowing me to see him. He's so big and tall, he gives me upside-down Spiderman kisses while he thrusts into me.

A few minutes in, I'm wondering if in spite of all Carter's talk, he might fuck sweetly, if his speed is any indication. He slowly draws in and out, seeming to relish the slow movements.

Then he stops, with his cock fully inside me, whispering close to my ear.

"I've thought about this for so long, Laces. You have no idea."

"Actually, I do," I whisper back.

I don't want to admit to him that my college roommate had Carter's picture as a poster on her wall.

But that I was the one who used the visual for my late night fantasies. Which are coming true, right this moment.

My mind melts to mush, and he speeds up his thrusts, grabs my hips, and fucks me like I've never been fucked before.

I clench around him.

He's a wild bull.

I don't feel like me anymore. He spanks me and pulls my hair from behind.

The pleasure is so damn intense, but I hold back my orgasm. I try to.

He runs his hands over my tits again and I can't hold back anymore.

"Gonna . . . come . . . now . . . please . . ." I manage to blurt out.

Instantly, he pulls out from inside me, flips me over onto my back, and my legs press against his shoulders.

My eyes bulge out of my head as he pushes inside. Carter thrusts into me again and again, skin slapping as he hits deep.

His head hangs just out of reach for a kiss, our skin sweaty as it slaps together.

"Come baby," he says in my ear. "I want you to let it all out." The throaty tone of his voice undoes me.

I scream as I clench around his cock, and scrape my nails against his back so hard I think I might be drawing blood.

Carter doesn't seem to care. His response is to grab my hips and plunge deeper with every stroke.

My orgasm crashes through me with the force of a thousand giant waves crashing onto the beach.

A sprinkling thought of the wrongness of this whole hookup only adds to the intensity. Carter squeezes my asscheeks and pins me down as his cock twitches inside me. Sliding his tongue along my neck, he sucks on my skin as he holds himself inside me. His thumb lays across my windpipe.

He lets my legs down from his shoulders as we both come back to the sphere of reality, still panting hard.

I rest my hand on his ass, wishing he would just stay inside me. When he pulls out, this whole moment is going to fade away like a figment of my imagination.

His mahogany eyes hold on me for a moment, and he pulls out.

We lie on the bed, chests heaving, fresh lake breeze rolling in from the open door, we stare at each other in the dim moonlight, and I feel like I'm seeing Carter for the first time.

He doesn't say anything either. He's looking at me with the same wide-eyed tension.

I run my hand over his abs and bring it up to his chest. Did I have this man pegged all wrong? No one who fucks like that can be all bad.

"Well," he says. "We should get you back to your boyfriend, Laces, shouldn't we?"

❧ 15 ❧

CARTER

I walk a step or two in front of Lacy as we stride down the narrow hallway of the bottom deck of the yacht.

"Carter!" Lacy yells from behind me, in a huff.

I'm not surprised she just can't stop yelling my name. I turn my head to take a look at her but I don't slow my step.

She pulls the strap of her dress over her shoulder while her heels click on the ground; she's making skip steps to keep up with me and my giant strides.

I examine her eyes. They've still got the laziness of her post-coital haze, which makes sense. How many times did she come just now? I lost count.

But she's also exuding this worried intensity. Like maybe she thinks we've just done something shameful. Her tone is biting when she finally starts to speak. "Really? You're just going to keep walking. Well that's precious. Just fucking typical of you."

I glance over my shoulder. "I like the sound of you saying 'fucking.'" You should say it again.

"Fuck you!" she yells.

Rage swells through me, and I halt us at the end of the

hallway before we head up the stairs. I grab her by the waist and press her against the wall with my hips. Taking hold of her hands, I spread out her arms behind her head.

With every breath, her chest presses into me again. I smirk down at her.

"You're serious right now, Carter? 'Time to get you back to your boyfriend'? That's all you have to say post-sex? You're unbelievable. You don't think we need a little debriefing after what just happened?"

I'm pretty sure I can still make out the points of her hard nipples through her dress. A smirk tugs at the sides of my mouth.

"Nothing to say? Good God, Carter. I'm still shaking from . . . what we did back there."

The less I say, the more she confesses. I like this. Although I'm still a little confused by the whole her-and-Lance-fucking-in-her-room thing. Was Lance just two-timing his boyfriend and hooking up with Lacy? Maybe he swings both ways.

I bite my lips as I stand still, staring at her. It's her scent. It's the way she moaned. It's the way her body molded to mine. All of those things combined leave me feeling a very mixed up emotional combination of love and hate.

What do you get when you combine those two? Hove? Late?

No. You get *Lacy*.

"You're thinking—what are you thinking?" she asks.

"Just that you're even more attractive when you're all worked up like this. And you have sex hair."

"Goddamn it, Carter. Enough with the dirty talk."

I don't budge. Instead, I wait until her wandering eyes find mine and lock on them like a guided missile.

"You want to call that dirty talk? I can get much dirtier.

And we both needed that. We've been carrying around a lot of tension."

She blinks a few times and her jaw falls open.

Clearly I've struck a chord. She shakes her head. "This is just like you. As soon as we get on a sensitive topic that would be good to talk about—like your father—you change the subject one hundred and eighty degrees. I told you, I'm sorry for how I accidentally lied to you."

"'Accidentally' lied? That's classic. I think I'm going to start using that one."

She averts her eyes, turns her head, and swallows. Her hips gyrate just the slightest bit.

I narrow my gaze at her. "And you. What are you thinking about right now?"

"None of your business."

Collecting herself, she shakes her head. She's about to say something, but she bites her lip and heads back up the stairs.

I follow her up the steep staircase. I do wonder what's going on in that pretty little head of hers.

Maybe she thinks I'm unfeeling because I don't want to cuddle and have post-sex pillow talk with her. And maybe she's right about that. But if there's one thing I've learned in my years of dating around, it's that I'm rarely in the right state of mind to have an objective discussion after sex. If that's unfeeling, well, I am callous. But I'd rather not say some stupid bullshit and have it come out the wrong way.

Plus, call me a sadist, but I want to see her try and explain what just happened in front of her "boyfriend."

Why doesn't she just come clean with me at this point?

Lacy looks hauntingly beautiful and graceful as she glides up the steps. We reach the lower deck, and she turns into the next staircase that heads to the top deck outside.

Just before she gets to the top of the upper deck, she turns and looks back at me.

I realize the moon is full, casting a shimmering light over her profile. She's glossy-eyed as we make eye contact.

For a moment, some foreign emotion wells up in my gut, inside me. It's fleeting, but I feel something I've never felt in my life. It's chemical, a strong undercurrent of desire, and I have no idea what to do with it.

I keep my gaze leveled on hers, not giving anything away with my cold, heartless facial expression. I swallow, my skin prickling with intensity as we hold onto each others' gaze.

I clench my fists and my whole body tenses up, from my gut to my jaw.

She speaks. "I never thought our first time would. . . never mind. Better get back to my boyfriend."

I cock my head a little at the 'boyfriend' remark, and squint as she disappears from view.

Now she's really fucking with my head.

Before I ascend to the top of the boat, a whoosh of thoughts whirl through me. What if Amy was wrong about Lance being gay? It's not like I have the best gaydar, myself. I've met straight guys who do modern dance. Maybe he's just a nice guy.

I try to get a hold of my wandering thoughts, but they just keep coming.

Am I the guy Lacy is using for sex behind her boyfriend's back?

No. Amy said she saw Lance making out with his boyfriend.

I grip my forehead as I try to steady myself.

Just then, Amy walks up the stairs.

"Hey Carter! Where have you been? We've been missing you. Great party!"

"Hey Amy," I grumble. "I've been . . . getting a drink."

"Oh. Where is it?" she asks, looking down at my empty hands.

"Silly me. Looks like I've finished it. I'd better go back down to the bar and get another one."

"Better hurry!" Amy says. "We're almost out of alcohol."

I chuckle. "That's impossible. I ordered twice what I thought we'd need."

Amy shrugs. "Never underestimate a crew of drunk twenty-somethings, I guess. Mind if I slip by you?"

"Sure."

I turn my body sideways so Amy can get by on the narrow staircase.

I head back downstairs, and see Chandler at the bar.

"Hey!" he yells over the music. Where have you been?"

I shrug. "Nowhere."

Chandler squints. I signal to the bartender and order a vodka soda.

"I'm gonna call bullshit on that one. You have post-sex face written all over you."

The bartender slides me a drink. "Fuck off. No idea what you're talking about," I counter.

Chandler wraps his lanky arm around my shoulder. "Okay buddy," he winks. "I have no idea what you're talking about either."

He laughs heartily and takes a sip of his drink. "Honestly man, you don't have to bullshit me. I used to be in your shoes before I was with Amy. I know how it goes at these sorts of events. Women basically throw their panties at you. I get it. All I'm saying is, no sense in lying to me about it. You can't be honest with your teammate about getting laid? Come on now."

And I have no problem being straightforward about who I am and how I behave. But for some reason, in this case, I can't quite bring myself to talk about Lacy. What we have is just between the two of us.

Some foreign feeling inside me bubbles up.

I take a swig of my drink. "No idea what you're talking about. Let's head upstairs and get some fresh air. It's getting a little stuffy in here."

"Don't want to talk about it, eh? Hey, I get that too." He takes his arm off me. "Let's head upstairs then. Amy's up there."

Chandler's toothy grin is comforting. I shake my head a little and let out a sigh.

It's almost a little disgusting to me how much Chandler and Amy are in love. Both always looking for each other at parties like these. I try to think of any girl I've ever felt remotely like that about, and draw a total blank.

"Bro." Chandler punches me in the shoulder, not too hard. "What's the matter with you?"

"Nothing. You and Amy are cute, is all. And yeah, I just saw her as I came down here. She was looking for you."

"Upstairs it is then."

16

LACY

My hair blows in the wind as I stand on the deck looking out over Lake Michigan.

The moon is full, illuminating the numerous skyscrapers up and down the shoreline in the distance. It's a beautiful sight.

I wish I could enjoy it. Instead, all I can think about is Carter.

I fight not to think of him, because I refuse to give my energy over to assholes. But my mind is like a Chinese finger trap. The more I fight to clear him from my mind, the more he's all I can think about.

His ability to dominate me like no one else has.

The feel of his rock hard body pressing into me.

The flecks of darker brown in his eyes as I clenched around him.

My inability to control myself as he made me come multiple times.

Last but not least, Carter's distance after we finished.

Not like he's ever been one to be emotionally vulnerable. I, of all people know that. But telling me he had to get me back to my "boyfriend" seconds after we finished? It's as though Carter relishes in torturing me, which makes me so damn conflicted.

I'm inescapably attracted to him. Yet, I have my doubts that he could ever show his tender side.

Plus, I have a sinking feeling in my stomach that I was just a quick fuck for him. The girl from home who he was never able to conquer.

Until tonight.

And damn, I'd be lying if I say I don't love how I feel when he conquers me.

When Carter wants something, nothing stands in his way. Even when a girl he wants has a boyfriend, apparently.

His words ring in my ear. *That wasn't a question, Lacy. Come with me, now.*

I heave a deep sigh as I swig from my beer. It's not even that cold, but it was unopened when I found it on the top deck of the yacht. And that's just the kind of mood I'm in right now.

I run a hand through my hair.

And the worst thing about it all? Even if I deny him with my words, Carter knows how badly I want him. When he pressed me up against the wall and interlocked his hands with mine, I had to fight to stop myself from moaning again in his grip.

From one asshole—who dumps me the day I finally decide to move to his city—to another.

Straight-up asking Carter to be nicer to me has been one big fail. The man does not respond to requests. And then *he* has the balls to tell me I'm the one who has a questionable character?

I jump when I feel a hand on my shoulder. I whip my head around.

It's Davina.

"Hey," she says, her voice soft. I do my best to relax my body and play nice. "How's it going?"

"Good," I say. "Just getting some air."

"It's a beautiful night out," she says. "You sure you're okay? You look stressed."

I clench up. Is her whole reason for talking to me just to comment on how out of it I currently seem? On the other hand, it's not like that's an inaccurate comment. My stomach is in knots.

"I'm fine," I shrug. "It's been a fun night."

Davina leans next to me on the railing. Her blond hair blows in the wind. Even when her hair is messy, she's totally gorgeous.

"Well, I just want to let you know. I've heard you're from a small town. I'm from New York, so Chicago is like a play town to me. Don't take this the wrong way, but I've watched you dancing over the last couple of weeks. And you're really good. But I feel like you aren't sure of yourself. If you had a little more confidence, I think you'd have one of the top spots, easy."

"Really?"

I'm suddenly struck by Davina's niceness. Maybe I've misjudged her all along.

It's not her fault she looks perfect all the time, even when her hair is being blown every which way by an open lake breeze.

She nods and takes her hand away. "I do. By the way, have you seen Carter?"

My smile fades as I wonder if she came up to talk to me for the sole reason of finding out about Carter.

"No, I haven't seen him lately," I lie. "Why, are you looking for him?"

"It's just . . . it's weird," she says. "I was talking to him a little while ago, and when he found out Lance was gay, he stormed off."

My heart skips a beat. "Oh."

She grins. "Yeah, weird, right? I mean, Lance is here with his boyfriend. I'm pretty sure they were making out earlier. Does it get any more obvious?"

My blood boils. So when Carter told me he'd better get me back to my boyfriend, he was just toying with me? And he didn't exactly give me a whole lot of runway to explain myself and why I decided to fake things with Lance.

"Yeah," I joke. "Well that's funny! I . . . gotta go to the bathroom. I'll be back," I say, taking off.

"I have to go to the bathroom, too," Davina says, following after me.

"Okay," I say, stepping quickly to the stairs. I take a step down and my phone buzzes. I stop and check. It's Lance, telling me he's on the top deck and asking me where the hell I am.

"You know what, Davina? Come with me. Let's play a little trick on Carter."

Her eyes light up. "What did you have in mind?"

"Just follow me. I'll explain."

"Guys!" I yell, throwing up my hands. "What happened to fake boyfriend mode!"

Lance pushes off Joseph, and then gives anyone in the vicinity—which is no one—a confused look. "Oh my God! That was weird."

I roll my eyes, holding back a slight smile at his antics. "It's okay. I'm glad you're having fun. But—we have a situation. And I need your help. Both of you."

Joseph's arm is still wrapped around Lance. "What's the matter, honey?"

I normally don't kiss and tell. But on the other hand, I have rarely had much to kiss and tell about. And something is gnawing at me to confess what Carter and I did, if only to one person. Or two people, in this case.

"I kinda . . . slept with Carter."

Davina's eyes widen. I shrug and look at her. "I might as well let you into the circle of trust at this point," I say.

Joseph and Lance's jaws drop. "Just now?" Lance asks. "Like on this boat?!"

I nod. "He has a room on the bottom deck."

Lance frowns. "What happened to your boyfriend, though?"

"He apparently doesn't care that I have a boyfriend."

"Wow," Davina nods. "You were right. He really does have some issues."

"Holy shit, that's hot," Joseph blurts. "And speaking of bottom decks, I wish I could see his bottom deck."

Lance frowns. "Honey. Really?"

"What?!" Joseph quips. "You're the one who said he was hall-pass worthy."

"Hall-pass worthy?" I question.

"Yeah. You know," Joseph answers. "Like a guy . . . or girl . . . who is so hot that if you had the opportunity, your significant other would grant you an, ahem, exception." He wiggles his eyebrows. "A hall-pass."

"Ohh," I nod. "I get it."

Lance frowns at Joseph. I have a feeling hall-pass is one of those 'better in theory than in practice' types of situations.

Lance grabs his drink from the arm of the couch they're sitting on, takes a sip, and when he puts it down his expression is inquisitive.

"Wait a second," Lance says, and holds one finger up. "So you're telling me that Carter was under the impression that you had a boyfriend, and hooked up with you anyway?"

I sit down next to them. "I'm not one hundred percent

sure. I think he may have somehow found out you two were gay."

Joseph shrugs. "Honestly, we've been a little careless with our makeouts tonight. But we're on a yacht!"

"I know," I sigh. "It's okay. But something is messed up with Carter. The very first thing he said to me after we were done having sex was 'I better get you back to your boyfriend.'"

"Ohhh! He was totally fucking with you!" Lance practically yells.

"Yes. He was. And now I want to fuck with Carter. But I'm going to need you guys to play pretend for one more hour. Think you can do that?"

"Ohhh," Joseph says. "She's got a plan! I'm excited! What do you need from us?"

"Well, it involves you pretending you're straight—hardcore straight—for one more hour." I put my hand on Joseph's forearm. "I need you in on this too."

He laughs. "Honey, I pretended I was straight for my parents for twenty-one years. I think I can handle one more hour."

"Wow. That's unexpectedly dark."

Lance rubs his back. "It's all good, Lace. We enjoy helping you. And Joseph never gets to utilize his theatre minor these days. He's too busy using his Ph.D in Psychotherapy."

"But tonight, I forget everything I learned in psychotherapy school and return to my acting ways in college. I can be straighter than a Boy Scout at summer camp."

I run a hand through my hair, slightly unsure of what he means by that. "Anyways, when we're done, you're released from being my fake boyfriend with whom I have loud sex."

Lance frowns. "Can I still come over and make you and Carter bacon and eggs some mornings?"

I roll my eyes.

"Just kidding," Lance adds. "Bad Lacy is coming out of her shell. I like where this is heading."

So Carter wants to mess with my head on purpose? Two can play at this game. Time to give him a taste of his own medicine.

Shewolf by Shakira comes out of the speakers, and I smile devilishly at how appropriate a song it is as I look up at the full moon.

"Just do me a favor," I say, lowering my voice and looking to see if anyone's around. "When Carter comes by, let's play a trick on him. Lance, pretend we're dating. Joseph, act like you and Davina are together. Have some fun with it."

Davina bites her lip. "Oohh, I like games like this."

"What's in it for us?" Joseph quips.

I scrunch my face up. "Helping a friend?"

"How about you tell us what happened with you and Carter," Lance begs. "The real story. I want to know, where did you and Carter go wrong?"

Looking down at my full drink, my mind floods with memories. The warm wind brushes my face, and I feel my body buzzing.

"I'm glad this boat isn't docking tonight, because this story is going to take a while."

"We're all ears," Joseph says, sipping his drinks.

I draw a circle in the air. "Circle of trust, guys. Do not tell anyone this story. It's between us only."

17

LACY

Ten Years ago, Junior year of high school

"HEAD TO BED, HONEY," MY FATHER SAYS, SHOOING ME UP the stairs. His breath smells like whisky, and he's still got a flask of Wild Turkey in his hand, waving at me as I go up the stairs.

My sister is already fast asleep, and I should be too, except when you're sixteen and you hear your mother outside crying with her best friend, your ears perk up.

"Why, Dad? What are Mom and Mrs. Flynn talking about out there?"

We both get to the top of the stairs, and he pauses, floating his eyes away from me and taking another swig of his bottle.

He's never been the same since he lost his job two years ago.

"Some things, honey, ain't for little girls to know about. You'll grow up and have your own problems some day. But let Mrs. Flynn and your Mom talk it out in private."

"Fine," I mutter, crossing my arms and stomping to my room.

I wish Carter were here. Our Moms are like two peas in a pod when they get together, gossiping about things from the town and reminiscing about their glory days in high school. I love when Mrs. Flynn brings Carter along, because he always finds something to do to entertain the both of us.

We've been hanging out together since I was a little kid, and he even taught me to tie my shoe laces. *Laces*, he called me after that. "I'll help you with anything else you need," he'd say with a wink. I tried making fun of him back, calling him "Lil Carter," but the name didn't exactly stick after Carter hit his second high school growth spurt.

Cartwheel stuck, though.

The truth is, I enjoy when he calls me Laces.

In my room, I close my door and open my window. We live on the outskirts of the town, and the sound drifts, so I can pick up snippets of their conversation.

Between sobs, I hear one word many times over. "Carter...Carter..."

Furrowing my brow, I turn my ear to the window, straining to hear the conversation. The wind picks up, howling, and I can't hear a thing.

I head out of my room, and down to my parent's room. Creaking the door open ever so slowly, I see what I expected: my father passed out in the room, with lights on, snoring. The Wild Turkey is on the desk next to him. I sigh. It's sad to see him like this, when even just three years ago, he was the most disciplined man I knew, waking up at four thirty A.M. to head to his shift at the tool and dye factory.

Now he can't even stay up ten minutes to keep his curious daughter from eavesdropping on her mother.

Tip-toeing downstairs, I head to the front of the downstairs. Cracking a window ever so slightly--and slowly--I press my ear to the screen and listen.

"He's been threatening me again," Mrs. Flynn says. "He called me the other day. Sometimes I'm afraid, I'm afraid he'll come here and do something crazy."

I bite my nails, feeling my heart palpitating deeply.

"Something crazy? Like what?" comes my mom's voice.

There's a pause, and I hear them pouring more wine.

"I don't know. Like . . . something menacing. I don't think he's got it in him to kill us, but who knows? Carter's father is a sociopath. He'd do anything to get what he wants. He didn't even want me to have Carter."

"So what did you tell him?" my mom asks.

"I told his father to mind his own asshole business. That I want nothing to do with him and his double life. That the decision to find him will be up to Carter when he turns eighteen, if he wants to seek out his father."

The hair on the back of my neck stood up when I heard that. Carter's dad--as far as anyone knew--had been dead since he was one year old. Mrs. Flynn said he'd suffocated on a pillow in freak accident, and we'd never thought to question it, it's not the sort of question you ask politely.

I keep eavesdropping, hanging on Mrs. Flynn's every word.

"I just . . . sometimes I hate this life, you know? But Carter's the best thing that's ever happened to me. I wish things could have been different."

My mom starts to cry too. "It's my fault. I should have never decided to go to Vegas for my stupid bachelorette party."

Dalila shook her head. "Not your fault. That was a fantastic weekend."

"Aside from the fact that you happened to meet the craziest, most psychopathic liar that the world has ever known."

"And the best looking. And most charming. It's my fault I couldn't see through that."

"No, honey," my mom says. "It's not your fault. How on Earth could you have known? You've always thought the best of people."

Mrs. Flynn's sobs grow louder. "I've never done that. I've never had a one-night stand in my life! I've never even thought about it! And then, the one time I do it, poof!"

"Do you feel safe? You know you can stay here with Hank and me." My mom raises her eyes to the sky. "God knows we have our own problems, though. Since the tool and dye factory closed down, Hank hasn't been the same."

"Still drinking?"

"Too much. He's so up and down. He'll make it a few days sober and be on an upswing, maybe even get a temp job. Then after a few days he'll get taken off of his job and start drinking again. He's just been bouncing from construction company to company now. He's not the same. I'm afraid it could rub off on Lacy and Eliza."

A silence overcomes the two of them. For the first time, I see my mom and Mrs. Flynn as fallible humans. My mind is totally blown.

I sit down on the couch, trying to process all of this new information. My heart beats a mile a minute. I start to cry. Not like a sob—more of a glazed over, stoic bawling. A cab comes and picks up Mrs. Flynn, and when my mom came into the house, she slaps her hand over her heart, shocked at seeing me in tears on the couch."

"Honey," she gasps. "What are you doing awake?"

A tear rolls down my cheek. "Mom, is Carter's father alive?"

She sits down on the couch next to me, her expression shaky, her eyes glossed over. "It's complicated, honey," she says as she takes my hand.

"No it's not," I said, wiping a tear away. "Is Carter's father still living? Is his heart still beating? It's a yes or no question."

My mom's voice trembled as she spoke.

"Honey. You're young. But life can sometimes get very complicated when you're older. Carter's father was not a nice man. For all our purposes, he's dead."

"But his heart is still alive and beating. In the world," I counter.

With tears in her eyes, my mom nods. "Honey, some day I'll explain all of this to you. But right now, I have to ask you something very important. I know this is all probably very shocking to you to find out. But there are some things that are between mother and son. And you can't tell Carter about this. It's up to his mom. Can you keep that secret?"

"I don't like keeping secrets. I'm not good at it."

"Please, honey. As much as I know you like Carter, it's not our place."

"Not our 'place?' What is that supposed to mean?"

She swallows, then puts her hand on my shoulder. "Honey, when Carter turns eighteen, he'll have the option to know all of this. Until then, it's none of our business."

I swallowed the lump in my throat. "Okay," I agreed reluctantly.

"Good girl," she said, caressing my hand. "Do you have any other questions?"

"Where is Carter's father? Is he going to hurt Carter?"

She heaved a deep sigh. "Carter's father lives in a town far away from here. For a long time, he didn't know that Carter was alive. But now that he knows, he doesn't like it. He won't hurt Carter though, I promise."

"So why did Carter's mom get scared tonight, all of the sudden?"

"Like I said, honey, it's complicated. And there are times in life where ignorance is bliss."

"Ignorance is bliss," I repeat. Swallowing, I vow not to tell him.

❦

I SEE CARTER A FEW TIMES LATER THAT WEEK, PASSING HIM in the gym when I'm doing a summer dance camp for kids, and he's running the basketball camp. He notices I'm acting weird and he asks me about it.

"What's the matter, Laces?" he asks, grinning widely. It's a true grin, from eye to eye, and I wonder if maybe my mom is right. Maybe Carter is better off not knowing. "Forget how to tie your shoes again? You know, I can help you with that."

"Yeah," I say sheepishly. "No actually, I was wondering if you want to get some ice cream after camp is over today? It's so hot out."

"Hell yeah, you know I do. Gotta run. Catch you after."

Thinking it's just a little white lie,

I swallow the truth, and ignore my instinct to tell him.

Little do I know how badly that decision will come back to haunt me.

❦

NEXT SUMMER, JUST AFTER CARTER'S EIGHTEENTH birthday, we'd played basketball in the park. He asks if I would go home with him to chat for a little while.

When we got back to his house, I can see his eyes gloss over.

"Lacy. I just found out something wild."

"What's that?" I croak, hoping against hope that somehow, my prediction that he's thinking about his father is wrong.

"My dad didn't die by suffocation of a pillow. He's alive. My mom told me yesterday."

Carter brings his eyes to mine. He looks like he just saw a ghost.

"Oh," is all I can say.

I want so badly to make the pain in his heart go away.

"Oh?" he raises an eyebrow.

"I mean, uh, that's crazy," I say, sounding insincere.

Taking a step back, he gives me an ugly, mean look. "Lacy, that is a weird as fuck reaction to some very personal information I just told you. What's going on with you."

He has black rings under his eyes, like he hadn't slept for days. My mom's words ring in my ear.

Ignorance is bliss.

Pandora's box has been opened, and it's not coming back. "I know he's alive," I whisper.

"What?!"

"I heard from your mom last summer," I admit.

His eyes practically bulge out of his head.

"You fucking *knew?* You knew and didn't tell me!"

I break down, fully sobbing. "I thought ignorance was bliss. I figured this was between you and your mother!"

"You didn't think, I would like to fucking know that my own father was alive?"

I swallow, words escaping me. "Please, Carter. You know I care about you more than anyone."

The angst in his tone when he says the next words is palpable.

"I thought I cared about you, too. I cared about you a lot more than you can even imagine. I thought wrong. Get away from me."

"Please, just give me a chance, Carter. Let me explain."

"You've explained enough," he growls. "Now get the fuck out of my house."

18

CARTER

Present

CHANDLER AND I HEAD UPSTAIRS TO THE TOP DECK, FULLY armed with drinks. I, for one, can't wait to get shitfaced and forget about life for a little while.

Upstairs, we lean against the railing and let the warm Lake Michigan air brush across our faces.

"It's fucking hot," Chandler says as he takes a swig of his beer.

I nod. "Makes me think of warm summer nights in Blackwell."

"Blackwell is downstate, right?"

"Yeah, pretty much dead center in the southern midwest. It's a tiny town, though. You've probably never been there."

Chandler rakes a hand through his hair. "Your folks still live there?"

"My mom does."

"Not your Dad?"

I shake my head, and let a little huff escape me. "No."

Chandler furrows his brow. "Oh? Where's he live?"

I tense up. This isn't a subject that I like talking about. Especially while I'm trying to process what just happened with Lacy.

And even moreso when I'm actually trying to have a good time.

"No fucking clue," I say simply.

Chandler nods. "Seriously? I can relate."

I scoff. "Dude. Fuck you. You don't know shit about me. You can't relate." My blood boils. Chandler may be a good teammate and friend, but he doesn't know shit about my life.

Growing up, I believed my father was dead, only to learn when I was eighteen that he was very much alive. And that he didn't want anything to do with me. I was his bastard baby.

"Fuck me? Dude, you don't know shit about me," he replies firmly with an icy cold glare, the moonlight highlighting his profile.

I tense my jaw, and stand up, realizing he's right. Chandler could have an absentee father just like me for all I know.

He stands, and we lock eyes. We both take sips of our beers, tension thick in the air like there's a Jell-o mold of it all around us.

"Do yourself a favor. Don't ask about my father again," I growl.

Chandler smirks. "Alright, pretty boy. Whatever you say. I don't want to get your panties in a bunch. Seems like you've got some unaddressed shit there, though."

I grab him by the collar. He puts his hand over my wrist. "Don't. Fucking. Touch me," I growl.

We stare into each others' eyes, neither of us backing down. We're a similar height. Lean build. I look down on his hand.

"Touch you? You touched me first. And you want to punch me?" Chandler baits. "Go ahead. But I can tell it's not me that you're mad at. You don't trust me? That's fine. You have no reason to. I'll just tell you my story and you tell me if you think it's bullshit."

I let go, trying to calm myself and listen.

"Two years ago, I was playing ball in Europe, sleeping with basketball groupies left and right. Amy came to Barcelona on a chance visit. She helped me realize I'd never even met my own father. So I finally found him. He was living in squalor and filth. A total loser. I left his house and vowed never to speak to him again. And I haven't. Because fuck him. And he had control over me until I met him. I'm getting married to Amy this summer—as you know—and I couldn't be fucking happier. I wasn't going to let that fucker affect my life any more than he already had."

I clench my jaw listening to Chandler's monologue.

I let my shoulders drop a little, and let go. "I didn't know all that."

"Because I don't like talking about it. Probably less than you do, actually."

I rake a hand through my hair, a brick forming in my stomach. "Let's not talk about this right now, man."

"Right," Chandler says. "Let's talk about how you banged Lacy."

"It was unexpected."

"Ha! I fucking knew it. Got ya," he smiles.

"Motherfucker. Not a fucking word to anyone," I say, poking him in the chest.

Just then, Amy approaches. "Hey you two! I've been looking all over for you!"

"Hey baby." Chandler wraps her up for a big hug and a kiss.

"You guys are gross."

"Aww. Is Carter jealous, baby?" Amy giggles into Chandler's chest, then whispers something into his ear.

"What's that?" Chandler says in an exaggeratedly loud voice. "You want to fuck on the yacht tonight?"

She punches his chest. "Not so loud. Besides. I meant later. Right now, the birthday girl just invited us to play some truth or dare with her boyfriend."

Chandler spits out his drink. "Did you just say . . . Lacy's boyfriend?"

"Yeah. With that guy Lance. Honestly, I thought he was gay, but apparently he's not! And apparently they are dating. Did you know that, Carter?"

Chandler shoots me a wide-eyed glance.

I rub my head. Was my intel false that Lance was gay?

Did I hook up with Lacy on the same boat as her *boyfriend?* Maybe he's bisexual, and in an open relationship.

I decide to play it cool. "Yeah. Of course I knew that. They've been over to my place a few times. They're always working on new moves in my living room."

"Ohh, that's so cute!" Amy giggles, rubbing Chandler's shoulder.

We head around to the other end of the deck, and see the crew of four sitting there. My heart drops to my feet when I see Lacy wrapped up in Lance's arms.

So she did have a boyfriend. She wasn't lying. I swallow a hard lump in my throat.

And it's definitely not a lump of indifference.

❦ 19 ❦

CARTER

I stare at the four of them. Joseph, Lance, Davina, and Lacy.

Their expressions are blank yet stressed, as if someone just killed a puppy.

Chandler, Amy, and I take a seat around the table, my mind swimming with muddled thoughts.

Now I feel a pang of guilt for sleeping with Lacy and ruining her relationship with this poor, happy guy who has no idea I was inside his girlfriend not one hour ago.

She'll never be able to be totally truthful with him again.

"Oh good, you found them! We wanted to play some couples truth or dare," Lacy says, brushing her hair behind her ear. "And we supposed we could invite you too, Carter."

I scratch my head. What the fuck is going on? Am I living in the twilight zone? I plaster a giant fake smile on my face. "Leo. Jacob. Good to see you again."

"I'm Lance, actually."

"And I'm Joseph. You seriously haven't learned our names by now?"

A smirk tugs at my lips.

"Carter! Have you had too much to drink? Forgetting my boyfriend's name?" Lacy flips her black hair in my direction and and gives me a positively devilish grin.

The way she says 'boyfriend' sends a wave of chills over me. Maybe it's time for me to stop fucking with their names.

"You just don't look like a Lance," I shrug.

Drinking down the rest of my beer in a few large swigs, I reach in the cooler under the table and grab another.

"Whoa. There is beer in there?" Lance asks.

"Yep. One of the secrets you only know if you own the yacht," I wink.

"Secret stash, nice."

"You like secrets, do you?" I say.

Lance clears his throat. "What do you mean by that? Do you know something I don't know?"

"Here, have one," I say, reaching in and grabbing a few.

And I'm going to need it, watching Lance with his arm wrapped around Lacy.

Davina's long legs rest on top of Joseph's thighs.

I clench my fists as I watch the scene.

"Davina, is this your—" I start.

"Boyfriend? Yeah. Joseph moved here from New York. I guess we really put one over on you with that bit about him being gay, didn't we?" she winks.

My heart drops.

"Oh. Yeah you did. Is that your thing, you like your girl to flirt with other guys and see how they react?"

Joseph smiles, putting his arm around Davina. "It is. I guess you could say we like to get in a little . . . freaky. Can I ask you a question, Carter?"

"Go ahead," I say, rubbing my forearm.

"Do you eat a lot of pineapple?"

"It's my favorite fruit. Why do you ask?"

He shrugs. "No reason. Just curious. I've heard professional basketball players eat them."

I squint. "What the hell? I've never once heard that in my life. I mean pineapples are delicious, sure.

"Did you know that when European explorers first encountered the fruit in the Americas, they called them 'pineapples' because of their resemblance to pine cones?"

"Joseph, stop being so silly," Davina says, sounding a little drunk.

I turn to Amy and Chandler to see if they're sensing something weird going on too, but they are making out.

"So. Truth or dare. Let's fucking play," I say. "I'm pumped."

Lacy blinks a few times, appearing thrown off by my intensity.

"I'll go with dare," I continue. "Who's asking me?"

"I am," Lance says. Slowly, he runs his eyes over me. "I dare you to take off your shirt, Mr. Pineapple."

I hammer on my drink. Hell, if they're going to fuck with me, I might as well make things interesting. I smile broadly. "I'll one up you. How about I dance around a little bit while I take it off? I'm sure the, uh, *ladies* would appreciate a little showtime."

"Yes," Lance says, rubbing his hands together. "I'm sure the *ladies* would."

Lacy leans her head against Lance's shoulder. I glare at them, then turn up the music.

"Well, this escalated quickly," Amy says as I do a little spin move and whip off my suit jacket.

When I untie my black bow tie, and start to undo my white button-down shirt, I carefully note the expression on all of their faces.

A smile surges through me. I have a perfect idea of what this entails.

I twirl in a circle, busting my best hip shake as I take down the buttons. I especially note the faces of Davina and Lacy's boyfriends.

They're fixated on me.

Taking my shirt all the way off, I dance around Magic Mike style to a techno song that comes on. I swear, I see one of the guys' cocks move in their pants.

I squint at Lance. "Satisfied?"

"Very," he chokes out.

"Your turn," I say, turning to Lacy.

She hesitates, and I take advantage of her brief hesitation to select for her.

"I think you'll take truth," I say.

"I think—"

"You'll take truth," I reinforce, taking a swig of my drink.

Everyone looks at me, a little awkwardly. Like I give a shit.

She wants to put one over on me? Make me watch her with some other guy's hands wrapped around her?

"Did you or did you not fuck Larry—I mean Lance—in my house the other night?"

They look at each other and hesitate, telling me all I need to know.

Lacy hunches her shoulders, tensing up. "I think I'm going to be sick," she says, getting up, and hustling toward the railing of the ship.

I wiggle my eyes at Lance. "Better run after her," I say.

He pinches his expression, then scurries off.

I want to run after her, too.

At least part of me does.

But after this shit she's pulling right now, I need to set the record straight once and for all.

✺ 20 ✺

LACY

When I wake up the next morning, the yacht is docked, and I'm passed out in my clothes on a bed in one of the private rooms with Lance, Joseph, and Davina.

My head throbs.

Not surprising, considering the amount of alcohol I drank last night. And the emotional drain from refreshing my memory about Carter and me, and where we went wrong.

Though it did feel good to get out of my system, I must admit.

Drunken story therapy. I'll have to ask Joseph if there is any research to support that as a practice.

Suddenly I flash to a weird dream I had where Carter and I were hooking up.

I breathe a huge sigh of relief about how impossible that is, and step into the bathroom, leaning in to look in the mirror.

What's that mark on my neck?

I squint to see, looking a little closer.

Is that . . . *teeth?*

I greedily suck down as much water as I can handle.

Advil. Where is it? I'm going to need it.

Lance slowly saunters into the bathroom.

"Good morning you sexy bitch," he says, drawing out every word in an extremely groggy voice.

"Morning Sunshine," I echo, my voice similarly dreary, and definitely not sunshiney.

"I feel like I got run over by a train," he sighs.

I giggle. "Probably because you and Joseph sneaked off for a little while."

"We did?"

I shrug. "Honestly, I'm not sure. I guess I'm assuming. Also, why is Davina in our bed?!"

"Beats me," Lance shrugs, peering through the open bathroom door.

I run my hand over my hickeys again. "And I have these! We didn't make out, did we?"

Lance furrows his brow. "How drunk were you?"

"On a scale of one to ten?"

"Sure."

"I'd say like a twenty-four."

Lance puts his hand on my shoulder. "I'll take the blame. I was the one who said we should do those extra shots at the end of the night."

"It's okay. I just—I don't usually have dreams when I'm drunk. But I had this weird dream last night that I hooked up with—get this—Carter! Can you believe that?!"

Lance spins my body toward his. "Honey. You *did* hook up with Carter. At least you told me you did. And I could see the soft glow of your skin in the moonlight."

My eyes widen, and I put my hands on my hips. "Liar."

"You seriously don't remember last night? How you and Carter sneaked away!? And then you tried to play a trick on everyone so he still thought you were. Which seemed to be going fine, until Carter destroyed all the fun."

My eyes widen to the size of walnuts, and a rush of adrenaline flows through me as the night comes flooding back to me.

I lean against the sink to keep my balance. Lance holds onto my hips.

"Oh my gosh. I *did* hook up with Carter."

Heat flushes through me as I remember all the things we said and did. How his hands were everywhere on me. How hot it was, and how he dominated me.

How badly I wanted more.

"He just shoulder-tapped you and swooped you away. I don't think anyone would have predicted that move. He's a wild, wild man."

I swallow, feeling my face reddening. "Yeah. And an asshole. An asshole who made me come harder than anyone I've ever been with. Oh. Shoot. Did I just say that out loud?"

Lance nods. "It's okay. I assumed he fucked you better than I did."

I muster the slightest giggle. My stomach quivers.

"I think I'm going to get out of here, take an Uber home from the dock, and get some actual, non-drunk sleep."

"I'm no doctor, but if I were, I think that's exactly what I'd prescribe you," Lance says.

❦

BACK AT HOME, I COLLAPSE ON THE BED, BARELY MAKING IT out of my clothes and washing my makeup off. I fall into a deep slumber.

I wake up to the sound of singing in my shower.

Carter's voice, singing along to what sounds like some old Beastie Boys song.

My blood curdles just picturing him.

Singing. In the shower. Being frivolous. He's crawled into me like some kind of virus who I can't get rid of.

I shut my eyes as hard as I can and pretend he's not there.

Carter's not singing in the shower.

Last night didn't happen.

Those hickeys on my neck don't exist.

Part of me wants to believe those things, because my life would be a whole lot less complicated without them.

Carter belts another note of the song. I pull my pillow over my eyes and ears, hoping to blot out reality.

What am I going to do, go after him right now and have another naked shower confrontation? I sit up in bed, put on my headphones, and listen to my own music, *Maroon 5, A Girl Like You,* for a few minutes until I hear the water stop. Once I hear footsteps on the ground heading back to his room, and his door shut, I grab my towel and head to the shower.

The hot water feels amazing on my body. I wash my hair, and then just enjoy the feeling of the stream of water hitting my skin for a few minutes.

I get out, wrapping my hair with a towel and another one around my body.

As soon as I step into the hallway, I see Carter.

He's staring at me while he eats peanut butter out of the jar with a spoon.

"Hey," he says in a low voice, tipping his forehead. "Oh. You're not decent. Never mind."

I squint at him. "What's that supposed to mean?"

"You don't have any clothes on. Put some clothes on, and then I would like to talk to you."

"We have nothing to talk about," I scoff, feeling my heart beating harder than I ever remember.

Except for maybe last night when Carter made me take my clothes off.

"Oh? So we're just going to walk around like last night didn't happen."

"I'm perfectly willing to write off last night if you are. Honestly, I'd prefer it didn't happen."

He saunters toward me slowly, smirking a little. I tense up as he brushes his mouth against the towel on my head.

"Really? You want to forget?"

"Yes."

"So you want to forget about the way your body caved to me. You want me to forget how sweet you tasted. And we especially should forget how much we both loved what we did."

The hair on the back of my neck stands up. "Carter. Stop talking like that."

He pulls back away from me, and lets his head fall to one side of his shoulder. "Why don't you make me?"

My blood boils. "Just stop!" I move to push him out of my way, and I do move him, a little.

Like half an inch. Pushing Carter's lean, athletic frame is like trying to move a wall.

Frustrated, I look him in the eye. "Yes I enjoyed last night with you. Yes you gave me toe-curling orgasms. No, I've never been with a man who I've been so dirty with—and liked it. And I hate—*hate*, with all my heart—the fact that it's you who I happen to have this stupid chemistry with. But I can assure you, that was a one time thing. It's not going to happen again in a million years. Are you fucking happy now?!"

I feel my body throbbing with heat as the words spew out of me.

Carter's expression barely alters during my diatribe. He smirks as he pulls out the spoon out of his mouth with a little less peanut butter on it than when it went into his mouth.

He shrugs. "I appreciate you being mostly honest."

I arch an eyebrow. "What do you mean, *mostly?* That was pure, one hundred percent honesty. *Cartwheel.*"

"That last part. About it being a one time thing. And not happening in a million years. That's a big fat lie if I've ever heard one."

"It's not a lie." I tip my chin up. "How would you know, anyway?

"Because I know what a one-night stand feels like. And what we have definitely isn't a one-night attraction."

"It was a mistake!" I yell back, starting to tremble.

Heat flashes through my body thinking about Carter with other women.

He shakes his head a little, frowning. "Or could it be that you wanted to lie to me? You wanted me to hurt?"

He twists the spoon in his mouth.

I belt out my response with my hands on my hips. "You really think I would hurt you on purpose? If that's what you believe, I'm done talking to you."

Turning on my heel, I start to leave.

Carter speaks in a slow, low voice. "Don't you dare leave this conversation right now. We're not done," he growls.

I freeze in place. There isn't an ounce of joking or sarcasm in his tone.

"W-we're done," I stutter, but I try to stay steadfast. "Last night was an outlier."

"So you didn't like the way being with me felt last night?"

I freeze up. My legs suddenly feel like Jell-o. "I faked it," I lie. "I'm not attracted to you in the slightest."

My mouth moves before I can think, again. I feel a little bad for lying to Carter, but I'll say whatever I have to so that we don't hook up again. It's not about attraction. It's about self-preservation.

Carter's reckless, and I can never hand my heart over to him. I have to protect it. I remind myself that as much as I wish he could be the Carter I used to know before he found out his father was alive—he never will be that carefree again.

"You faked it?" He chuckles, his voice low. "Look me in the eye, and say that again."

I feel frozen to the ground. He takes a step toward me and, brushing his finger across my face, tips my chin up at him.

"I'm not denying that any of what I did was right. It wasn't. But I'm not going to let you skewer me like some stupid sucker. *You* were the one who started lying. Not me."

I swallow, and my heart starts to beat like crazy. "C-Carter. You know I didn't mean to hurt you."

"Oh yeah? You just figured I would find out on my fucking own that my dad wasn't dead like my mom had told me all those years! You fucking *heard* your mom and my mom talking about how my dad tried to contact her. Why didn't you come to me? That was when we were dating, for God's sake!"

I well up with emotion, and my vision clouds. "Carter. You know that's not fair. I was sixteen years old at the time! When my mom realized what I had heard, she swore me to secrecy. What else was I supposed to do? And if I'd told you, you would have gotten mad at me anyway!"

He clenches his jaw and locks his eyes on mine. His tone is serious, his voice gravelly. "You were supposed to fucking tell me the second you found out, that's what you were supposed to do."

When he averts his eyes, a tear streams down my cheek.

And it's not for me.

It's for him.

Here we are, almost a decade, and he's still grinding his teeth over the actions of some teenage girl who was torn over who to share which secrets with.

I run one hand along the stubble of his cheek, and press another into his heart.

"Carter," I whisper.

"Yeah," he chokes back.

"I'm sorry," I whisper. "I probably didn't say it back then —or say it enough—but I truly am."

I hear him swallow, but he doesn't say anything. I rest my head on his bare chest. I feel his heart beating as loud as a bass drum. And fast.

He wraps his big, long arm around around me, and I let myself fold into him.

We stand like that for a few minutes in total silence. His breaths get bigger and deeper, until he reaches his hand to my head, pulls the towel on my hair off, and chucks it on the ground.

"I need you right now, Laces," he growls, as he attacks my lips with his.

He's broken down my heart's defenses, and all I can do is eagerly accept his assault.

21

LACY

"Carter," I mutter between desperate breaths. The two syllables barely escape my mouth in between his kisses. He's so tall he has to bend down almost awkwardly to kiss my neck, reclaiming the territory he marked just last night.

Feeling the heat growing between my legs, I try and keep the last bit of resistance up.

If Carter and I hook up one time, we can write that off as an outlier and a mistake.

A drunken mistake on a yacht. Albeit a steamy, hot mistake.

But if we do it again, who knows where it will end.

He lets his fingers fall around my neck, so I feel the weight of his hand. I get an up-close view of the veins in his forearm.

I breathe desperately, like every gasp of air could be my last.

He rips my towel off and lifts me onto the marble kitchen countertop. The feel of the cold surface on my bare skin sends a chill reverberating through my whole body, but that's quickly offset by feeling Carter's firm, hot hands all over my ass, hips, and back as we make out ferociously.

It's a battle of wills as our lips press into one another.

Heat wells through my whole body. All of the pent-up emotions I've channelled into Carter over the years run through me.

Last night was one thing, in the dead dark of the night, on the yacht. But this feels totally different. In the middle of the day in Carter's penthouse, the light streaming from the balcony windows. I can see every rippling muscle in his body. Or I would, if he'd stop kissing me for one second.

Through his mesh shorts I feel his throbbing package against my thigh. I reach a hand down and run it over the outline of his cock.

He pauses for a moment, tipping his chin up and his eyes down. "I fucking need you, Lacy. I don't want you, I need you. Do you understand?"

"Yes," I mutter against his ear when he brings his cheek back to mine. I add, "I need this too."

The word 'you' escapes me.

I bite my lower lip waiting for his response.

He runs his eyes up and down my body, his gaze landing between my legs for a solid five seconds. I lean back on my palms, watching him with interest.

Focusing his pupils on me again, he brings his hands to my thighs and spreads them open a few more inches.

Carter's expression of need is like a drug. I've never felt so wanted. Yeah, he is a drug. I want to bottle him up and pop a pill of him when I need it.

"Oh, and one more thing," he says, hesitating before he goes down on me. "You don't come until I say so. Or there will be consequences. Understand?"

I nod, exhaling a hard breath. "Is that the game you like to play with me now?"

He gives me a look, leans down, and licks from just above my opening all the way up my stomach, between my breasts, up to my neck, until his lips land on mine again. "It is. No more lies, Laces."

"No more lies," I groan, echoing him.

An instant later, his tongue lands on my clit. I wriggle and shake as he eats me out like he's starving, gripping my hips with his hands to hold me in place. I glance through the window, out at the city and the lake. I'm thankful his hands are wrapped around me because if they weren't, I think I might just float away into the skyscrapers, I'm so high.

Pleasure ratchets through me, and after only a few minutes I feel myself on the brink of orgasm. "Carter . . . gonna come . . . so close. . ."

Quickly, he stands up, running a hand through his hair. "Good girl."

I swallow, not wanting to admit how close I came to coming before telling him. I'm not sure what sort of 'consequences' he was referring to, but something tells me I might not be ready for them just yet.

He pulls down his basketball shorts and boxers at the same time, revealing his erection.

The height matches so perfectly, I wonder if he had the island constructed specifically to fit him. Probably, knowing Carter.

Grabbing the base of his cock, he runs the fleshy head of his dick up and down my opening, teasing me.

I flutter my eyes, completely wet with desire. "Carter, just fuck me already," I beg.

He smirks and shakes his head a little. "When are you going to learn that ordering me around doesn't do you any good? Now let's make some use of that dirty mouth of yours. I want you to lay down across the marble, on your back, so just your head hangs off."

His tone and his eyes don't leave room for argument. I obey, positioning my naked body as directed.

The first thing I feel are his hands rubbing me from my breasts, down my stomach. I watch his abs as he leans over me. Then he lifts his hands off my shoulders and I feel the flesh of his hard cock across my face. He doesn't have to ask me. I know what to do. I open my mouth and stick out my tongue, taking him inside my mouth.

I close my eyes and focus on the sensations. How wide I have to open for him. How the head of his cock feels as he runs it over my tongue, back and forth.

I squirm, rotating my hips around while he fucks my face. I've never been this wild with a man. Never allowed it of myself.

But with Carter, I yearn for it.

Desire pools in my stomach in spite of the slight awkwardness of the positioning with my neck hanging off the edge of the island.

A low, throaty growl escapes from Carter, spurring me on.

I'm ravenous for his cock. I try to take in as much of him as I can stand for as long as I can stand it.

Another muffled word from him tells me he loves it. I lock my lips around his cock and run my tongue over his skin as he touches the back of my throat. I gag, and press into his legs with my palms. When he pulls away, I'm left gasping for air like there's a hole in my lungs. "Carter, please," I mumble. "I want to feel you inside me so bad."

Something coils inside me. Every square inch of my body throbs with want for him and the release only he can give me. It's not about the act. It's about ten years of pent-up tension begging for release.

He pauses, not quite grinning as he runs a hand through my hair. "Stand up," he orders.

I obey, sitting up and then sliding my feet to the ground.

I walk back around to his side of the island. I quelch the resistance in my head that wants to disobey him. My need to have him is stronger than my want to be disobedient, for once.

"Turn around," he says.

I do.

"Arch your spine and stick out your ass. Like this."

I reach my hands onto the marble for balance, and Carter presses my spine down and my ass up.

Pulling my hair out of my eyes so I can see him, he says, "You're gorgeous, Laces. Remember that. I love the way this pose accentuates all my favorite parts of your body."

He sweeps behind me and, holding onto a clump of my hair, he guides his cock into my pussy.

I lean my elbows down onto the countertop, my neck pulled back by Carter's strong grip on my hair. I let out a desperate moan as Carter thrusts into me and pulls, a tingle running down my spine at the dual feelings of pleasure and stimulation at the base of my scalp.

His motions are slow and deliberate at first. I'm finely attuned to the hand he rests on my back, running back and forth over my skin while he thrusts into me. Letting go of my hair, he grips my hips with both hands as he pushes deeper into me.

Even though I was on the brink of orgasm not long ago, I find myself resisting.

So much between us is still unresolved, up in the air. I want to get more in depth with him.

Or maybe we should just succumb to the healing properties of sex.

I blink when I feel a slap on my right buttocks, followed by a soft rub.

I don't just like it.

I *love* feeling his power.

I rock my hips in tandem with Carter's thrusts and we find our groove.

Slap again. Left buttocks. Then he softly rubs the tender area.

Why the hell is Carter the man who can make me feel more than I've ever felt before?

I should hate him for never giving me a chance to explain myself.

But it's hard to hate him fully when he breaks me down like this.

The feelings swell inside me, a confused stew of pleasure, anger, and lust.

The pleasure as I clench around him, holding onto nothing and everything as he slides in and out of me.

Slap. Rub.

The anger that I've submitted to him.

Slap. Rub.

My stomach lurches knowing how badly I want him, and what I might be willing to do to get this feeling again.

Slap. Rub.

Fuck. He's going to leave a handprint. The way his hand connects to my skin undoes me. The pain and pleasure mix together, and my mind fades to mush as pleasure override kicks in, nothing making sense.

". . . I'm going to. . . come. . ." I mewl, barely lucid enough to remember Carter's rule.

My words are a last second ditch effort to gain his permission as my orgasm crescendos. For a moment, he doesn't say anything and I try to hold back from coming. But everything about this is too much.

His huge hands on my hips. His big hips and the skin-on-sweaty-skin slapping noise every time he thrusts into me. The way his powerful, hard cock spreads me out and touches deep inside me. Pushing down on the countertop, he presses the weight of his whole body into me.

Grabbing my hair as if it's his anchor, he speaks, his voice a gravelly growl. "Come, Beautiful. Don't hold back. Come all over my cock, Laces."

Laces.

It's my childhood nickname that sends me right over the edge.

A subtle reminder that this isn't some one night Tinder date with a random guy.

The man I've both idolized and hated for years is the one who can give me this sort of pleasure. I let out an awkward cry as I clench around his cock and come so hard I wonder if Chicago might be having its first earthquake.

My toes shake, my calves quiver, and my thighs tremble as the heavenly feeling takes over my whole body.

I scream again—nearly in tears of pleasure—and turn my head to look at Carter. His eyes are as wide as mine as we lock onto each other.

With my free arm, I reach back and slap him on the side of his butt.

He blinks—shocked, perhaps?—and then smiles ever so slightly.

Wrapping his fingers around my neck, he leans forward and growls as he kisses me, pounding me all the while. He pulls back and his eyes flutter. I love the way his eyelashes look. His breath is short, and he slides his hand up my neck to cup my cheek.

I whisper in his ear. "I want to feel you come now."

Carter screams so loud, I flinch.

"Holy fuck," I yell, as he shoves me down on the countertop and fucks me like I'm his last. He runs his hands over my tits, my hips, my ass. I feel his cock twitch as he shoots bolts inside me.

I rest my head on top of my forearms while I pant to catch my breath. When Carter pulls out of me, I can feel the emptiness he leaves behind. Totally destroyed, I glance up at him with one eye from my resting position. His body glistens with sweat. "I hate you, Carter Flynn," I mutter.

He swallows. "I hate you too, Lacy Benson."

But as he drags his hand across my thigh and my stomach flips, I know that's a lie.

This isn't hate at all.

It's something else entirely.

22

CARTER

I'm jolted out of a deep sleep when I hear the sound of my own voice trying to speak.

My palms are sweaty, and I have the sensation of being on edge. Taking a few deep breaths, I attempt to still myself.

Hints of nightmares nip at me, but they fade away into the backroads of my subconscious.

I open my eyes, and a surge of adrenaline rushes through me when I see Lacy lying face-down, stark naked, in my king sized bed.

Late evening rays of golden sunshine seep through the blinds in my room.

The heat of what Lacy and I did in the kitchen this afternoon comes crashing back to me.

I'm naked too.

Although we were both wrecked when we finished, I can feel my hard-on returning as I watch her gorgeous body while she sleeps.

Sitting up in bed, I blow out an audible exhale.

So we fucked each others' brains out. Holy fuck, did we ever.

I pull strands of Lacy's dark hair out so I can see her ear. I contemplate whispering a sweet little nothing into her ear.

Like, *sleep in your own damn bed.*

I don't let girls sleep in my bed. Especially late on a Saturday no less. I'm tall with long appendages, and I like to starfish when I sleep.

But this isn't just anyone. This is Lacy, my original inspiration. I listen to her breathing pattern, watching her back gently rise and fall.

She's damn gorgeous, I'll give her that. Supple skin, toned legs from years of dance. That fucking attitude of hers has got to go, though. From watching her sleep, you'd assume she was a proper fucking good girl.

In truth, she's the first girl I've been with who seems to be able to stand up to me.

Running my gaze from her heels, thighs, the small of her back and neck, I want to kiss her everywhere. Just because I can. Because even though I still can't stand the way she's acted in the past, I can't deny she's sparked something in me. What that is, I'm not sure yet.

I could never get past what she did to me my senior year of high school.

Lacy knew my dad wasn't dead like my mom had told me all those years.

She knew, but never told me.

Lied to my face for an entire year while I was falling deeper in love with her.

That was silly love though, teenage stuff. I knew in my heart that she was the One with a capital "O." I had this picture in my mind of us taking it slow, dating throughout our college years, before we would finally get married and have beautiful children.

I just *knew*.

But then my mom told me--well, more like sobbed to me--on my eighteenth birthday in early May of my senior year that my dad was alive, that he was a powerful man and that I was essentially his bastard child who he wished was never born.

That hurt.

But I'd had so much love from my mother and my friends in Blackwell, I brushed it off at first.

I told my mother everything was going to be fine. God had given me the strength to make it through my first eighteen years of life and get a scholarship to play basketball. I knew He had eyes on me, and I was blessed.

But when I saw Lacy on my birthday, I broke down.

I told her everything.

Only she barely reacted.

She didn't even seem surprised.

Because she *knew*.

She'd overheard that my father was alive, and she fucking knew all along.

I'd trusted her with my heart, and she'd chosen allegiances. She kept a secret for her mother instead of being honest with me.

My chest tightens, and I swallow a lump in my throat as I replay the movie of my birthday in my head.

I know my father's out there somewhere, but just doesn't give a shit about me as a son. Sometimes I wish I still thought he was dead. That ignorance was blissful.

Though I've never had the motivation to seek him out. I've shunned it. I don't want to know who the fucker is.

I grind my teeth and try not to think about him. Luckily there's a beautiful distraction on the bed right in front of me. A grin spreads over my face.

Goddamn, she has really grown into herself. Mentally, I

never remember Lacy being so headstrong. And then there's how hot she's gotten. Wider hips. Is her ass slightly more bubbly?

I snort. Bubble butt. I'd love to shake the hand of the man who invented the term.

I think about how good it felt to be with her last night.

This was beyond sex. With other women, we'd had no connection. It'd been mechanical. I always knew something was missing with them.

And now I know exactly what I was missing: Lacy.

I swallow, and without even trying, I realize I'm at full mast again.

I get onto my knees and straddle her, pumping my hand over the fat tip of my dick.

A low growl escapes my lips. I want to kiss her. I want to fuck her again.

Why the fuck can't I stop with Lacy?

She shifts a little bit in her sleep, wiggling her ass, and it damn near sends me over the edge.

Her phone buzzes on the nightstand close to her head. She stirs and I think she might wake to see who texted her, but then she just scratches her little nose and puts her cheek on the pillow again. Well goddamn if that wasn't the cutest thing I've seen all day.

Still naked, I check her phone to see who's texting her.

The name shows. Some guy named Norton. Wasn't that her ex who she came here to live with originally?

Now I use both hands on the phone. I'm interested to know what this fuckhead has to say.

Number locked with five digits.

First, I try the numbers that correspond with 'Laces.'

No luck.

Then I try 1-2-3-4-5. Nope.

Hmm.

Lacy, five digits.

A memory of pulling up to her house in Blackwell when I was a kid flashes in my mind.

10439 Country Road C.

Bingo.

Time to mess with people for my own enjoyment, one of my favorite activities of all time.

I pull up Norton's text.

NORTON: HEY HONEY, JUST WANTED TO SAY HAPPY BIRTHDAY! That party looked fun yesterday, too bad I couldn't come. WYD tonight

Hey, Honey?

I narrow my eyes, somehow angry at the text message. What the fuck is going on with this guy? I guess I'll play along. I text back.

Lacy: Wow! Things got pretty wild last night. How have you been honey?

Norton: Good to hear. So, I was thinking, what are you up to tonight?

Lacy: Oh idk why

Norton: Well obviously you moving to Chicago caught me off-guard, but I was thinking. . . we could just hang out tonight and do whatever

Lacy: Whatever. . .?

Norton: lol like you don't know. . . don't act all innocent

My blood boils. What the fuck is going on with this guy?

Lacy: Norton you're just going to have to spell it out for me.

Norton: lol. Ok. . . DO YOU WANT TO HOOK UP TONIGHT?!

I take a deep breath and try to calm myself. I know Lacy didn't hook up with Lance, now.

But could she have hooked up with this Norton Mother-fucker while she was here?

Jealousy courses through me, and I can feel blood pumping straight to my balls.

I look down.

Even while I'm concentrating on sending this text, I've got a hard on as straight as a flag pole. Must be the pheromones she gives off or something. I can't *not* be hard around her.

A devious idea creeps into my mind.

"Carter Flynn, you're a real dick," I say in a low voice. Still straddling Lacy's body, I land in a sitting kneel position so my cock lays across her supple ass.

I snap a picture with Lacy's phone and send it to Norton along with a text.

Lacy: Hook up? No, I'm actually taken care of in that department tonight :)

I smirk to myself, wondering what that turd will think when he sees my fat, hard cock on top of Lacy.

I snap my finger. Damn. Should have taken a fucking video. I pull up Lacy's messages again when a text from Lance comes through.

Lance: Hey Sexy Bitch, you alive after last night?

I shrug. Well, when in Rome. . . might as well troll him too. Especially since he was willing to play a devilish prank on me with Lacy.

Though to be honest, I actually like and respect the guy that he had the balls to do something that wacky.

Lacy: I crashed so hard. We have a lot to talk about

Lance: lol I'm sure. Have you spoken with Carter since last night?

I think for a moment. If Lacy said something to Lance, he'd just reflect that back via text messages now, right?

Lacy: I just didn't know what to tell him. What do you think I should say?

Lance: Tell him the truth. That you hate him but no one can make you come like he does. And can you please turn him bi? Lol

Lacy: lol you're funny

Lance: I'm serious. So you never told me, is his dick as big of a dick as he is? I always assume the more of an asshole, the bigger the equipment. It's sort of an informal survey Joseph and I are running

Lacy: lol that's none of your business

Lance: Come on you sexy bitch I faked sloppy slappy sex with you I deserve DETAILS!

I grin at Lance's response, thinking about how I can have some more fun when Lacy stirs and seems like she'll really wake up.

Fumbling my hands, I aim to send one more text to Lance.

But what I actually do is send the dick pic to him.

Oops.

Lance: holy Chicago Sausage King who took that picture though?!

Lacy starts to rotate around in bed, and I toss her phone onto the ground just before she opens her eyes.

And sees me straddling her.

"What are you doing Carter? You creep," she says, her eyes sleepy.

I clear my throat. "Just, ah, you know. Stretching."

Squinting a little bit, she throws her arms behind her head. She looks like a damn mermaid. Or a siren, sent straight from heaven to seduce me.

"It looks like you're stroking yourself to me while I'm sleeping," she says in a sultry voice.

"You're not sleeping anymore."

She bites her lip. "Were you going to fuck me in my sleep?"

I wink. "I already did."

She rolls her eyes, speaking playfully. "Carter. That's not funny. Do you ever stop being an asshole and take things seriously for like two seconds?"

I shrug, trying to keep a straight face as I consider the dick pic I just sent her ex.

Instead of answering, I grip my cock at its base and thump it on her abdomen and use my best caveman voice. "Carter Hard. Carter Smash."

She can't hold back her laughter. Sitting up, she pushes into my chest. "I still hate you. I do, you know."

"So if you hate me you can't laugh at my jokes?"

She bites her lower lip and stares at me. "You're very hard."

"I know."

"How are you that hard again?"

"I'm no doctor, but I think it's something to do with testosterone and being close to you."

"Close to me? Like specifically?"

"Yes. You're. . . what, a Gemini? I'm pretty sure Taurus's get hard naturally when there are Geminis in the room. Plus, you're just plain hot."

She furrows her brow and snorts. "I'm a Cancer, not a Gemini. And you're wrong—I'm not hot."

I clench my jaw. "What the fuck did you just say?"

"I said I'm not hot. Come on. You know it's true. I'm okay. I'm no *Davina* though."

Without thinking, I reach my hand out and hold her. I stare at this mystery of a woman in all her naked glory. Her thick black hair. The natural hue of her pink lips—her makeup is faded away by time and kisses.

"Carter," she gasps, and I forget how I'm holding onto her even harder than when we were fucking on the kitchen island.

I swear I see her wipe away a tear from under her eye, but it could just be sweat.

She straddles my stomach and lowers her head to mine, whispering in my ear. "One more time, Carter. And I want to be on top this time."

I put my arms behind my back. The corners of my lips quirk upward in a curious grin. Who is this girl, sitting on top of me?

I've known her for more than twenty years. I've seen the good and the bad develop in her from a young age.

But right now—she seems like a stranger.

A hot-as-hell stranger who wants to fuck.

And wants to be on top.

You know, there are some moments in life where you have to just sit back, be grateful, and thank God that he put you on Earth and gave you life and a cock so you can enjoy moments like these.

Lacy wants to do the work? Yes motherfucking please.

"You've got that look," she shakes her head as she grinds the outside of her pussy against my cock. "What devious thoughts are you thinking?"

I shrug, as much as you can shrug lying down. "Nothing much."

She rolls her eyes. "Goddamn it, that's like my all time least favorite reply for a guy to give."

Smiling, she leans closer to me. She raises her ass, grabs my cock and guides it into her. "This time, you don't come till I say."

"Oh no?"

She smiles, "No. You think you can do it?"

I grin back. "I'll take you up on this challenge. But honestly, with you, I never know what I'm going to do."

Our dialogue stops, fading into action.

Planting her hands on my chest for balance, she rides up and down the full length of my cock, slowly at first.

For the first few minutes, I just lean back, grin, and shake my head ever so slightly.

Here's a girl who can't even classify herself as 'hot.' Pleasure floats through me, and I can't help but wonder why she holds onto this belief.

I do my damnedest to search for her imperfections.

Well, at fifty percent brainpower, I do.

Is it the little sequence of birthmarks close to her belly button?

Because those are the hottest fucking things ever. Cindy Crawford wishes she had birthmarks like that.

The scar on her hip? Wait, how the hell did she get that?

Before I can think more, my thoughts drift away to the sweet winds of fucking. She leans back, and I'm about to come. The way she looks arched backwards. The way her swollen pussy grips my cock. How her supple breasts bounce every time she lands deep on my cock.

I grab onto her hips. She may be on top. She may want to be in charge. But her flesh calls to me, aching for me to grab it, to dig my fingers into her ass.

We find our rhythm. She bounces in tune with my strokes and now we're fucking like animals.

I feel her tense and shake, her pussy tightening around my cock.

Spurred on, I reach up and grab her neck and a clump of hair. I pull her face into me for a messy kiss.

"You came, didn't you?" I growl into her ear.

"Mm-hm," she purrs.

"Well that's the one time I'll allow that. Now it's my turn."

"But I didn't say you could yet," she whispers.

Oh. This woman doesn't know how this shit works.

Time to show her.

With a roar, and not pulling out of her, I flip her around onto her back.

Her eyes widen a little, and I lift her legs to my shoulders, then plunge inside her.

"Fuck, Carter!"

"Yeah? You like it when I go deep, don't you?"

"Yes," she swallows, furrowing her brow. "That hurts. . . almost."

I grip her legs as I pound into her. Her screams get louder and louder.

Yes.

Yes.

Yes.

I open my eyes again. Hers are lit up.

"Harder, Carter, deeper!"

Holy fuck.

Dirty Lacy has arrived.

And I fucking love this side of her.

Her pleasure is so intense, she seems as though she might cry.

I grab a bunch of her hair and fuck her so hard it's a wonder the headboard doesn't fall off.

She pushes her hips against me and holds onto my neck as I come, bolts of pleasure blowing through me as I orgasm.

I rest my head on the pillow close to her shoulder when we're done.

"Dear God, Carter. You're going to ruin me."

Sliding out of her, I can't hold back a grin. "I tend to do that."

She bites her lip. "You know. I could get used to this. Maybe I don't hate you as much as I once thought."

Before I can respond to that, her phone buzzes.

"Oh, my phone is on the floor."

She picks it up, and her expression shifts one-hundred-eighty degrees.

"What. The fuck. Did you text Norton? You fucking asshole!"

She rakes a hand through her hair and waves her phone at me.

"He wasn't getting the picture, so I thought a visual would help. Anyways," I say, getting up. "I'm hungry as hell from all this fucking. I'm going to make some steaks. You want in?"

Her jaw is wide open. She palms her forehead.

"I cannot believe you. You're unbelievable! Just when I was thinking you might have, you know. . ."

Her sentence drifts off as I towel the bodily juices off me, and throw a towel at her for the same purpose.

"Toned it down? Is that what you're thinking?" I shrug. "Tell me something useful. Like how you prefer your steaks. Trying to be a nice guy here."

She shakes her head. "You—nice?! You know, screw you. For a lot of reasons. Screw you for texting my ex a dick pic. And also fuck you for besting the best screw ever. And for being nice sometimes." Her voice softens during her last point.

Scrubbing my hand over my face, I nod blankly. I swallow the lump in my throat and the pang in my stomach telling me that this is something much, much deeper than a roommate with benefits situation.

"So. . . medium rare?"

❧ 23 ❧

LACY

I lay in Carter's bed, staring up at the ceiling. Still naked. Exhausted from the sex and from the battle with this man.

I feel exhilarated from our burgeoning romance, but nonetheless I bite the inside of my cheek, running through the entire text conversation he had with Lance pretending to be me.

Why can't he just be a normal guy for two minutes?

No, instead he's got to send a picture of his johnson to Lance and Norton.

My chest tightens as I reread Norton's response. Lance will get over it—quick. He'll probably just think it's funny.

Tossing my phone on the nightstand, I tilt my head in thought. How the hell did he know the code to my phone?

I throw on my pink shorts and a tank top, the smell of steaks wafting into the room. My stomach grumbles. I haven't had a solid meal all day. And I've definitely been taking part in an array of physical activities.

I swallow a lump in my throat. Why does he have to be the one who turns me on the most? I shake my head. Sometimes, I have doubts about our creator. Is God just playing some sick joke on us?

My phone buzzes and Norton's name pops up on the screen again. I feel my empty stomach curdle a little as I go to grab it. The truth is, since I arrived to Chicago a couple of weeks ago, I've been completely ignoring Norton.

After he got cold feet initially about me moving in with him and broke up with me, he started texting me every couple of nights. The texts would come in at night, when I assumed he'd been drinking and was horny. It's so ridiculous what that one appendage between their legs has the ability to do to a man. I swear, Norton seemed like the greatest guy in the world the week I met him. But when he was drunk, horny, and lonely?

What a weirdo.

I exhale a hard breath, and unlock my phone to see what he was texting me. When I press on Norton's message thread, the dick pic Carter had sent is at the top, followed by a string of texts from Norton.

I pull the picture up again and just stare.

Pinching the bridge of my nose with my forefinger and thumb, I look over the text thread.

NORTON: LACY. WHAT THE FUCK.

Norton: *Real fucking mature. And you want to say I'm the immature one? You're such a damn hypocrite. Screensnapping videos of porn to get back at me? Real classy*

Norton: *Are you going to respond? You always were such a bitch*

Norton: *That cock wouldn't even fit inside you anyway, you're such a tightly wound cunt*

Norton: *I'll take that as a 'yes, I like screenshotting random porn video I see online and sending them to my ex*

. . .

"Fuck, Carter. You've got to be kidding me," I mutter, staying strong with my policy of not sending him a message.

I don't bother replying to Norton, because I don't even know what I'd say. Plus, I don't want to reignite our text thread. I should probably block him, but I don't have the heart.

And I have to admit, seeing Norton so pissed off is a touch satisfying.

Because forget him and his cold feet.

What would he say if I texted him that *no, that's not porn, you asshole. It's one-hundred percent real.*

Counting to ten, I face my palms up, and take a deep yogic breath. I feel a little better, think better of responding, and pull up Lance's text message.

I look at the picture Carter sent again, shaking my head. The man has absolutely no shame. I'm almost surprised he didn't snapchat it to all of my contacts.

A brick forms in my stomach and I check my Snapchat app.

No, he didn't send it to anyone else. Thank God.

I smile just a tinge reading what Lance has to say.

Lance: GIRL, YOU DONE LOST YOUR MIND!! (EGG-PLANT EMOJI)

Lance: ok sorry about the caps. Is that. . . Carter?? For real?? Is that your ass? Wow, you look good girl, no lie. You sexy thang

Lance: So. . . can I show this picture to Joseph? He's asking me. But I assume this was. . . for me? Wait, WHY ARE YOU SENDING ME DICK PICS OF CARTER?

Lance: This is Joseph. I wrestled the phone away from Lance.

Lance: All I can say is, WOW.

Lance: So. . . you're not responding. I'm assuming you're a little busy? I'll let you and Carter do whatever you're doing. I mean I know what you're doing. More or less. I understand how sex works.

Lance: Have you and Carter tried anal? #Askingforafriend

Lance: Sorry boo. Just realized I might have gotten a liiiitle personal with that last text. Joseph and I may or may not have been day drinking to get rid of our hangovers from last night.

Lance: It's Joseph again. I'm sorry, too. We're inappropriate sometimes. But I'm still curious. And it's fun. Trust me. Oh and we have definitely been day drinking. There is no may or may not. Okay we're going to stop texting and start interacting like human beings again. We're becoming "those people" who just sit at dinner and text on their phones. But we made an exception for you

Lance: Also, you want to get brunch tomorrow? We should talk about our variation this week

Lance: LMK you sexy bitch <3

Lance: Tell Carter we say hi, too

Lance: :D :D

Lance: Or should I say 8======D

By the time I'm done reading Lance and Joseph's string of ridiculous texts, I can't help but smile a little. Those two are keeping me sane in a city where everyone seems to be plotting against me.

Feeling a little better, I head out of Carter's room, following the delicious smell of the steaks. I hear heavy metal coming from the balcony, and my jaw drops at what I see. I actually close both of my eyes, really hard, and open them again.

Carter stands out on the balcony facing the grill, and he's totally naked except for his apron. He's got his sunglasses on and he's singing along to the song.

I pause for a brief moment before joining him. In spite of how much of an asshole Carter can be, this is what I admire about him. He's so unencumbered. Sure, maybe he rubs a lot of people the wrong way, but I don't think he acts for one second how he thinks people want him to act. His will is totally his own. He does what he wants. When he wants.

A chill runs through my body as another thought crosses into my consciousness, involuntarily. I don't want to think the words, but I do.

Carter does WHO he wants.

So what does he want with little old me?

He turns and sees me.

"Hey Laces, can you grab the wine bottle and a glass and bring them out here? We can eat out here on the balcony. It's a gorgeous night."

I feel my stomach tighten.

He definitely saw me staring at him. I should have known. He is a professional basketball player, after all. Aren't basketball players known for having spectacular peripheral vision?

"Oh, you already have a glass?" I say, trying to divert attention from my staring.

"Yeah," he turns around, holding tongs in one hand and a glass of wine in the other. I almost roll my eyes at the text of his apron, which says 'kiss cook here' with a down arrow pointing right to his dick. I giggle a little, thinking back to the breakfast when Lance wore the same thing.

I grab the bottle of wine, a glass, and slide the screen door open to head out onto his patio.

"I picked these up from this Spanish meat market this week. They are going to be amazing. And I've got fresh grilled local asparagus."

"Sounds healthy."

"And delicious."

"You need a refill?" I ask. He nods. I fill up his glass, then glance out at Lake Michigan. The sun sets on the other side of the building, but the sky still fills with a beautiful orange-red glow.

"You're not worried that people are like, staring at you out here?"

He winks. "Mrs. Englewood always stares. I don't mind giving her a show, though."

He waves up to a woman who is on a kitty corner balcony. I can barely make out her grey-blonde hair. She waves back.

"Full frontal is extra!" he shouts up to her. "You knew that though, Mrs. Englewood!"

I laugh. "I want to tell you that you're being ridiculous, but I'm realizing there's no changing you."

He pinches his forehead into an accusatory look as he takes the steaks off the grill. "Her husband just died a few months ago. She could use a little pick-me-up."

I shake my head, tensing up.

My mind shoots to the two-piece of naughty lingerie I brought here, wanting to surprise Norton. It's in the bottom of my suitcase still. I haven't touched it.

I should probably burn it.

"I don't think so. Can you please put some shorts on?"

Carter sighs. "You're such a buzzkill. Please get the table ready. I'll be right back."

I line up the knives and forks, and put some asparagus onto both of our plates along with mashed potatoes from a bowl on the table.

When he comes back, he's got basketball shorts on. "Alright, let's eat some steaks! You hungry?"

"I think my stomach is literally trying to eat itself right now. So yes."

A soft grin tugs at Carter's face. He touches my shoulder and massages it slightly. "Thanks for setting the table, Laces."

"No problem," I say, and a strange warmth spreads through my chest. The moment is over as quickly as it passes.

Carter sits down. "Shall we say grace?"

I roll my eyes. "You don't say grace."

"True. I don't know why I even said that, to be honest. I haven't eaten dinner up here with a girl yet."

Snorting, I cut into my steak. "Yeah, okay, Mr. 'All I do is hook up with girls.'"

He shrugs, not looking at me. "First of all, why would I lie to you about that? What a silly, white lie. Second, I don't have to make dinner for girls to get laid. That's ridiculous."

I roll my eyes. "So I'm the first girl you've ever cooked for?"

"I don't know about ever. It's been a while though."

I bite into my steak. "Mmmm. This is so good. The Spanish Market, you said?"

"Yeah, some old guy with grey hair and a thick Spanish accent. Grew up in Spain, lived most of his life in Argentina. He always gets the best, thickest cuts. Glad you like it."

A warm summer breeze rolls across my face. Carter seems fixated on his steak and nothing else.

"So how does it feel?" he asks.

"Um. What do you mean?"

"Being twenty-six."

"Oh. That." I shrug. "I don't know. I guess I always looked at twenty-six as the the wrong side of twenty-five. I guess I feel like I haven't done enough. In life as a whole."

Carter sips his wine. "Elaborate."

"Well, like I'm doing this whole modern dance thing this summer. This is really my last shot to do this. I'm old in dance years. Most modern dancers get their break earlier. . . shit. They break in at like age eighteen or nineteen. If I don't get the spot this time, I don't know what I'll do. Move back to Blackwell and work in the studio again, I guess? Stay out in Chicago and get a waitressing job? I don't know. I just feel. . ."

I trail off, and stress rolls through me. My throat clamps up.

"Tell me," Carter booms, as if reading my mind.

"When I was eighteen, I thought I'd have a family by now. I thought twenty-six was old. That I'd be settled down. Have a couple of kids and live on a farm, maybe. Teach some dance during the day, have a garden. I thought I'd be satisfied with my life. Instead, I feel like a total hack. I'm ranked like thirty-nine out of forty at camp and I'm probably just wasting my time here. My ex-boyfriend dumped me as soon as I decided I would actually live anywhere near him. Ugh, why am I telling you this?"

Carter leans in, his eyes intense. "You're not a hack. Don't ever think that."

My chest hitches, a heavy feeling coming on in my stomach. "How do you know?"

"Because I know."

"I'm too old to get it, though."

He shakes his head. "Lacy, you know how old you're going to be next year if you don't make it onto Blue Illusion?"

I furrow my brow. "Twenty-seven. What's your point?"

"Okay. And how old are you going to be if you *do* make it onto that team?"

"Twenty-seven. I still don't see your point."

He finishes a bite of asparagus, then locks his eyes on mine with a seriousness I don't think I've seen in him yet. "The past is done. You weren't like some of these girls who lived in the city when they were sixteen and could practice with the best dancers all the time. But you're here now. And next year, you're going to be older whether you like it or not. So you damn well better do what makes you happy. Don't let the ghosts of the pasts kill your dreams of the future."

I swallow down a healthy gulp of wine as I process Carter's rather poignant advice. I'm not used to such wise words coming from the man. Some mix of emotion wells inside me. Carter stays on the surface so often, but once he goes deep, he goes really deep. "More wine, please," I say. "And why are you you being so nice to me?"

The ebbing sun reflects off a building onto his face, giving him golden-brown skin. "I'm not being nice. I'm just telling you the truth."

I stop chewing mid-bite as a realization hits me. One of the few benefits of Carter being so harsh most of the time is that I know he's not bullshitting me. If he thought I sucked, he would just give that info to me straight.

"Fine. You want to know how I know? I know because you *love* what you do. You were a dancer before you even knew what it meant. Remember in the park, after we played basketball that one day—I don't remember how old we were. But you insisted on teaching me the dance moves you'd learned. That was pure passion."

"You remember that?" I breathe, my vocal pitch rising.

Carter nods. "Of course. I told you how it changed the way I played forever."

I shake my head. "We were just kids then."

"Yep."

Swallowing a lump in my throat, I breathe out and consider not saying what's on my mind. But I must. I brace myself. "So, if you can admit we were just kids then, why do you still hold a grudge against me?"

Carter's entire posture instantly stiffens. "I still can't get over some of the stuff you've done. I don't know if I'll ever make it past that."

"So," I swallow. "What are we doing, then?"

Taking a long sip of his wine, Carter looks away and then brings his gaze back to me. "You've got this energy to you, and it's fucking magnificent. You know why I cooked for you tonight? Because I wanted to spend a little more time with you. This may make me an asshole, but you know as well as anyone I don't like wasting time with girls. There's something about you that drives me up the fucking wall and back down. But I also don't think you let everyone see this side of you. You walk around with your guard up.

And that's fine, I guess. But for fuck's sake. You're ranked thirty-ninth of forty? I call bullshit on that. I'm guessing that dance, like basketball, is a lot more mental than you'd like to think. And something's blocking you. That's clear as day."

I twist around in my seat, suddenly uncomfortable. My wine buzz hits me a little, and I feel bold.

I pinch my eyebrows together. "Carter, who the hell do you think you are?"

Carter leans back. "The fuck is that supposed to mean?"

"You're telling me I have something blocking me from the past?" I bite out. "Talk about projection."

"I don't follow," he says evenly.

I heave a deep breath. "I don't really want to go here, but I have to. This is what you do! Any time—like today—you're getting anywhere near addressing your father issue, you change the subject."

"That is not true."

"Yes, it is! You've been avoiding that subject for almost a decade. And now you're just going to keep avoiding! I keep trying to bring it up with you and you keep dodging my questions."

"I don't think now is the time to address my stupid dead-beat dad."

My whole body feels heavy, hearing his excuse. "Oh! So when is? You've got some real problems, Mister. Do you think it's fucking normal to send a picture of your cock—along with my ass, which I did not consent to, by the way—to a person's ex? Is it?"

Carter stands up. "I don't know why you give a shit about what that guy thinks any more! How long did you date? You planned your life in the city with him, and he bails at the last second! Sounds like a real piece of work if you ask me! I didn't include your face in that picture on purpose, by the way.

You're fucking welcome. I mean, sure, I could pick your ass out of a lineup. But no one else is going to know that's you!"

"I just don't like the idea of a naked picture of me being out there! Wai. . . did you just say you could pick my ass out of a lineup?" I stand up, and through my anger I stifle a giggle.

Leave it to Carter to insert comedy even into this ridiculous situation.

"One-hundred percent. I'd bet my life on it. I have every nook and cranny memorized. You have a little birthmark on the side of your right cheek," he winks.

"Nook and cranny?! What the fuck is wrong with you!" I shake my head.

"Well it's true! Try me."

Standing up, I bite my tongue.

I think back to Norton's message.

He honestly thought Carter had just taken a screenshot of a random girl and guy from a porn site.

I mean, Carter *does* have porn-worthy equipment.

But also, it's clear that Norton couldn't pick my ass out of a lineup.

A strange warmth spreads in my heart. And even that warmth angers me.

Why am I so into the man who's also the most emotionally unavailable? It's ridiculous.

I clench up, feeling like a wind-up toy about to explode.

I step up to Carter. "And Lance!? Really? Why did you have to send a picture to *him*?"

Carter shrugs. "For comedic relief because I knew you'd be pissed about me sending one to Norton. And also, because I knew Lance would appreciate it."

I open my mouth to speak again, but nothing comes out.

He's so openly ridiculous—and unashamed, it's just impressive.

I want to slap him. And I want to jump him.

"Carter," I say through gritted teeth.

"Laces." He imitates me, giving me a sideways grin.

"If we were playing kill, fuck, or marry right now, you'd win two out of the three options. You want to guess which ones?"

He flashes a cocky smirk, then brushes my hair behind my ear. "You know I'd pick the same two for you."

I rest my hand on his abs, heaving heavy breaths. "This isn't over," I say softly.

"I agree." He brushes his lips against my ear. "But right now I'm feeling a lot like I need to fuck you so hard I might even stop hating you for a minute."

"Shut up. You don't still hate me. I don't believe you."

He tips my chin up toward him. "Shut your mouth and get in the damn bedroom," he growls.

I run my tongue over my lips, and swallow. "Yes, Sir," I say, my tone just a smidge below mocking.

Lifting me over his shoulder like a fireman, he carries me to the bedroom.

❧ 24 ❧

CARTER

Thankfully, Lacy doesn't interfere with my starfishing in bed. I don't think I've slept so soundly in months.

Mindblowing sex has the tendency to launch you into that deep R.E.M. sleep, so I'm not surprised.

When my alarm goes off at six A.M., I silently curse my coach out for inventing early morning Sunday practices, especially in the off season. Supposedly, they're meant to keep our team from partying too hard. Like that's ever stopped a group of twenty-something guys.

I rouse myself from bed and steal a glance at Lacy while she sleeps.

This time, she's sleeping in one of my Chicago Wolverines jerseys. An urge wells up in me to kiss her on the cheek before I go, but I squash it.

Glancing at the time on my watch, I realize something.

My twenty-four hour rule. She's coming damn close to breaking it. We've been hanging out non-stop since yesterday afternoon. Does the clock still run on the twenty-four hours if she's sleeping in my bed, but I'm not here?

I sling the strap of my gym bag over my shoulder, when another realization crosses me that Lacy's getting into my head. The twenty-four hour thing isn't real. It's an arbitrary rule I made to kick girls out when I feel like it.

And I hope she's still lying in my bed like this when I get back.

Not in the mood to drive, I call a Lyft and head out the door to practice.

After our warmup, we head to the gym for an early morning lifting session, then to the court for a scrimmage. I wonder what exactly we're supposed to be simulating with a scrimmage at eight A.M., since all of our games are at night.

I ask the coach a simple question about his early practice philosophy, but he takes it the wrong way.

"Alright, you don't want to scrimmage? Get on the motherfucking baseline, then," he yells.

"That's not what I—"

"Baseline!" he quacks, louder this time.

Everyone on the team mean-mugs me, and I shrug.

"The fuck's the matter with you?" Chandler quips. "We all went out last night until like four A.M. Where the hell were you anyway? You didn't answer a single text."

I shrug. "Dinner with Lacy."

He stares at me, shaking his head. "I knew it."

Our first wind sprint interrupts the flow of our conversation, and to be honest I'm thankful for the break.

Probably since I'm the only guy who wasn't out all night for the second night in a row, I come in first easily. Although I was certainly doing some cross-training of my own with Lacy last night.

She really is a naughty girl. You wouldn't know it from looking at her from the outside though. Or maybe she's only like that with me.

Before we can fully catch our breath, we do another

sprint. To half court and back. Then full court and back. After several more, some of the bigger guys are wheezing.

"That's fine. You guys weren't ready to play today anyway. And as you all know—"

"Champions are made in the offseason," we complete Coach's often-cited motto.

"Right. Now get the fuck out of here."

On the way out, Chandler pulls me aside. "Hey man. We're going to breakfast. You coming?"

"When and where?"

"We're going to The Big Fork. In Lincoln Park."

"Oh, nice place. Yeah. I might make it," I say as we start our stride into the locker room.

"Might make it? What the fuck does that mean?"

I shrug. "Just what it means. I'm not sure."

"Don't give me these bullshit halfway millennial answers, Cart. The fuck's up with you? It's a yes or no question."

I don't say anything as we arrive at our lockers. The truth is, I'm picturing Lacy back in my bed. I've been thinking about what Lacy said to me about my father. And she's right. I've got a big hang up when it comes to the man I've never met.

For once, I think this morning actually might be the right time to talk with Lacy about that. And there's no one else I can talk to on the same level. Chandler's the only one on the team who has any clue about my fucked-up past.

So this is one morning I'd prefer to spend with her.

I wrap a towel around my waist and eye Chandler.

I don't say any of that, though. Because it's not relevant to the discussion.

"Okay. No, I won't be coming to breakfast today."

His gaze tells me he's disappointed.

"It's not a team breakfast, right?" I add. "So what's the big deal?"

"It's not *not* a team breakfast. But do whatever you want man."

⚜

ON THE WAY HOME, I HAVE MY LYFT DRIVER STOP AT Dark Matter Coffee.

I get a black coffee for me and a Cappuccino for Lacy. Part of me thinks I'm nuts. I'm not the guy who gets coffee for a girl. But I've got this picture in my mind of Lacy and I sitting out on the balcony this morning, sipping our coffees and getting our caffeine buzzes rolling.

Maybe we'll even get into some deep conversations.

I ride up the elevator with the two coffees in hand.

A cute brunette who once tried to flirt with me at a building party gets on as well.

"Hi Carter," she says.

"Marisa," I say dryly.

"Two coffees? I thought you don't let girls sleep over."

I pinch my eyebrows together. "What makes you think this coffee is for a girl?"

Rolling her eyes, she responds. "So you get Cappuccinos for your guy friends? Give me a break."

I nod. "You're good."

She puts her hand on my wrist. "I used to work in a coffee shop. You know you can depend on me if you ever need me to come up and," she wiggles her eyebrows, "make an espresso. Or anything like that."

"No thanks. I'm good."

Thankfully, the elevator dings at my floor, and I get off.

A sigh of relief escapes me at being out of Marisa's reach.

I guess she's sort of right. I have cultivated a reputation as the guy who will give girls a night of pleasure they'll never forget. Right now, I just want to relax, though.

Opening the door to my penthouse, I call out. "Lacy? You awake yet?"

I set our coffees on the island and walk down the hall toward my room. I smile, pausing before I head inside. For once, I feel ready to talk about my dad with Lacy, like she's been asking at me to do.

My body tenses. What if she's right? What if I have expended years of energy hating her for how she lied to me, when she was just a pawn in the grand scheme of things? A pawn—just like I was.

I open the door.

She's gone, although her scent still lingers in the room. I check the shower. Her room. Her shower. Gone.

I dump the cappucino in the trash and dial up Chandler.

"What the fuck do you want?" I can hear him smirking through the phone.

"Is it too late to come by?"

I park, get out, and walk to The Big Fork, where I see Chandler and Amy sitting at a table. I pull up and sit next to them.

"What happened to team breakfast? And hi Amy," I add.

"Good to see you again, Carter," she says sweetly.

"After you bailed, everyone else did too. See, this is why I wanted you to come. You're the glue of the team, man! Why'd you change your mind anyway?"

"No reason," I lie. "Just got hungrier than I thought I'd be after that workout."

"You're telling me. I could eat like two omelettes."

The waitress comes by, and we order a ridiculous amount of food for brunch. She scribbles quickly, and I think lingers an extra few seconds to make sure we're serious about how many sides of bacon we ordered.

"Yes, four sides of bacon," I confirm. "We had some rough workouts this morning."

She gives us a funny look and then walks off to put in our order. When she leaves, a silence falls on the table for a minute. It's not awkward—Chandler and I are beyond that. But we all notice it, I think.

Amy breaks it, looking at Chandler. "So . . . how's Lacy? Did you invite her?"

"Oh, I figured this was a team thing," I lie, omitting the fact that she was nowhere to be found in my apartment, and had essentially ditched me.

"Oh, that's too bad. I like her. We should do a double date or something or. . ."

"They're not dating," Chandler cuts in, then looks at me. "Right?"

"Right. Definitely not." And that's not a lie. We're sure fucking, but we haven't been on a date yet.

"Ah. Okay. Hard to tell with you two."

I sip my water, trying to think of a subject change. "So what's the deal with Coach Fable? Like he's got a stick up his ass, right?"

"No idea." Chandler squints, then looks at me. "Hey. Did you think about what I said the other night? I couldn't tell how drunk you were."

"About the genes ancestor tree test, you mean?"

"Yeah. You should do it."

Amy rubs Chandler's back. "It helped Chandie a lot, seeing what a loser his Dad was."

I squint. "I do remember you saying that now."

"I'll send you the link to the test I did," Chandler adds. "It's totally fucked up—people like you and me—who don't know their real father, but I think closure is important. It's a loose end you need to tie off."

I swallow a lump in my throat. My nostrils flare, and I clench my fists. "If I ever meet my father, I don't know what I'd do. Knock him the fuck out, maybe."

"Like that song, a Boy named Sue."

"Exactly."

Chandler puts his hand on Amy's knee and leans back in his chair. "It's our job as men to be better than our fathers. I'll tell my son that some day."

"Your. . . son?"

Amy rubs her tummy. "He says it's a boy for sure. Too early to tell, though."

"Holy shit. Guys, congratulations!" I cock my head. "Wait, what about the wedding?"

Amy smiles. "I'm tiny as it is. I figure maybe being pregnant can add some curves. Maybe my boobs will get bigger."

Chandler rubs the back of her neck. "Shush, Squirt. You know I love your. . ." he stops himself, and looks at me. "I was just about to say something very inappropriate, but I didn't. You're welcome, Carter."

"Seriously, congratulations, guys. And also, you still disgust me with how lovey dovey you are."

"Thanks!" Amy says, and I'm not sure what else to say. "So are you going to take the test? You should find out about your family! Oooh, what if you two are brothers?!" She says, joking.

I laugh, and our food arrives.

Amy lets out a screech of joy and claps quietly.

Chandler reaches across the table and grabs Amy's plate from the server.

She locks eyes with him as he hands it to her, and her hand lingers on his forearm. "Thanks, Babe," she whispers softly, in a voice not meant for me to hear.

"Thanks," I say, turning to the waitress, who glances

passive aggressively at the four plates of bacon on the table, as if to prove she got the order right.

As we dig in, an emotion sets in as I watch Chandler and Amy that I've never felt for another couple in my life: envy. I want what they have.

Maybe not today, but someday. And I've never wanted that.

It would take one hell of a woman for me to fall in love, though.

25

LACY

The morning light streams into Carter's room, making me stir. I'm sore all over.

I'm a flexible girl, but my legs are sore, and I've got an idea why. That's what happens when you get pretzeled into an array of different positions over a marathon fucking session into the wee hours.

Not to mention how sore I am between my legs. I might have to ice myself down.

Also, good thing Carter's bed is king size, since he sleeps so spread out.

And now, I think I deserve a little morning cuddling time for putting up with him all night. I spin away from the window, toward Carter's side of the bed.

My heart drops when I feel nothing on his side—though it's still warm. I swallow, rushing to check my phone.

Barely past seven A.M. on a Sunday. Where would he go?

I bolt up and look around the penthouse, but there's no trace of him. Almost without my consent, rage fills my heart, along with foolishness, and a realization. I'm just his little plaything, aren't I?

"Fucking asshole," I mutter out loud.

No girl he's met in his entire life has been able to change him. Why should I be so cocky as to think I could? My mind floods with more thoughts.

What am I even saying? *Change him?*

But why must the most satisfying sex I've had in my entire life be with a man who is quite possibly the most emotionally distant in the universe?

Yet that undercurrent of 'Good Carter' is in there, somewhere.

I shake my head, shower off, and give Lance a call.

"I was worried you'd be with your boyfriend all morning," he says.

"Boyfriend? Pssh."

"Right. What's that word even worth these days?"

"Preach."

"We're going to Thirteen Eggs at eight-thirty for breakfast. You in?"

"It's early. But I'll make it. See you there."

AFTER WHAT TURNS INTO A MULTIPLE HOUR EATING marathon, I walk home through the city streets of Chicago for hours. I figure I should walk off my buzz so I'm not totally hungover come tomorrow.

Lance and I make a no-drinking pact—that starts tomorrow, naturally—and I resolve to fully concentrate on dancing. No distractions.

But is Carter a distraction?

Maybe.

A beautiful distraction.

I walk along the Chicago river, then head under the bridge and make my way along the Lake Michigan beach.

People are out in droves sun-bathing, playing volleyball, and swimming in the lake.

My stomach is in knots thinking about Carter. Plus all the stuff I admitted to Lance and Joseph. I just needed to tell someone about my situation.

All along the beach, I see happy couples walking hand in hand. Others lie on the beach. I pass a giant boat on North Avenue, and see a guy picking up a girl who I assume is his girlfriend and threatening to throw her in the lake in spite of her protests.

A smile pulls at my lips. That would definitely be Carter and I. Even if we ever did become something more, I don't think he'd ever let up on me. That asshole side of him is too strong.

And I'm headstrong too.

A young dad and mom walk by with their toddler, each holding one of his hands. The kid laughs, letting his feet off the ground as he pretends to air walk, holding on to his parents for support.

If Carter and I ever become a couple, that would be us. In spite of everything, I just know it. I know Carter's a good man underneath his hard shell.

My heart drops a little. We'd never make it as a couple. I stop dead in my tracks, and reconsider the thought, almost trembling.

A couple?

What does that even mean? Why on earth am I considering Carter as boyfriend material after one weekend of sex?

This is a whirlwind romance, and I need to stay focused on dance, anyway. To take my mind off him, I pull out my phone and text my mom to see how she and my dad are doing.

She texts me back quickly, and I let her know I miss her.

She texts me some smiley emojis. Moms are so cute when they text emojis.

Feeling slightly better—and less buzzed—I start to walk in the direction of Carter's apartment using the GPS for guidance.

As I'm walking, I notice a funny-looking storefront, with a blank door. I head inside, curious.

As soon as I'm in, I realize why the storefront was blank and the windows dark.

It's a sex shop in the middle of Chicago.

I'm shocked at what I see.

Plenty of porn dvds, sex toys, and lingerie. Lace, satin, leather.

I sheepishly maneuver around the store to look at everything.

In one of the corners, a certain piece of lacey lingerie sticks out.

It's bright red set of a thong with a strap, a braless thing that goes around the breasts, and a freaking set of devil horns.

It's also waterproof, according to the label.

I bite my lip, looking at it, and my thoughts are of Carter.

I bet I could surprise the hell out of him if I used these for him.

And I sure am not going to use the tainted lingerie I have that was meant for Norton. I should just throw that out, anyway.

Sheepishly, I buy the lingerie set, not looking the cashier in the eye as I take it.

When I get back to the apartment, Carter's still not home.

I dig deep into my suitcase and pull out the set of white lingerie that I'd bought for Norton.

I shake my head and stuff the thing into a white plastic bag. I spent days researching this piece for him online. I was so nervous when I ordered it that my mom would find it, I began racing home after teaching my dance classes in Blackwell to beat my mom to the house and see if it had been delivered.

All that meticulous research out the window.

I pick up the red devil lingerie. Carter would freak if I wore it for him.

I shake my head thinking of all the things I've done for him. Would do for him.

Sighing, I walk the plastic bag to the main trash bin in the dining room. I need to get rid of the evidence, and preferably push it so far down in the trash, Carter would never think to find it.

I fling open the trash with my foot.

I hesitate before I throw it out, because the first thing I see is a Dark Matter paper coffee cup right on top of the trash. It seems to be leaking.

It's not even dirty, so I pick it up. The order label is from this morning, and it's still half-full. And it looks to be a cappuccino.

I furrow my brow, as a strange feeling overtakes my gut.

Why would Carter order a cappuccino? He hates cappuccinos . Or so he said.

Did Carter come back with a coffee for me this morning?

It makes no sense. Why would he do that? He wasn't even here when I woke up. Weird. Probably a mistake from the coffee shop?

I shrug and throw out the bag of lingerie, making sure it can't be seen from the top of the trash.

Tired, and possibly still a little buzzed, I head into Carter's room to make sure he's not there.

He's nowhere to be found. I grab my ereader and head to my bed.

I SLEEP STRAIGHT THROUGH THE NIGHT, WHICH IS GOOD.

Because on Monday, we start twelve-hour rehearsals to get ready for the show.

Carter texts me saying that he has to travel to Philadelphia for a charity tournament, and to take care of the place until Saturday night when he gets back.

The man is still an enigma when it comes to communication. You'd think he'd put his schedule on a calendar or something. Then again, before I moved in with him it was just him in his apartment, so it's not like he needed to communicate with anyone to let them know he was going to be out of town.

I breathe a sigh of relief knowing he's gone, although I miss him at the same time.

I miss him a lot, actually.

Part of me wonders—considering the timing of his travel —if he didn't just get freaked out that I was going to finally try and talk to him about his father—which I am. From what I gathered, the tournament was a sort of optional thing for the team.

Heading into the big bed in his room, I lay on the bed, starfish, and think about him.

For a guy who is such an asshole up front, Carter has a surprisingly soft and tender side. Oddly, his pep talks have made me more confident when I'm on stage.

Or maybe it's the post-sex glow that makes me feel more confident.

I take a deep breath. I could use some post-sex glow tonight. Eying my dresser, I have a naughty thought.

Maybe I'll put on the lingerie I have and do a sexy photo shoot for him.

Just the thought of him getting turned on turns me on.

❧ 26 ❧

CARTER

All week while I'm away, she's all I can think about.

I've never been consumed by thoughts of a girl. But as I'm staying in the hotel room in Philadelphia for a summer charity tournament, I'm tormented by thoughts of Lacy.

Then I remember she ran away Sunday morning. I got a fucking cappuccino for her and she wasn't even there to accept it. Maybe for some guys, that's a small gesture. Not for me.

I thank God I have basketball to take my mind off life. But this has been, honest-to-God, the weirdest week of my life.

First, I resurrect a relationship I thought was long dead.

Second, I just sent in one of my hairs to a genealogy company.

I float on a raft in the hotel pool, soaking in some rays of sun as Chandler explains the test, since he already did it.

"The way it works is that they'll tell you what your genetic make-up is by origin of country. And if you have relatives who have also taken the test, they'll be able to let you know who those people are by cross-referencing their database."

"Sounds creepy and intrusive, in a way."

He shrugs. "It is, a little. If you've got something to hide."

"So you found out who your father was by running this test?"

"Yep. A little over a year ago. Me and Amy went down to southern Illinois in some little podunk town, Murhpysboro. I tell you man, I was both pissed and relieved once I finally knew."

"What if the results come back and I still don't know?"

He pauses, taking a sip of his cocktail. "Man, I don't know. Maybe ask your mother."

A chill rocks through me at that. "No. We don't talk about those things."

He raises his eyebrow. "Hey I get it. Touchy subject."

"You have no idea, man."

"Try me," he scoffs. "If you can top my own fucked-up story, go for it."

"Alright," I say, my skin starting to tingle a little bit. I realize there is not one other person in the world who knows the full version of this story, other than me.

And Lacy.

"Up until I turned eighteen, my mom told me my dad had died, and that he'd suffocated on a pillow when she was pregnant with me. I thought it was a weird story, sure, but I guess I just went along with it. Kid stuff, you know. The day I turned eighteen, I heard her talking to a man on the phone late at night. She sounded scared, so I asked her what was the matter. Tears in her eyes, she said 'nothing.' I got angry all of the sudden. I told her she needed to tell me right now. That she needed to stop lying. She straightened up, pulled out a cigarette, and started to smoke. She only really smoked when she was stressed, you know? And she told me the whole story about how she met my father. She said she had a one-night stand in Vegas. That she'd gotten pregnant—with me—by the man she was talking to on the phone."

Chandler stares at me, wide-eyed. "That is fucked up, man."

"That's just the beginning. So apparently, this guy—my father—had demanded my mom not have me when she was pregnant."

"He wanted her to—"

I hold up my hand. "Terminate the pregnancy."

Chandler nods slowly, and swallows. The look on his face is dark as what I say sets in.

I continue. "To him, I was some aberration from a one-night stand where he didn't wrap it up. He would have preferred I had never been born. I was a mistake baby. My mom told me all of this that night, tears in her eyes. She must have smoked half a pack of cigarettes while she did. She said that my dad had some very powerful friends protecting him. And that now, since I was turning eighteen, my dad was worried I would try and find him and his family. This could cause a life-altering scandal for him, apparently. I think he works in politics--or business, maybe."

"My fucking God. What a fuckhead."

"Yes. That's one of a few words I've used to describe him over the years."

Chandler shakes his head slightly. "Who the fuck is he, that he's so worried about a scandal he can't acknowledge his own son?"

"No fucking clue. I never sought him out."

We both fall silent for a few moments. There's only the gentle sounds of the pool water lightly running around us.

Finally, I go on. "My mom showed me the text messages. They were only labeled *Him*. I didn't even learn his name. I didn't ask. I didn't want to know. He threatened my mom. So

I called him up. I told him I didn't want shit to do with him, and called him some more names. I'd only heard him answer with one word. 'Yeah?' That voice still haunts me to this day. After I'd gone off on him, he just hung up."

Chandler leans in, then glances at some of our teammates who are lying on the side of the pool.

"Carter, this is fucking mind blowing. Have you ever told anyone about this?"

"Not a person. Only Lacy knows." I said.

"Lacy? Why does she know."

"Because she found out before me, when my mom was at her house."

Chandler's eyes widen substantially. "And she didn't tell you?"

"No." I continue. "So anyway, I sent in the test. I'm excited to find out what kind of ancestry I have. But mark my words: I don't ever want to meet my father. Fuck him. I'll never forgive him, no matter what. He never wanted me to be born."

"Fuck him," Chandler agrees.

I look off into the distance, staring at the Philadelphia skyline. "Lacy had known for an entire year. And we were..." I swallow. "We were dating at the time. I flipped out on her. After that, I wanted nothing to do with her."

Chandler nods. "Man, I'm no doctor, but you have some fucking issues. You should probably go to a therapist or something."

I run my hand over my throat. "So did I beat you?"

Chandler rolls his eyes. "Yes, you beat me with your messed up story, Mr. Competitive. I admit it. And I'm going to beat your ass tomorrow in the dunk competition."

"Not possible."

Chandler splashes me. "Come on man! Give me a fighting

chance. I've got a kid on the way now. That does something to you, man. Trust me."

I shudder. "Not to everyone, apparently."

"By the way, are you coming to the wedding? You know you have to send in the paper RSVP. There's no special treatment for you. Amy asked."

"Of course I'm coming."

"With a plus one?"

"I didn't know I had one."

"Well maybe if you ever read your damn mail you'd know. Honestly though, please don't bring one of your French model slampieces. If you bring Lacy, that's cool. Amy said she has good vibes. But I don't want to have another fiasco like at the Wilson wedding last winter."

I scrunch up my face. "Hey, it's not my fault my date thought she could consume alcohol on par with a man twice her size."

Chandler shakes his head. "Watching her get drunk and make a scene was like watching the Titanic go down. It was also like the Titanic in that we'll never again let that happen! Besides, what's the deal with you and Lacy?"

I tense up. "What do you mean?"

"Don't be a dense dipshit. You know what I mean."

"Can't say that I do."

He shrugs. "Well when you get a clue, let me know. Preferably by next week, considering RSVPs were due a month ago and Amy has been asking me about yours every other day."

I slide off my float. "Oh, has she?"

"Don't you fucking dare. I'm finally dry."

I wink as I flip his floaty and dunk Chandler.

He stands up in the water, hair like a wet dog's and shakes his head. "I thought we were having a moment."

I shrug. "I don't like to have moments."

"I'm serious about that therapist. Amy's got a good one."

"I don't do therapy."

"Yeah, yeah, yeah, it's for pussies. And so is yoga. Got it. Like I said, you win the award for most fucked-up father and upbringing. Congratulations. I'm pretty sure that also comes with a few years of therapy as the prize."

❧ 27 ❧

CARTER

I text Lacy on and off during the week, to see how she's doing. And how Smokey is doing. By the time Friday rolls around, I've had my fill of the hotel pool. The team jet is heading back on Saturday morning, but I ask the coach's permission to head back late Friday after the game, citing the fact that I need to deal with some personal family stuff.

He doesn't have to know that by 'personal family stuff,' I mean I miss the fuck out of Lacy.

I get into Midway airport around ten on Friday night and take a Lyft to my place.

I stop at the front desk before I head up, to pick up my mail. The attendant tells me that my roommate already picked up the mail, so I head up the elevator. I burst through the front door, and once inside I notice that there is a cluster of mail on the marble countertop. I thumb through the stack, looking for Chandler's wedding invitation, when a piece of Lacy's mail falls out, already opened.

Narrowing my eyes, I pick it up and look at it. I blink a few times when I see that it's a credit card bill for Lacy with well over five figures of credit card debt.

Well this is news.

I hear a faint noise and glance up.

"Lacy? You here?"

My voice echoes through the house, and for a moment I think it might be empty. I drop my bag on the floor in the living room and stand silently for a moment.

I hear music on the balcony. And the low rumble of the hot tub jets bubbling up. She's on the balcony. Probably in the hot tub.

Wasting no time, I grab two glasses and a bottle of wine. I'm going to need it for this conversation.

When I slide the door open, I can't help but stare at Lacy for a few beats.

She's wearing one of my bath robes, and she stands with her back to me as she spreads her arms out, gripping the railing and looking out over the city. Her hair blows in the wind.

She doesn't even notice me as I approach her, and when I make it to the railing and see her face, I understand why. Her eyes are closed as she belts out the lyrics to Taylor Swift's *Will you Remember Me*, which is playing loudly.

And looks like she's already got the bottle of wine covered, judging by the half-drunk bottle in her hand. I don't even see a glass.

"Happy Friday, Laces!" I belt out. "Nice to see someone's celebrating!"

She opens her eyes wide, and clutches her heart, then grabs the ends of the bath robe to pull them in before I have a shot to see what she's wearing underneath.

"Carter," she says, swallowing. "You're here!"

"Laces," I say casually. "I'll admit it, fine. I missed you. Came home a day early. Mind if I join you?"

She blinks a few times and stares at me. "Yeah, sure," she says, breathlessly.

"I brought an extra glass out," I say as I turn on the jets to the hot tub. "Were you just drinking from the bottle?"

She clears her throat. "It was just me, so I figured why dirty up a glass."

I shake my head and spin around to check the temperature settings.

Lightning quick, she slips into the hot tub and slinks lower into the water. The white bubbles cover her body all the way up to her neck. I silently lament I didn't even get to catch a glimpse of her beautiful body on the way in.

I slip all the way down into the hot water, the jets soothing my muscles. "Fuck, that feels good. How was your week?"

"It was okay."

"So okay that you're drinking wine by yourself. . . from the bottle?

"Okay it was pretty good, until today."

A shiver runs through me thinking about the news I saw about her debt. I can't believe she hasn't told me. But on the other hand, maybe it's none of my business. "What happened today?" I ask.

She averts her eyes. "It was just a relentless day. I needed some hot tub therapy. How about you, how was your week?"

"I've been doing a lot of thinking this week," I say.

I dart my gaze around the balcony. This isn't a conversation I relish having. But like everything in life, once I've decided to dive balls first into something, that's what I do. And with the results of the test coming back in a few weeks, I'd better start considering their implications.

"About what?"

I suck in a deep breath. "About everything. You, me. My past. Our past. Chandler convinced me to do a genealogy test to see what my genetic make-up is, so I sent in the sample. And if any relatives of mine have taken the same test, I'll be able to see who they are. Cousins—siblings, of course I don't have any of those, though. Aunts and uncles. That kind of thing."

"Fathers," she says, and covers her mouth as soon as she says it, her face filling with fear as she notices how I visibly stiffen at the word.

I cringe a little at that F-word, like I always have. But I've vowed to face the truth and stand up to my past. I've done enough running.

The heat of the water feels damn good on my skin as it heats up my body.

Lacy hits the jets behind us again, starting the timer for another ten minutes.

"It's okay. You know, I need to thank you. I wouldn't have gotten to where I am if it wasn't for you. From here on out, Lacy, no more secrets. Not from you, at least. I'm done with secrets, and I'm done running. What you said to me last weekend struck a chord. You're right."

Her jaw falls open. "Did you just say, 'I'm right?'"

"Yeah. You were right. About a lot of things."

"I always get suspicious when you're being nice to me. Like it's a trick."

I laugh. "No trick. Just want to ask, though. Is there anything you have to tell me?"

I picture the piece of mail I just looked at. And now I know that Lacy's got almost thirty thousand dollars in credit card bills that she's making minimum payments on.

She glances at me, and averts her eyes. "Some things are just my problem, Carter," she swallows.

I nod and take a sip of my wine, looking out at the vast expanse of Lake Michigan. So this is how it's going to be.

As long as I've known Lacy—she has to know that in spite of any ill will I've harbored for her I'd wipe that debt out in a fucking heartbeat if she came clean to me about it. She's a family friend, and an old friend.

Most girls just excuse away my bad behavior, letting that shit fly because they know they won't find this type of dick anywhere else.

Not Lacy.

Even right now, she's acting odd. Standoffish and squirmy and I can't quite tell why.

Maybe she doesn't trust me. I can't say I'd blame her, given my track record for fucked-up behavior. I think back on the piece of mail I just saw. Technically, I shouldn't have looked at it. Her credit card debt is none of my business. But I'm done with secrets now, even ones that might seem insignificant.

As blunt of a guy as I am, maybe ten P.M. on a Friday after she's drunk half a bottle of wine isn't the time to start chatting about finances. I exhale slowly and let it go.

Scanning the edge of the hot tub, I notice a strange object from the side of the hot tub. I pick it up and hold it in front of my face.

"Are these. . . devil horns?"

Her face turns beat red. "Maybe."

I narrow my eyes. "That's hot."

"Thanks," she swallows.

"So why are you acting so weird?"

"I didn't know you were going to be home tonight," she says.

"Don't dodge my question. If you don't answer, I'll have to assume you were planning on having some kind of angels and devils orgy. Seriously, what are these things?"

She swallows. "This is silly, Carter. But...I just didn't have a swimsuit. I wanted to get in the hot tub."

"You didn't want to give my neighbors a nude show? They don't mind."

She rolls her eyes. "I had this devil lingerie lying around, so I put it on."

I cup Lacy's cheek and stare into her eyes.

"I want to tell you everything I've thought about this week. How the thought of you has turned me on so much this week, every night. How this is the first time in a long time I've fantasized about the same woman every night. I haven't felt like this since high school."

She nibbles on her lower lip. "Oh? And who were you thinking about in high school?"

Smirking, I cock my head. "You really don't know?"

"No."

"You."

She freezes up, not moving, and I see her swallow slowly. "Seriously?" she whispers.

I nod.

"We were dating. Why didn't you just make a move?"

"I wasn't in a rush. I thought we had our whole lifetimes."

"I didn't want to lie to you, Carter. You have to know that. My mother made me swear I wouldn't tell you, and swear to respect your mother-son relationship. I wanted to respect your family. It wasn't about keeping a truth from you. It was about respecting your mother."

I feel the rush of emotion roll through me as I recall that day she told me she was lying.

"I know. But it hurts, and it made me think everything that happened between us that year was based on a lie."

Putting a hand on my shoulder, she whispers, "We can still make up for lost time, Carter."

She leans toward me, and her nipples press against me. Her very hard nipples.

Desire ratchets through me, along with confusion. I pull back and hold her shoulders, staring at her.

The jets stop.

My jaw drops at what I see through the water.

She's got on a bright red lingerie piece. Noticing how my eyes are tracking her, she wipes the tears away from her cheeks, and stands up shyly.

She puts the devil horns on her head.

Her expression turns positively devilish. "I was thinking about doing a photoshoot for you."

I turn my head so we're facing each other, our noses barely inches apart.

She runs her hand over my chest.

Her eyes flit up to me, and she smiles. "Because I like being a little bad, with you. Is that wrong?"

The water splashes as she stands up, giving me a full view of the lingerie. Her ass juts out of the back of the tiny little thing. It barely covers her pussy. Her nipples, hard and pink, point attentively at me.

Adrenaline pumps through me and my cock hardens, half with desire. And half with rage.

Straddling my lap, she pulls on the back of my neck to bring my ear down to her mouth, and whispers.

"I was thinking about you, Carter. I bought this for you. Do you like it?"

My nostrils flare, and my body flushes with desire. Want. *Need.*

She bats her eyes, bringing her full gaze to mine. Her lips hover, a paper's width from mine.

I lick my lips, and heat consumes me.

I come home after a week of reflection. I try to confront my feelings—for the first time in my life—and she distracts me like this.

I grab a fistful of Lacy's hair. "Come with me," I growl, and lead her out of the hot tub to my bedroom.

❧ 28 ❧

LACY

"Lie here. And don't move," Carter growls.

My entire body charges with desire as I lie in Carter's bed on my back. He rummages around in the top drawer of his dresser while I stay still.

My eyes flit to Carter without me moving my head even an inch. He looks so incredible from behind—he has the back of a body builder, and the sexiest ass I've seen in my life.

I'm a ball of tension as I lay, waiting for him to do with me as he wants. I've never felt such a confused stew and litany of feelings running through me all at once.

I want Carter to have his way with me. Make me his . . . his property? No, fuck that. Women didn't fight for independence for hundreds of years to have me desire to be a man's whore. In my mind's eye, though, I imagine Carter's body pressing down on me. I feel him pressing all of his weight down on me as he penetrates deep inside me, and whispers against my skin.

"Lacy. You're mine, and I don't care what you think. You can't hide the desire in your eyes. I said, no more secrets."

My heart speeds as though I'm about to go out onto the stage and begin the most challenging variation of my life.

I close my eyes, summoning all of my effort to keep my body still.

I want to run away, far from here. Part of me still feels like once I hand over control to Carter, he'll just hurt me. But I love the way he makes me feel.

I open my eyes, and Carter is standing still, to the side of the bed. I turn my eyes upward toward him.

"No more secrets between us, Lacy. So here's a secret of mine: I like to play."

I swallow a lump in my throat. "Play with what?"

"It's better that I show you."

"Right now?"

He smirks. "You want to do this, Lacy?"

"What are we doing? And yes."

"Then close your eyes and trust me. If you want to stop, just tell me."

"I want it all, Cartwheel."

He secures the black blindfold around my head, blotting out my world.

Instantly, my senses of hearing and touch heighten.

Carter's fingertips run along my jawline, down my collarbone, teasing the skin around my areolas. My skin tingles, my nipples hardening.

"What are you going to do to me?" I ask. I feel the absence of his fingers on my skin. My heart lurches.

"I'm done being nice to you," Carter growls.

"Being . . . nice? When were you nice?"

"Turn over," Carter says, ignoring my question.

I do as he says. He pulls my arms behind my back, and wraps them with something.

"Are you going to answer my question?" I ask, my cheek turned against the sheet.

"I don't answer stupid fucking questions," he growls. "So you might as well stop asking."

I clam up. I feel Carter's strong hands as he fastens my wrists together. I can't tell what he's using except for the fact that they're not handcuffs.

"These are bondage cuffs. You won't be able to move your arms with them."

"Oh really? I hadn't noticed."

He grabs my hair, then pulls my hips up so I'm on my knees, but I can't use my arms to balance myself, so my head smashes into the mattress. I keep my head to the side a little so I can still breathe.

My heart pounds as his hands run up and down the backs of my thighs.

"Gorgeous. Just fucking gorgeous. A gift from God, really. I could stare at your creamy skin all day. I love how it contrasts with your black hair. Have I ever told you that?"

"No," I say, blowing out a breath of relief.

Too soon.

A second later, I feel a smack on my ass.

With something light.

"Oww," I mutter, swallowing as the sting rolls through my body.

Carter's palm rolls across my ass, rubbing the hot skin.

"Carter," I protest. "It hurts a little."

He chuckles. "You want me to stop?"

"No. Keep going. Punish me, Carter."

"What did you just say?"

"Keep going Carter," I say with a hushed breath. "I want it all."

He rubs his hand in a circular motion on my ass, and I take a few deep breaths.

A wave of anger pulses through me, my chest swelling. No man should have this kind of control over me and my desire.

Especially Carter.

But you know what I hate the most?

I hate how much I love what he's doing right now.

"Screw you," I mutter. "You always have to get some snide comment in. Get the last word. You think you've grown in the last week? I doubt it."

Carter grunts, and I feel another slap on my other cheek.

"You don't like it?"

I let out a little air this time, but not as much as before. I embrace the pain.

Carter caresses the spot he hit with his bare hand. And then strikes me again on the other side.

"Yes," I grunt lightly. "I do like it. But screw you, Carter."

Yes. Screw you and how good you make me feel.

Continuing with this pattern, he does each side six times.

I stay silent, as the endorphins pump through me, making me feel high. I refuse to give Carter the satisfaction of showing how much I love this.

I love him.

Fuck. No.

I love what he can do to my body. Love the way he takes control.

And I'm not telling him.

He spanks me once more and can't stop the purr of pleasure that escapes the side of my mouth.

"Ohh, God yes," I murmur, and as soon as I do, I want to cover my mouth. But I can't move my arms. He lifts up my torso until I feel the heat of his cheek against mine.

"Are you enjoying this?" he growls.

"No," I lie.

"Good. And now, if you come before I say, I swear to God, Lacy."

I giggle. "You swear to God, you'll what?"

He huffs. "For a girl who wants to be punished, you've got a smart, smart mouth. Don't you?"

I don't say anything. I feel the bed shift as it loses Carter's weight.

He slides my legs to the side of the bed. "On your feet," he says.

I do as I'm told, and stand up on his carpeted floor.

"Kneel," he growls.

I balk. "On my knees?"

I hear him huff. "You've got three seconds."

I clam up.

"One."

Why would he ask me to do this? Of all the things he's wanted of me. I blink a few times underneath my blindfold, wishing I could see him. What's his expression right now? Playful? Mean? Blank?

"Two."

I swallow, tension rocketing through me.

"Three."

My knees hit the carpet just as he says the first syllable of the number.

He steps toward me, I know because I feel the heat emanating from him.

I crave his warmth.

Running a hand along my jaw, he speaks again. "I'll be back. Don't move."

I hear his footsteps moving away, and a weird feeling of panic sets in. "How long will you be gone?"

"One minute. One hour. It doesn't matter to you."

I'm still as I kneel. I feel throbbing between my legs at the commanding tone of his voice.

I flinch when I hear him slam the door shut. My whole body tenses, and I wonder if I'm an insane woman for doing this with him. I close my eyes. Not that it makes a difference with my blindfold.

I've given Carter the power to destroy me.

And what's more, I ache for him to follow all the way through to the end of . . . whatever he's got in mind.

I want to show him how strong I am. I can take whatever he has to give me. And in another way, I wonder if he's getting pleasure out of this night. Seeing me all bundled up and vulnerable.

He must know how badly I want him. Before I knew he was coming home tonight, I was just planning on sitting in the hot tub in the devil's outfit I got for *him*, for God's sake.

He was all I could think about all week.

I wanted to wrap my legs around him and feel him inside me, loving how deep he goes.

Hold onto to his arms, his sides, as he thrust into me so fucking powerfully.

"Mmm," I mutter, so hot and so wet for him.

I open my eyes and I'm slightly surprised when all I see is black. Suddenly I'm irritated that he's left me alone like this.

What if he's gone for an entire hour?

What if he leaves for more time?

How long has he been gone?

And what's he doing out there anyway?

Making fucking dinner? Some sort of food smell wafts into the room. My stomach rumbles.

From in the kitchen, I hear Carter clear his throat.

He even does *that* with power.

I blow out a hard breath. What am I even doing with my Friday night?

I'm tied up, submitting my will to this man who might do God-knows-what to me. I should get up and leave. Go to Lance's. Watch silly rom coms and eat popcorn.

I swallow the lump in my throat, recalling the brunch

conversation I had with Lance and Joseph. How I'd been holding something back. What that something is exactly, I can't quite put my finger on.

I don't know what Carter's planning on doing with me tonight. But I'd rather feel a burn than feel nothing at all.

My hands clam up, and I part my legs a little more, feeling the heat building between my thighs. My skin is flushed, and my ass tingles from the blows I received from Carter's paddle.

I wonder how far into this stuff Carter's gotten. Clearly he had that toy box ready to go.

My skin feels hot yet chilly all of the sudden. What is Carter capable of?

Finally, I hear Carter's footsteps coming down the hallway. The door opens, and I stay silent, kneeling at attention.

"My my. Looks like someone's finally been a good girl."

"I have?"

"Yes. Time for your reward. Open your mouth."

I part my lips, and listen to Carter step toward me.

"Very good girl," he says as I take him into my mouth.

I brace for his his size, but when I wrap my lips around his tip, I realize instantly he's not fully hard.

Instinctively, I try to pull a hand out to grab the base of his cock, forgetting my hands are tied up.

"Nah-ah, baby girl. You're going to have to learn how to do this with just your mouth."

He pulls back for a moment, and I suck in a breath. Heat pools between my legs as I wonder what he'll do next.

I feel a guiding hand on my head as he wraps my hair up into an improvised pony tail, guiding me back onto his tip.

Tenuously, I lick. Running my lips along the sides of his shaft, I feel him growing, the flesh hardening.

"Do you like how that feels, Lace? Do you like how hard you make me?"

"Uh huh," I mutter, hungry for the rest of him.

I hear a short breath escape Carter's mouth, and it spurs me on. I lean my neck forward and take him in my mouth, as deep as I'm able.

"Fuck," he utters in a wispy grunt, and I feel his body shift somehow.

I ask myself what he's doing, and a second later I have my answer when I feel a slap on my ass. I try to moan, but I'm stifled by my full mouth, and instead let out an awkward grunt-sounding noise, like I'm trying to say something but just bit off more than I could chew.

Carter's soothing hand runs along my back and up to my neck.

"So fucking hot," he mutters, then pulls my head away from his cock, leaving me gasping for air.

My eyes drift upward, naturally, and all I see is the black leather of the blindfold. I want to see him so bad. See the want in his eyes. His need.

Focused on *me*.

"Come on," Carter says in a low voice, guiding me up to my feet.

"Where are we going?" I breathe. Carter pauses. I feeling his presence behind me, his breath on my neck.

"I said stop asking fucking stupid questions. Haven't you figured it out yet, Lacy?" he growls, his breath soothing my neck. "I'm in control. I'm taking care of you."

Picking me up, he places me back on the bed. As he props my back up at a forty-five degree angle with a few pillows, I can't help but repeat his words in my mind.

I'm taking care of you.

As gruff and unfeeling as Carter often seems to be, it feels like an odd choice of words. They help to relax some of the tension I'm feeling from being unable to see anything.

I listen as Carter gets up from the bed. It sounds like he's picking something up from his dresser, and a few moments later I feel his weight pressing into the mattress again.

Then, I feel leather straps being tied around my ankles. I open my mouth to ask Carter another question about what we're doing, but I close my lips as fast as I opened them, knowing his response. Instead, I say something else.

"Hey Cartwheel," I say in a raspy tone. I feel his motion pause. That gets his attention.

"Laces?"

His tone is surprisingly caring, throwing me off again. I feel like I'm grasping at straws for words to express what I'm feeling.

My heart pounds like crazy. "Nothing," I say. "Never mind."

I suddenly get the feeling like I'm putting my life in this man's hands. Carter, who's hated me for so long. What if this is one elaborate plan to exact some sort of screwed up revenge on me? What if . . .

I hear a noise like an umbrella snapping open, and at the same time I feel my legs jut apart.

"Leg spreader," Carter chuckles.

"Why do you need that?!" I retort instinctively.

"You'll see."

My adrenaline spikes, when I feel a tender kiss from Carter on my inner thigh, sending chills over my skin.

"Oh, Carter." I'm about to relax into the pillows behind me when I hear him flip a switch, and a buzzing noise starts, sending my heartbeat racing again.

Carter shifts on the bed until he's at my side. He kisses me on the cheek, his stubble brushing against my skin.

"Is that a—"

"Vibrator. Time to see what you can handle, Laces."

"See what I can—oh, dear God!"

Heat rushes between my legs as he presses the vibrator

against my clit. I squirm and want to twist my hips, as the waves of pleasure burst through me.

Carter kisses me on the forehead, then on the lips.

He feels like two men as he covers my mouth with his, kissing me with force and using his free hand to rub all over my hot skin. He runs it along my jawline, my nipples, my stomach.

"What does Lacy want?"

"You," I say without thinking.

"Good. Now arch your back and put your ass in the air." Carter's tone is unmistakably dominant.

I do what he says, even though it's a little bit awkward and difficult with my hands behind my back. Using the pillow behind me for leverage, I arch my back and lift my hips.

Just then, I feel the absence of Carter's touch as he lifts his hands and mouth away from me, and the vibrator on my clit is the only point of contact between us.

My skin flushes and I hold in a breath. My body feels like a firework starting to go off.

"Tell me when you're getting close," Carter says.

"Okay," I say, swallowing. Not this game again.

My face tightens, and the pulse in my clit throbs.

It's not fair.

Under my breath, I mouth his name. I want to reach out and grab him, touch his face.

I shake nearly uncontrollably, light-headed as my orgasm builds. I want to tell him, screw his game, and screw his control over my pleasure.

But somehow, if I *don't* tell him, he wins. And if I *do* tell him, he wins, too.

I clench my hands and release them, feeling utterly powerless and at his mercy.

The pulse on my clit is too much, too intense. Clenching up, I move to close my legs, but I can't.

"Now, now," he says, stroking a hand through my hair. "You're getting close, aren't you?"

"So close," I admit, craving the ability to touch him.

Pulling the vibrator off of my clit, I feel him switch positions to the base of my legs. The straps on my ankles detach, and he pushes my legs straight up into the air, onto his shoulders.

The weight of his cock falls on top of my belly, and he pauses. I feel him reach behind my back. He pulls the string of the leather attacher, and my arms hang free, blood rushing into them.

Instinctively, I reach out and run my hands across his chest muscles, greedily feeling what I'd been missing.

I brace as he pushes his throbbing cock into me with one big, long stroke. He holds inside of me, and the buzzing of the vibrator starts again.

I tremble as he presses it into my clit, and my eyes roll into the back of my head.

"Carter, what are you doing to me?" I mutter.

"I'm ruining you for other men," he says in a cocky growl.

"Holy fuck," I mewl.

Holding onto my legs, he fucks me and presses the vibrator into me.

Carter *is* two men.

"I need to come. Please, Carter." My chest flutters and I writhe, hyper sensitive to his touch as he brings a hand to my face and lifts off my blindfold.

When I open my eyes, he's squinting at me with a tight expression as I run my gaze over his beautiful face. He thrusts faster, and grips my my jaw tightly, his thumb brushing my throat. I bring my eyes down to his chest and perfect abdomen.

"Look at me," he demands, his tone not leaving a single inch for dispute.

I flit my gaze back to his dark brown eyes, my whole body tingling like I'm a bomb about to go off. "Carter . . . can I . . ."

"You can come."

I shiver, not wanting to give him the answer, even though I know it's true. "I know," I say desperately, still keeping my eyes locked on his. "I'm all yours."

I run a hand through his thick, brown hair as I orgasm desperately, never having needed the release so badly in my entire life.

I flood with warmth as the pleasure ratchets through my body, my cunt tightening. Managing to hold onto his gaze somehow through the fog of sensations, I see his face tighten as he growls.

"Fuck, when you get so tight like that . . ." he trails off.

He chucks the vibrator and grabs hold of my hips as he pumps into me, his eyes like a predator's.

We both pant as our sweaty skin sticks together. My heart is a mix of rage, surrender, and relief as he pulls out of me. Taking my hand in his, he kisses the side of my neck, sending goosebumps over my naked body.

🌿 29 🌿

CARTER

Lacy and I settle into quite the routine over the next few weeks.

I would have never guessed she'd be able to keep up with me, but I notice the usual suspects have stopped texting me for hookups.

Lacy handles everything I can throw at her and more.

One weekday in late July, about a week and a half before her final performance, I get back from an an evening workout with Chandler and she's sitting on the couch, surfing the web on her iPad.

She lifts her head up and smiles at me from over the couch. "Hi," she say sweetly and simply, her smile soft.

I can't help but grin back. "Hey."

The truth is, she's softened me—if only a little—these past couple of weeks.

"I picked up the mail," she says, looking back at her iPad. "There were a couple of things for you."

"I arch my eyebrow. "Fan mail?"

She rolls her eyes. "No. Looks like the results from that ancestry test you did finally came in."

"Oh." My heart starts to pound, and I glance at the envelope on the counter.

Putting down her iPad, she rests her arms on the top of the couch, and cocks her head to the side a little.

"Come look at it over here?" Her tone is tentative. It's not an order, more of a invitation.

Still, she of all people knows how badly I've struggled with wanting—and then not wanting—to know the details of my past over the years.

I walk over to the couch and join her, envelope in hand. Kissing her on the lips, I sit down.

"Oh," she turns her head a little. "Are we . . . kissing hello now?"

My stomach twists a little bit. As much as we've been hooking up lately, we still haven't had much discussion about our status beyond the bedroom.

I shrug. "I just felt like kissing you. So I did. Don't read into it too much, Laces."

She lowers her eyes to the envelope in my hands. "It's okay. Sorry. We should focus on this now, anyways. Are you nervous?"

She brings her gaze back up to mine, a cheerful smile masking the topic we are obviously both avoiding talking about: any sort of relationship status update.

Putting my hand across her thigh, I swallow. She leans her head into my shoulder.

"You know I don't get nervous," I lie, passing off the heat in my head as nothing.

The smell of her hair makes my heart warm a bit. For once in my life, I'm happy I have something more than just a hookup here to share a moment with.

"You don't think it could change things for you?" she offers.

I close my eyes and suck a breath deep into my lungs.

"According to what Chandler said, the results of this test totally altered his perspective on life. Then again, he was able to find out who his biological father was based on the results. Since it's crowd-sourced, the only way you can tell if you have other relatives is if they've taken the same test. That way, they have the other genetic code on file. Otherwise, it just lets you know your ancestry. Eastern European, Greek, or whatever."

"Your mom is a mutt right?"

I chuckle at her choice of words as I run my hands over the envelope.

"Yeah. A mutt. Part Spanish, part Swedish, part German. And part North African—according to her great grand-mother who was from the south of Spain."

She grins up at me. "I'm getting anxious. Open it!"

My palms sweat as I stick my finger into the slit and rip it open.

Lacy rests her hand on my thigh and reads over my shoulder with me.

I've never read so fast in my life, racing through the components of the letter.

"Looks like she was right about the North African," Lacy says.

"Yep," I swallow, and flip to the next page.

My jaw drops at the words I read.

RELATIVES WHO HAVE ALSO TAKEN THE TEST AND CONSENTED *to be connected to their relatives on Long Lost Ancestor Tree:*
  -4 distant cousins
  -1 sibling

FREAKED OUT, I STAND UP, MY HAND ON MY FOREHEAD.

"One fucking sibling?!"

"Holy shit," she mutters, her eyes wide.

I hold the paper in my hand, and it shakes.

I look down at Lacy and she's got the same expression as me. Her eyebrows are pinched with worry and her face tinged with confusion.

"How the fuck is this possible?!" I say. Getting up off the couch, I start pacing through the living room. "My mom . . . my Mom kept some things from me, but she sure as hell would have told me about a sibling!"

I pace back toward Lacy, and she puts her hand on my chest, stopping me.

My heart drops to my feet as a scary thought crosses my mind. "You don't know anything about this, do you? That you overheard from your mom?"

She pinches her expression, narrowing her eyes at me. "You're not fucking serious, are you?"

I shrug. "Just had to ask."

She shakes her head. "Maybe . . . it's on your dad's side?"

My chest coils up. I've come to hate that word, *dad*, with a passion. Especially when it's referring to my shitbag of a deadbeat father.

"Don't say that word again," I growl.

Lacy puts her hands on her hips as I glare at her. "Sorry. Carter. It's going to be okay." She rushes toward me and wraps her arms around me as I let my arms fall at my sides.

I'm not used to being comforted like this. My eyes well up, and I rest my head on top of hers as I wrap my arms tightly around her body, pulling her into me, saying nothing.

We stay just like that for a few moments, until I pull back, staring at the paper in my hand. My eyes zoom in on a set of instructions after the word 'sibling.'

To find out who your relatives are (if they have consented to be connected) log on to your online account.

My heart starts to hammer, practically jumping out of my shirt.

"Lacy, give me your iPad," I say.

She grabs it quickly, realizing where I'm going. We both sit back down.

I notice when she pulls up her browser that she was doing an apartment search on Craigslist in New York.

Although I have too many things cramping my mind right now, the thought of Lacy being gone makes me grind my teeth. I press the thought out of my mind and focus on the task at hand.

"Just in case I get the spot with Blue Illusion." She says the words shyly, like she's embarrassed about it.

"Of course," I say gruffly.

She pulls up a fresh browser page and hands me her device. Frantically, I type the login information I was given, and then into my gmail so I can verify my account.

I switch back to my Long Lost Ancestry account and pull up the *my family tree page*.

I read through the names like lightning.

When I reach the area that says 'siblings,' I feel the lump in my throat turn to a steel brick as I read the name.

"This . . . has to be an error," I say, my heart pounding.

Lacy's jaw is nearly on the couch. "Oh. My. God."

She turns her head, and runs her eyes over my face, and her hands over my jaw. "But you two do share a resemblance."

I rub my hand over my face, as I try to process this mind-boggling information.

If it's true.

Why wouldn't it be true, though?

I pull my phone out of my pocket and, my hand shaking, I dial.

"What the fuck do you want, asshole? What, one workout

wasn't enough of me tonight?" comes Chandler's gravelly voice.

"I need you to get the fuck over to my apartment. Right now."

He recognizes the serious tone, extremely unusual for me. "Holy shit. Everything okay?"

"No. Everything is not okay," I swallow.

"I'll be there," Chandler says. I hear him drop a fork onto a plate. "What the fuck is going on?"

Heat flushes through my body. I've drained shots in front of thousands of people as time expired on the basketball court. But I've never felt this sort of nervousness cropping up in me.

Lacy, sitting on her knees, runs her hand on my shoulder, her worried gaze staying on me as I speak.

"I just got the ancestry test back. It says we're fucking siblings."

Silence on the other end of the phone. He takes a few deep breaths. "Be right over," he finally croaks.

I turn to Lacy. "I'm going to fix a whiskey. You want one?"

❧

LESS THAN A HALF-HOUR LATER, CHANDLER KNOCKS. WHEN he appears at the door, he's visibly shaken.

I am, too.

When we look each other, it's an odd feeling. Sort of like we're sizing each other up for the first time. Both wondering the same thing.

Is it possible that we're blood?

We shake hands and he breezes through to the living area, greeting Lacy as well.

Lacy hands him her iPad and he sits down.

"I logged into mine, too. It says the same thing now," he says. "Half-brother: Carter Flynn."

I rake a hand through my hair. "This is too crazy to be true, right?"

He shakes his head. "Get me some of that whiskey. And I don't fucking know, man."

I pour him a rocks glass full of the stuff. "I guess anything's possible," I say. "I called and emailed the service team at Long Lost Ancestry to verify."

"What are you verifying? That there's not someone at the company who is just totally fucking with us?"

I head over to the couch, and Lacy moves so I can sit between her and Chandler. I put my hand over her leg. "I guess you're right."

Lacy chimes in, squinting at her iPad. "I just checked your email, Carter, I hope you don't mind. Looks like their troubleshooting team got back to you. They say their process is 99.99999 percent accurate. And congrats on the new half-brother."

Chandler turns to me and shrugs. "Well. I guess that's settled, right? Cheers, brother."

We clink glasses and I have a long pull of the stuff, savoring the tingle in my throat as I swallow. My mind races with a thousand thoughts.

"You said before you met your father—our biological dad. Right?"

Chandler nods. "Yes sir. Amy and I drove down to good old Murphysboro, Illinois. Middle of fucking nowhere. Guy was a loser, apartment was filled with beer cans. Scared the shit out of me, if I'm being honest. I vowed I'd never end up like him."

"Damn. I was always under the impression that my father--our father--was someone important."

He puts a hand on my shoulder. "He wasn't. I know this is

going to sound crazy, but I bought a ring for Amy the next day. Because I just got this clear vision all of a sudden what I wanted my life to be like. And that sure as shit wasn't it." He rakes a hand through his hair. "Holy shit man, this is a lot to take in, though. I feel like the cosmos are really fucking with us today."

I unfocus my eyes, looking out through the balcony window on the city of Chicago. My chest still tingles with disbelief of this whole scenario. Lacy's voice rings in my ear.

Ninety-nine point nine nine nine nine percent accuracy.

I turn my head and look at Lacy.

Part of me is shocked she is being so low-key about the whole thing. I wonder if inside, she's thinking about running for the hills.

I think about what Chandler said. How—as depressing the confrontation was—he finally felt sure of himself and his path after he went down to Murphysboro.

I swallow. "I need some time to wrap my head around this whole thing. I'm going for a walk. You guys mind waiting here? You can call Amy over, too."

"She's already on her way," Chandler says. "She's coming as soon as she gets off work."

"You sure you don't want me to come with you?" Lacy asks, raising an eyebrow.

"I'm sure," I say as I leave.

The hot summer air crashes into me as soon as I burst through the revolving door. The people, the cars, the noises in the city are a blur. I head down my block, walking quickly and pumping my arms more than usual. I turn to cross State Street and head to the lake, and I'm so out of it. I almost walk right into incoming traffic, but a woman saves me, grabbing my wrist.

"Jesus Christ, Carter," she says, pulling me back onto the curb as a honking car whizzes by.

I glance at her through the haze of my whiskey buzz. She must notice how glazed over my eyes are, because she asks me if I'm okay.

"Fine," I croak, my eyes totally unfocused. But that smell. "Lacy?"

"Carter, you're not okay. Let's go back to the apartment."

"Leave me alone," I growl, brushing her hand off as the light turns green. I cross the street.

I walk briskly, and Lacy has to practically jog to keep up with me. "Where are you going?" she begs.

A bolt of rage flits through me, and I stop and grit my teeth. "What did I tell you about asking stupid questions?!" I seethe, the ire seeping into my tone.

Lacy wraps her hands around my forearm as she hustles, keeping up with my long strides.

"Please don't say that. We—I just want to be here for you this time, Carter."

I tense up at her choice of words. *This time*. "Oh yeah?" I grunt. I steal a glance at Lacy. Her expression is soft, and tears stream down her face.

"What are those for?" I ask, my eyes moving to her cheeks.

"Can't you just let me be there for you?"

I swallow. "What don't you understand about leave me alone?" I grit out.

Tears stream down Lacy's cheeks. She holds onto my arm tighter. We stop on a corner on busy Michigan avenue.

Her eyes sear into mine as she pleads.

"For God's sake, Carter. I'm just trying to be a good friend to you. No, I can't relate to what you're going through. But can you please let me be there for you?"

"I don't need anyone. I told you."

She uses her wrist to wipe away tears. "When I got to this city, I didn't know fucking anyone. Now, I'm on the shortlist for Blue Illusion. It's because of you, Carter. What *you* said to me. You gave me the confidence. You and your—fucking stupid cocky self gave me the confidence to actually let go for one summer in my life and enjoy myself. And dammit, I have. I don't even know what our relationship status is—and to be honest, I don't care."

With pained eyes, she examines me. "Carter it's not like I'm asking to get married. I just want to be there for you. It doesn't matter right now."

I shake my arm loose of her grasp, my mind racing with frustration and confusion.

"There are some things a man's got to do on his own. Just let me be right now. I'll see you in a couple of hours. I've got to clear my head."

She stops following me and I walk off.

Picking up my phone, I dial the number of someone I should have called a long time ago.

❦ 30 ❦

LACY

I wipe the tears from my eyes as I step into the elevator to head back up to Carter's penthouse.

I sigh. *Carter's Penthouse.*

Although I've lived here for almost seven weeks, I still have a tough time calling it 'my apartment.' Maybe that was because I still feel like a guest living here.

But it could also be due to the way Carter still seems to keep one odd degree of separation between us. As close as we've become, he still puts up this distance at times that I can't quite articulate.

We've been growing close, and I know he cares about me. I'm not imagining that.

But now, riding up the elevator without him, I finally have a concrete example in my mind of the things I've been feeling. It's true that I can't relate to the sort of anguish he must be feeling. I don't know what it's like to grow up without a father. I just wish he'd let me me be there for him. Walk with him silently. Be by his side.

The elevator dings as I reach the floor. The entryway door

is wide open, just as it was when I rushed out to catch up with Carter.

I see Chandler and Amy before they see me, and I stop my step to reflect on them.

They sit on the couch. Chandler is noticeably shaken, rubbing his eyes and forehead as Amy stares him dead on in the eyes, inches from him. Her hands are on his shoulders.

It hits me, and I swallow down a ball of tension in my throat.

That's what I want.

Sure, Carter is amazing in a multitude of ways. He's been opening up—albeit slowly—to me over these past few weeks. But could he ever truly admit it when he needed help?

I start to move again, heading into the apartment. Chandler and Amy turn when they hear me.

"Hey Lacy," Amy says, her tone a little somber.

I offer her a wave. "Hi."

"Did you find him?" Chandler asks, his voice sounding shaken.

I nod. "Yes. I was able to track him down. He wants to be alone now, though. How are you doing?"

Chandler shrugs, taking a sip of his whiskey. "I'm okay. Other than the fact that my half-brother apparently is so freaked out about me being related to him that he wants to run away."

I sigh. "You know that's got nothing to do with you, right?"

Chandler nods. "Of course. Honestly, I've been seeing a therapist since I moved here last year from Barcelona. Best thing I ever did. I know it's crazy—it sucks, in a way. But I'm done expending energy giving a shit what that shitbag—Jack Whitehead—did years ago."

Chandler squints and unfocuses his eyes, sort of staring into his drink.

I pinch my eyebrows, trying to piece together what he said. "Who is Jack Whitehead?"

Chandler pauses, his pupils dilated and his gaze still unfocused. Amy rubs the back of his neck. "Babe," she says softly. "Did you hear what Lacy asked?"

"Oh, shit. Sorry," Chandler says, shaking his head rapidly, almost like a dog does when trying to get rid of moisture. "I just had a weird thought. Jack Whitehead is the name of my father—I mean sperm donor, as I like to refer to him. And when I went to see him last year, he said he had seventeen children. Seven-fucking-teen. You believe that? Nuts."

My jaw slackens in disbelief. "That's totally crazy. That means . . ."

"There's more of us out there," Chandler says forcefully, taking the words out of my mouth. "It's just so fucking crazy —Carter was right under my nose this whole time and we didn't notice anything."

"What the hell was this Jack Whitehead guy?" I say, my voice stained with vitriol. I walk over to the couch and take a seat next to Chandler. "Was he a traveling milkman or something?"

I hunch my back, running my hands over my face.

"Honestly, I didn't even ask him. After we visited him, all I wanted to do was get the fuck out of there. Jack Whitehead I met didn't even keep track of his kids. That doesn't make sense to me."

"I'M OPEN TO IDEAS. HONESTLY, I THOUGHT WE'D JUST PUT it behind us and never wonder too hard about it."

"Obviously that's not likely," Chandler says, his voice gruff. "Somebody's wondering very hard about it right now." Tipping his chin in the direction of the balcony window, he flits his gaze to the city outside. The sky is a gorgeous red-orange hue as the sun breathes its last breaths on the horizon.

I inhale a deep breath, and look at the two of them. "Thanks for coming over so quickly you guys," I say. "And thanks for staying with me."

"No thank you necessary," Chandler grits. "I'm keeping a solid front but this is as mind-blowing to me as anyone. To find out that for the past year, I've been playing on the same basketball team as my biological half-brother? This is fucked. In the best way—I mean I'm pumped for whatever the future holds."

Chandler trails off. He opens his mouth like he's about to say more, but nothing comes out.

"What is it?" I insist.

"My biological dad said he had more. He said he had seventeen other kids besides me."

"Seventeen?! You mean there could be more of you out there?"

"I assumed he was bullshitting. I don't know. Goddamn. I always wanted a brother, too."

The gravity of his words hang in the air for a few moments.

"Well, you finally have one."

"So does Carter."

Amy and I exchange a glance. "We can stick around for the night," she adds. "Until Carter comes back. Want to cook something? Or order in?"

I smile. "That sounds amazing."

We end up ordering Chinese food—plenty for four. I set Carter's plate—and put a lid over it—so it's ready for him the moment he walks in.

Chandler, Amy, and I spend the night trying to come up with theories as to why Carter's mom would have freaked out

out of the blue one night when Carter was eighteen years old
.

My theory about a possible custody battle is still the best we can manage, even though Chandler brushes it off.

The night gradually creeps in, and around quarter to eleven Chandler and Amy rise up to leave.

The door is still wide open. I haven't closed it since I came in, hoping Carter would surge through it some time soon.

"You want us to stay here?" Amy offers.

"No, no. It's fine. Carter does have a key. And he's a grown man. I'm sure he'll be fine. He's just got to deal with this in his own way."

"Text me when he comes back," Chandler says as he gives me a big hug. Amy hugs me goodbye, too.

I feel a strong connection with the two of them as I wave goodbye and watch them walk down the hall, hand in hand.

When I close the door, I lean against it with my back and let my shoulders slump.

31

LACY

Sleep is hard to come by as I snuggle under the covers in Carter's room.

We've been sleeping in the same bed the last few weeks, but our night of sleep usually begins with a romp between the sheets before we shower—or don't—and pass out together.

So with him gone tonight, I feel a little off. Not that I should have to ask him at this point whether or not I can sleep in his bed.

Without flipping the light on, I grab my iPad from the nightstand and sit up.

I pull up the browser tab with the apartments in New York I was looking at earlier today.

Flipping through a few different options, I frown as I look at the prices. Rent in New York is twice as expensive in Chicago for half as much. And although I'm not spending any money right now thanks to Carter's generosity, I'm also not making any.

Shivers run down my spine as I see a studio apartment the size of Carter's walk-in closet—literally—for over two grand.

Should I just forget about New York right now and accept that, even if I do win a spot on Blue Illusion, I'm going to have to find a part-time job just to make ends meet?

I purse my lips. How do middle class people live in New York at all? You'd have to be making two-hundred grand a year before taxes just to afford your own normal-sized place. It makes no sense to me.

I suck in a deep breath, refocusing my eyes as I flip to another closet in manhattan that costs a ludicrous amount of money. I glance at the empty spot on the bed to my left, and my mind drifts to the giant elephant in the room.

What the hell are Carter and I going to do when and if I move to New York?

Since we broke the seal on our friendship and started sleeping together, we've not once had a conversation about our relationship status. It didn't seem right, anyway, badgering Carter about it when I'm the one who's going to be moving away.

But I can't help the little thought virus gnawing at my heart. With only one week to go before my big show next weekend—the final show after which I find out if I've made the company, the shadow of the future looms ever larger between us.

I close my eyes and inhale. There's no smell in the world like Carter's room. It smells like the woods and fresh rubber from the basketball next to his bed, and boy and sex, all combined to form one amazingly pristine scent. I wish I could bottle it up with me and take it to New York.

I wish I could take Carter to New York.

If I go.

There's another scent lingering in the room too—and the corners of my lips turn up in a slight smile as I realize what it is.

It's my shampoo. It's . . . *me*.

As much as he's rubbing off on me, I wonder if Carter has these same thoughts about me rubbing off on him. My smile broadens, and a wave of emotion flows through me.

As unlikely as we are, I can't imagine myself with anyone else right now.

Carter's cockiness has rubbed off on me a little in my personal life—even the other dancers have commented on a shift in me over the past weeks.

I wonder if my softness—my propensity toward empathy has rubbed off on Carter. I hope it has, but after today's events I'm not so sure.

Just then, I hear the sound of the front door opening. Keys rattling. Then a grunt, and the noise of the microwave turning on. I smile. He's eating the food.

Part of me wants to go outside and join him, but after our confrontation on the sidewalk I've left the ball in Carter's court. I don't want to push him any more than I already have.

I flip my iPad off, close my eyes, and try to sleep. It's hopeless, though. Every tiny noise Carter makes is magnified in the otherwise quiet night as it echoes down the hall.

Finally I hear him walking down the hall. Still, I feign sleep, curled up on my side as I keep my breath steady and slow.

His side of the bed caves in, and I hear him blow out a loud exhale.

I want to open my eyes so badly, to know what he's looking at. Is he just starting out into space? Looking at me?

I feel the sheet at my waist creep up toward my neck. He's tucking me in.

I try to breathe steady. At this point it would just be creepy if I opened my eyes all of a sudden.

Carter sighs. All of a sudden, I feel his lips on my cheek as he kisses me goodnight.

I hope to God he can't hear me sniffling as he lays back onto the bed.

I hold back tears with all my strength as I hear his breathing pattern ease into sleep. Warmth radiates through my body, and my heart drums.

Maybe there is hope for us after all.

❧

CARTER HOLDS THE WHEEL OF THE RED CONVERTIBLE, GLANCES over, and smiles broadly at me. We laugh as the summer air blows through our hair. I throw up my hands in ecstasy, but flinch when I look over the side of the car and see how close to the edge of the cliff we're driving.

Looking out, I see a vast expanse of endless ocean. And I notice that if we veer off the cliff it's a long, long, way down.

My breath hitches with fear and I grab onto Carter's shoulder.

"Cartwheel. You're driving so fast. Don't you think we should slow down?"

But Carter just laughs, smiling at me. God, he's so devilishly handsome. The weather is perfect, and I'm in a red bikini. Carter's not wearing a shirt, either.

"Baby, why are you so worried? We're going to be fine. I always drive this fast."

"Do you? Well, I don't know if I like it."

Carter oozes confidence, but it doesn't help the impending sense of doom I feel.

Suddenly, I look up ahead and, to my astonishment, see a giant, brick wall in the distance.

My heart drops to my feet. It's right out of the Looney Tunes scene where the Road Runner sprints into a huge wall.

"C-Carter," I stutter, grabbing onto him and pointing at the wall. How fast are you going? Slow down, for goodness sakes! There's a wall coming up."

"Laces," he growls, letting go of the steering wheel, and turning to me in the passenger's seat. "I said, don't worry about it. I've got this handled. You trust me, don't you?"

I avert my eyes, then look at him again. "I do."

He locks his amber eyes on mine. "Well trust me when I say I've got this handled. Fuck, you look sexy right now."

"I do?"

"Fuck yes. Come here."

To my amazement, he takes his foot off the gas pedal, but the car keeps hurlting down the road perfectly. Not running off the edge of the cliff. I take my eyes off the giant brick and soak in Carter.

My heartbeat starts to soar as he kisses me, then runs his hands all over my skin. Heat pools between my legs.

I moan, and he bites his lip, grinning.

He slides a hand slowly down my stomach until his fingers land on my clit.

Smirking, he licks his bottom and then his upper lips.

"So wet for me, aren't you?"

My eyes glaze over. "It's not fair."

He pinches his eyebrows together, confused. "Not fair?"

"It's not fair how you can do this to me. I hate how wet you make me."

Chuckling, he runs a hand through my hair, then takes my hand.

Holding eye contact with me, he places my hand on his cock over his jeans. My heart thumps as I feel the thickness.

"It's too bad you feel that way. Because I love how hard you make me, Laces."

Warmth radiates through me, most of it pooling between my legs.

I glance away from Carter and down the road. My eyes widen when I see how close we are to the brick wall.

I turn my head back to him, ready to beg him again to slow down, but I notice his attention is averted, his head jerked toward the back seat of the convertible.

He scowls, his eyes burning with that same shade of hate I saw the first day I arrived to Chicago. Growling, he doesn't look at me.

I turn to see what he's looking at, and my blood freezes when I see.

It's an older man, in his forties or fifties, with no eyes, nose, or mouth. Just a blank face.

Carter points as he snarls. "My fucking father!"

I gasp for air.

I WAKE UP IN A HOT SWEAT, AND CARTER'S GOT AN ARM wrapped around me as he cuddles me. I feel him flinching against me. His arm is heavy on top of me, and every time he flinches, he squeezes me tighter.

I swallow, blinking a few times while I think about what to do. Should I wake him up, or is it best that he sleeps through this? I remember the dream I just woke up from, and I wriggle as a shiver spreads over my skin at how appropriate the dream was for our situation.

Feeling the heat centering in my core, I slide my hand between my legs. I'm so damn wet and turned on.

The man even invades my dreams. It's not fair.

I start to wiggle my hips a little, trying to get out of Carter's grasp and maybe wake him up. His arm weighs a ton, which isn't surprising considering he's what—over two hundred forty pounds?

I wriggle a little and suddenly find myself in a strangely erotic position as I grind my ass behind me, Carter's cock pressing against my ass. My panties are thin, and I can feel the warmth of his body pressed against me.

It is a hot night, after all.

And Carter likes to go light on the A/C.

He expels a throaty grunt again, and I turn my head toward him.

"Carter," I whisper, running my hand along his side in an attempt to wake him up gently.

His eyes flutter awake, and I feel his muscles tense. He grips me hard, and I groan. "Ow, Carter, too tight," I say, grabbing his forearm.

"Oh," he says, blinking a few times. "It's you. Fuck, I just had the craziest dream."

"Me too," I say.

He loosens his grip, but doesn't let go, his lanky arm extending over all of my torso.

He moans as he grinds his hips against me, interlacing his fingers over mine. "Lacy," he whispers. "Fuck."

I wiggle my hips against him with desperate desire.

"You okay?" I purr, but he doesn't say anything.

Drawing his hand up to my neck, he kisses the back of it, sending goosebumps over my entire body. His hand finds my panties and he draws them down to my knees, where I finish the job, kicking them off with my feet.

Bringing his hand back up, he cups my jaw, twisting my face toward him so we can lock eyes.

I turn to butter as he slides a hand down my abdomen and lands it between my legs, not saying a word as he keeps his pupils locked on me.

My tongue darts out and lands on his lips. I press the flesh of my ass into his hips, feeling his hard cock slip between my thighs.

Arching my neck back, I reach a hand down and guide him between my legs and inside me.

I'm so wet already, there's no need for foreplay.

No need for the games we've had fun playing.

He grabs my hips as he presses all the way inside me, and I wince a little at his size like I always do as he takes me.

My pleasure crescendos as he thrusts, wrapping what seems like his whole arm around me.

Maybe there is hope for us.

But it damn well feels like we're speeding toward that wall with no plan of how to slow down or go around it.

❦ 32 ❦

LACY

When I get back to the penthouse after our dress rehearsal on Saturday evening, I hear some added voices inside. Female voices and laughter. My hair stands on end for a moment until I register whose voices I'm listening to.

My eyes widen when I approach the couch in the living room to find Carter's mom and my own mother sitting on the couch.

"Lacy!" my mom screams, jumping off the couch to hug me.

"Hi, Mom! What a surprise!"

My heart hammers hard, in shock. As I'm hugging her, I glance over at Carter for any insight into how we're going to handle this situation. Do we tell our moms we have kind of become hook-up buddies in the past month? That we could be more than that?

Carter's eyes evade mine as he sits by his own mother, talking in a low voice.

Then again, what's the point in telling them anything about Carter and my it's-complicated relationship status?

And it's even more complicated after the surprisingly passionate, sweaty sex we had last night.

My mom takes hold of my shoulders and smiles. "You didn't think we'd miss your big performance tomorrow did you? We wanted to surprise you."

"Well that, you did," I say with a smile plastered on my face.

Just then I hear the bathroom door open, and my little sister Eliza comes out. My body warms at her presence, and she skips toward me for a hug.

"Lacy! I'm so proud of you!" she says, gripping me tight. Mrs. Flynn gets up and hugs me, too.

Carter cuts in. "I was just telling them about how you're on the short list for the Blue Illusion."

"That's amazing. At your age, too!" my mom adds.

Her words twist into me a little, but in a way she's right. Twenty-six is old in dancer years.

"Just remember, honey," my mom continues. "If you don't make it to New York, you'll have a place to stay in Blackwell."

"I was looking at rent in New York," my sister blurts out. "As I try to convince Mom to let me skip senior year and move there to do ballet."

I shake my head. "You shouldn't do that, honey. It's important to finish high school."

"Right," she nods.

There's an awkward silence for a moment as we all sort of size each other up. I swallow. I have no idea where to start with everything that's happened in the past month.

Does Carter want to bring up the fact that he's found his father?

I glance over at him. He's in his typical outfit—black gym shorts, blue shoes, and and a grey v-neck T-shirt that emphasizes his rippling muscles. On the other hand, they're basically impossible for him to hide.

"I'm going to grill some chicken on the balcony tonight. That work for everyone?"

"Of course!" My little sister blurts out.

A little disconcertingly, I notice my little sister checking Carter out as he heads to the fridge and loads up a plate of raw chicken, then seasons it, totally oblivious.

"Can we help you with anything?" she says, perking up.

Carter shakes his head. "You ladies just had a long drive from Blackwell. I'll cook. Lacy, I'm going to have your mom and my mom sleep in my bed in the master. You and your sister can sleep in your room. I'll take the couch. Would you mind helping everyone to their rooms?"

"Of course," I say, my voice a little shaky as I picture the scene in Carter's room right now, which probably includes my underwear tossed to the side of the bed.

"Carter," I say, my voice laced with a secret intonation. "Are you *sure* you want to show your mom the room right now? Don't you have to clean it up?"

Carter turns to face me, his eyes locking with mine. "I cleaned it up this afternoon. It's totally and completely clean," he says, emphasizing the word 'clean.' "I even changed the sheets."

I breathe a sigh of relief that our secret code works in this instance, and I wave our moms to the room, grabbing their bags.

"How was the drive here?" I say, making smalltalk.

"Fine—until we got to Chicago! There's so much traffic here! I don't know how you stand it!" Mrs. Flynn says.

I open the door to Carter's master room and toss their bags on the floor.

"So it seems like you two have been getting along okay," my mom says. "At least from what Carter was telling us before you got here."

I smile, maybe a little too broadly. "Of course! I mean, Mom, you know that we've been best friends since always."

Mrs. Flynn and my mom make eye contact and roll their eyes.

"Yeah, okay," my mom says. Mrs. Flynn sniggers.

I pinch my face. "What's that supposed to mean?"

"We know the game you two always play when we'd get together in high school. And we always knew you two didn't *actually* like each other."

The pitch of my voice rises. "You did? But I thought—"

Mrs. Flynn sighs. "Lacy, we know you two had a lot of issues when you were younger—and I shoulder the blame for a lot of that. But now that you're older, it's nice to see you're at least being cordial. After all, you are both from the same small town. And you're trying to make it in the big city at the same time."

I pinch my eyebrows together. "So if you knew we didn't like each other, why did you recommend that I move in here!?"

They both glance at each other. "We just knew you were in a desperate place," my mom says.

I cringe, not wanting to even consider what they are referring to.

"Well, now that you're settled..."

My mom sees an object on Carter's dresser, and is drawn to it.

"What's this?" she asks, picking it up.

My eyes bulge out of my head as she picks up the vibrator from Carter's dresser. Cleaned the room well, my ass, I say to myself, my heart pounding.

"That's, uh . . .nothing."

"Oh my," she says, setting it down and placing a hand over her heart.

Mrs. Flynn, my mom, and I stand in a triangle of

awkwardness, all alternating making eye contact with each other.

I shrug. "I guess . . . Carter has a healthy sex life!" I mutter. "Let's head back into the living room, shall we?"

My skin is red hot as we make our way back into the living quarters. I glance at the deck, where Carter is grilling up a storm. He's taken his shirt off and has an apron on.

Thankfully he's otherwise clothed, but that doesn't stop my sister from sitting at the table next to the deck and shooting him google eyes as she leans onto her palm.

Dear God, I need to have a conversation with her about how to play it cool.

"That's like, amazing," she's saying. "I just can't believe you made it from Blackwell to be famous. There's basically like, no one who gets out of there. I want to get out of there, though."

I let my mom and Mrs. Flynn head to the balcony, then follow behind them.

"Hey B—Lacy, could you get some plates and stuff?" Carter asks, turning to me with a grin.

Did he almost just call me baby in front of our families?

"Of course," I sigh defeatedly, realizing it's back to a pretending act between the two of us. Except this time we're pretending that we haven't been having regular hot sex over the past month.

We make small talk for a bit, and I tell everyone about how the program has been. For some reason I feel like I'm giving a sports interview that lacks real substance as I tell them everything, but keep my responses vague.

"It's been good, I've made some friends, and the last month I've really put my head down and concentrated. It's now or never, you know?"

"I think you're going to get the spot in New York," my sister says confidently.

"Thanks," I nod.

Finally Carter finishes cooking and we sit down to eat, having a salad and some sweet potatoes to go with our meal.

Carter says he's got to go to the bathroom before we start eating, and gets up from the table.

"I'm going to get a drink of water," I add, getting up as well. "Anyone else need anything?"

They shake their heads, and I scurry off, stopping Carter before he gets to the bathroom in a whisper of a voice.

"Carter!"

He turns around. "What?"

"Are we going to—you know. Tell them?"

He raises an eyebrow. "Tell them what?"

"Uh, you know. About us." I shrug my shoulders and cock my head to the side.

"What's there to tell?"

I blink a few times and part my lips, but nothing comes out.

"Lacy, I know it's weird having them here, but it's just for one night. We'll be fine. No sense in getting into a whole thing about us with them here."

"It just feels weird keeping a secret from them."

His nostrils flare, and he averts his eyes from mine for a moment before bringing them back to mine. "So you think it's 'lying' if we don't tell them we're in a...What are we in, exactly?"

"I like to call it an 'it's-complicated.'"

"You're proving my point. We don't even know what to call what we have."

"Yeah, but still." I run a hand through my hair, feeling overwhelmed. I can't find the right words to express what I'm feeling.

Carter smirks. "Is this because your sister was checking me out?"

My mouth falls open and I stare at him, agape. "You did *not* just say that."

"Oh please. You were staring at her with devil eyes. The jealousy is written all over your face."

"My God, Carter. You're still—"

"An asshole. Is that what you're going to call me?"

I don't give him the benefit of agreeing with him, even though he's right.

He takes a step closer to me and speaks slowly. "I like to call it, 'someone who dwells in reality.' I'm going to let you know that your sister is checking me out, even though I can see this is making you uncomfortable."

I can feel my face heating up and tingling with anger.

Because he's right.

He glances outside, then pulls me by the waist into the hallway, out of view of everyone on the balcony.

Pressing his hips against me, he pins me against the wall and runs his hand along my hip. "You're the one who's suggesting a long-term relationship. And you can't even handle someone checking me out."

"Stop it, Carter," I say, seething, three inches from his face.

His body presses into mine, and I fight the feeling of arousal building in my core. I hate the fact that Carter has a direct line to my desire, just with a simple touch.

"The reason for telling our parents is not at all what I was referring to," I say, baring my teeth. "I just don't like lying to them. That's all."

His grin turns positively evil. Leaning his cheek against my ear, he whispers. "Don't look at it as a lie. Just look at it like an omission of truth. I know you've been good at that in the past. So why don't we just consider this summer our little secret until we figure out what the fuck we're going to do in the future?"

My hands move in jerks, and I avoid eye contact with him. My face heats as my ire builds the more I consider Carter's comment. "You have such a fucking double standard," I mutter. "I'm willing to forgive you for what you did, but you just . . ."

I suck in a big breath as Carter's amber eyes find my gaze, and he interlocks his fingers with mine. My blood boils at the fact that he doesn't even have to use words to present a counter argument without me melting in his hands.

But heat throbs between my thighs, and my pelvis curls up into him, almost involuntarily.

I feel his cock hardening into my leg as we grind together.

"Stop, Carter," I mouth, looking at him through half-hooded eyes. "They could come out and find us at any moment."

"Yeah, they could," he scoffs. "And you'd like that, wouldn't you?"

"Carter, please. Not here. We're . . . in the middle of dinner. And you can't . . . oh for the love of God."

My protests melt away as Carter kisses my neck. I rest a hand on his back, and arch my hip up as his hand slides down my panties and onto my clit.

I bite his shoulder.

"This is soo . . . wrong," I mutter as Carter curls his fingers into me, making me quiver.

"Want me to stop?" Carter smirks

"Screw you," I mewl between desperate breaths.

🎇 33 🎇

CARTER

Before Lacy's Sunday show, her sister and Mrs. Benson take the opportunity to go window shopping on Michigan Avenue. My mom is considering going with them as well when I pull her aside.

"Mom. There's some stuff I'd like to talk to you about. Just you."

She reads the tone of my voice, and nods. I'm not one to be serious for no reason.

We part ways and head next door to the bar at The Drake Hotel, one of those swanky joints where the drinks are overpriced. But I don't mind, considering it means less chance that some asshole will walk up to me and start talking about their hoops for next season.

My mom and I take a booth in the back, next to a window overlooking the Chicago River.

"This is nice," she says as our waitress brings us our drinks. My mom is drinking a gin and tonic and I'm enjoying an old fashioned.

"Cheers, Mom," I say in a low voice as we clink glasses.

Her gaze turns serious. "So what did you want to talk to me about?"

"About—" I swallow, taking a long drink. I hate even saying the word. "About my biological father," I finally say.

"Oh," she says, rubbing her arm and taking a pretty long pull on her drink, too. "That's . . . interesting. I thought you'd sort of let that one go."

I clench and unclench my fists, leaning toward her across the table. "I thought so, too. And then one of the players on the team suggested I get an ancestry test done. Just for kicks. So I did."

"Oh." Her gaze softens, and she lowers her eyes, her mouth slightly agape. "What did you find out?"

"Mom, I know this is tough for you to talk about. But— according to the test, I have a biological half-brother. His name is Chandler Spiros—one of my teammates."

Her eyes widen. "Get out."

"I wouldn't joke about this. I also talked with him, and it turns out our father—or sperm donor as Chandler and I like to say—lives in Southern Illinois, now. Did you know that?"

She closes her eyes and shakes her head. "I don't keep track of him these days, Carter. You know what I think of him."

"That he's a piece of shit. I've heard you say that, of course. I've just been having a little bit of a rough time dealing with the fact that, you know, he was sleeping around with so many women and having kids with them. Chandler is barely a year younger than me."

Her skin bunches around the eyes, and she gives me a pained stare. "What do you want me to tell you?" she asks, her voice quivering.

"For so many years, I've avoided even thinking about him. I've listened to everything you've told me about him, about how he was a horrible person. Is it all true about how bad he is?"

She turns away from me for a moment, pressing her chin down into her shoulder.

"I know this isn't easy for you, Mom. But I've got to know."

She brings her gaze back up to meet mine. "I hate the man so much, Carter. With all my heart. I've shielded you from the truth for too long," she says, sucking in a deep breath.

My heart starts to race as I consider that my mom might have withheld something else about him from me. I can feel my blood pressure rising as a surge of adrenaline spikes through me. "The truth? What truth?"

I clutch my phone in my pocket, thinking about the picture I have of Jack Whitehead in my phone. Chandler forwarded an email with resources that Amy had put together online of the man, and a recent picture that she snapped when Chandler and Amy went down to Murphysboro to visit him.

Her expression pained, she holds my gaze. She sucks down the rest of her drink, then catches the waitress's eye to bring her another. I do the same.

"That night, when I was in Vegas, I was out having the time of my life. Then, he caught my eye. Tall, dark, and handsome."

I pinch my eyebrows together, thinking about the picture of Jack Whitehead. That does not sound like a description of him, but maybe he's aged since then.

"Be blunt with me, Mom. I can take it," I say in a low voice. "I need to know. For my own sanity. Tell me everything."

She takes a deep, controlled, breath.

"I was having a great night and—yes, I was flirting with

him. He told me his name was Ryan. Didn't give me a last name. At the time I didn't care. And well, I had a lot to drink. He did, too. Next thing I know, it was morning and I was waking up in his suite as he was leaving. He said this was fun, but was I on the pill? I told him it was a little late for that. So he took me to get the morning-after pill, then we said our goodbyes before he went to the airport."

"So you took the morning-after pill?"

She nods. "But—and I thank God every day—it didn't work. So I ended up with you."

The muscles in my face tighten as I consider the philosophical conundrum of not existing. On the outside, I keep my expression steady, though. I can tell how painful this is for my mother to recount.

"Right. So that's it?"

"Well, not exactly. He had like, some kind of spy or something in Blackwell. Somehow, he found out when I was visibly pregnant and called me up. He told me to . . . terminate the pregnancy."

I clam up, trying to brush off the existential implications of this conversation. "Obviously you didn't."

"Right. But to throw him off, I told him that the baby belonged to someone else. He was suspicious, but let it go. Until you turned eighteen and became an adult. To this day I don't know how he did it exactly—but he ran a paternity test and found out I'd lied about you being his. He called me up one night—drunk—talking about how he was rich and he was going to kill me if I ever let anyone know you were his son. I told him I didn't want anything to do with him—and I hadn't for thirteen years—so why was he even bothering to call me now? I told him he could come to Blackwell and kill me himself if that's what he was planning—and that if he was cold-hearted enough to kill the mother of his son he'd better hurry up and do it."

She closes her eyes and clasps her hands together. The waitress drops our drinks off on the table for us.

"I remember you buying a gun that summer. Now I know why."

She tips her chin up. "You were so young. I didn't want you to worry about adult things."

"Mom," I croak. "I was eighteen. I needed to know."

"I know honey, I'm sorry. I thought many times about telling you, but I could never quite find the words. You turned out okay though, I'd say."

She musters a smile.

I try to smile too, but I can't. I run my hand over my face, the anger and the bitterness of the years swelling through my body. I suck down another swig of the whiskey.

"I'm thinking about going to see him," I say, ignoring her comment about me turning out okay. I unlock my phone and pull out the picture I have. "This is what he looks like now."

My mom takes out her bifocals and looks at the picture of Jack Whitehead that Amy took.

She squints. "Where did you get that picture? That's not him."

My heart speeds. "Yes, it is," I argue.

"No, it's not," she scoffs, waving a hand dismissively. "I could never forget the man's evil—although handsome—face. He had a little scar on the side of his cheek. Seriously, where did you get that picture?"

"My fri—my brother Chandler got it when he went to Murphysboro. He saw him."

"How did he find out that's who his father was?"

I swallow. "Uh, I'm not sure."

"Well you had better ask him." Glancing at her watch, she frowns. "Oh my! It's almost four o'clock. We'd better hurry."

My heart tumbles, and I silently curse myself for forcing

this conversation with my mom at a time when we were rushed.

"You seriously don't think that's him?" I say to my mom as we leave, feeling completely and utterly powerless all of a sudden.

"Carter, there are some people you have burned into your memory like a tattoo, and you'll never remove it. I've tried to forget what the man looks like." She stops me on the sidewalk and puts her hand on my shoulder. "But I see him in you, every day. And yes, I look at your picture every day. That man you just showed me—there's no way that's your father. Unless he had reconstructive facial surgery or something."

"But it was a test. It's scientific. It's got a ninety-nine point nine nine nine percent success rate!"

She must feel the tension rising in my heart, because she pulls me in for a hug. "You're old enough to make your own decisions now. I'll stand by you if you want to find that man. But I'm telling you, that picture you showed me is not him. Feel free to show me some other angles and I'll give it a shot. But I don't think it's going to change my mind."

We walk next door to the theatre, and my mind is everywhere but right in front of me. I feel like I'm a zombie as the attendant rips my half of the ticket and leads us to our seats.

I was finally starting to come around to the idea that I might have a brother. And one who I could see myself having a lifelong friendship with at that. Only to have my mom refute with total confidence that this man was my father?

We find our seats in the third row, where Mrs. Benson and Lacy's sister Eliza are already seated with big smiles on their faces. I blow out a deep breath as I sit.

"You must be pretty excited!" Eliza says.

"I am. Lacy's worked really hard on this. And to be honest, I've never seen her dance. Except in front of the mirror at my apartment when she thought I wasn't watching."

Eliza giggles. "You've seen that, too? I thought I was the only one."

Mrs. Benson leans over her daughter and catches my eyes. "Carter. I want to thank you so much for everything you've done."

I wave her off. "No thanks necessary."

She scoffs. "I'm serious. Who knows if Lacy will make it too New York, but either way—"

"She will," I cut in.

"How can you be so sure?" These are some of the best dancers from across the country.

In my mind's eye, I run through a montage of Lacy over the last few weeks.

A giant smirk broadens across my face, and I have to stop myself before inappropriate words come out. Because although what I want to say is one-hundred percent true, I can't say it in front of this crowd.

Because if Lacy dances as passionately as she fucks, she's going to absolutely crush this entire performance. I would know.

Luckily, I don't have to answer Mrs. Benson's question because the lights dim, and a spotlight hits the stage.

I bite my lower lip, and my cock twitches just thinking about all we've done. The look in Lacy's eye when I first touch her, when we're starting.

The delicate motions her body makes as I press further inside her.

The fire in her eyes when our gazes are locked, and she's coming.

I rake a hand through my hair and lean back.

The performance starts with a fast hip hop routine.

And through it all, I've treated her like not even a girl-friend, to be honest. Yet she's been there for me through one of the most tumultuous weeks of my entire life.

Her words flash in front of me like a marquee sign, all of

the sudden. *"Carter it's not like I'm asking to get married. I just want to be there for you."*

Just then, the first dance ends and the second one comes out. It starts with maybe ten dancers, and then suddenly it's reduced to two: Lance and Lacy.

I'm drawn to Lacy like a magnet. As she moves slowly and gracefully to the music, I can't stop thinking about the person behind the performance.

Just then, a surprising word that pops into my mind.

Love.

I love Lacy.

I clench and unclench my fists, fighting the thought.

No. No I don't. It's just a silly little infatuation. She's no different than any of the thousands of women you could meet in the city.

Lance takes Lacy in his arms as they do a triangular sort of pose, and my nostrils flare.

Maybe it's that first trick they played on me, but even knowing he's not into women, my throat runs dry as I watch his hands on her.

A desire courses through me, and I try to interpret it. I want to touch Lacy. I want to hold her. We're a couple of fucked up souls in our own ways, but together we're a beautiful mess.

The music fades and she's all I see. I can't focus on anything else, suddenly. I'm driven mad.

I have strong feelings for Lacy, and I want to be with her. And she's moving to New York.

I clear my throat and do my best to calm myself as I sit through the rest of the show.

Now that I've decided to say something to her, I feel like a clock is counting down, and I need to tell her before it's too late. Too late for what, though?

The show continues, and Lacy is in a couple more of the

group dances.

She totally blows me away. She blows everyone away.

At the end of the performance, they all come out for a curtain call and a bow.

When Lacy and Lance hit the stage together, they get by far the biggest cheer of any of the dancers.

I take a deep breath, trying to process the conflicting realizations in my mind. I love Lacy. And she's definitely going to New York. No doubt whatsoever.

But it doesn't matter if she's in New York.

I make up my mind—resolutely—I don't give a shit what I've got to do to be with her. I'll do whatever it takes.

We all stand, clapping. Mrs. Benson wipes away tears from her cheeks with a handkerchief.

"She really needed this," she says, clearing her throat.

"She's a lock for Blue Illusion," I bite out.

"How do you know?" Lacy's sister Eliza asks.

"Because she's magnificent," I bite out, but I can feel a queasy feeling in my stomach.

Today has been one hell of a day, first finding out that my mom doesn't think the test results have latched onto my real father.

And now, thinking about how Lacy's leaving, just as I'm beginning to feel something deeper for her again.

❧ 34 ❧
LACY

I lock arms with Lance and we bow, the applause of the crowd deafening.

Lance says something to me, but I can't hear him. I search the faces of the audience for my family and Carter but the lights are too blinding.

Once we head off stage, Lance repeats what he was saying to me on stage. "Holy shit, holy shit! You crushed it!"

"We crushed it," I correct him, holding up a finger.

We hug in the hallway, then head to the green room where everyone is undoing their costumes.

I put on flats and a skirt, since I'm meeting up with my family for dinner.

The buzz in the green room dies down for a moment, and I look to the entrance to see Georgina Fleming—the coordinator and woman who gets the last say as to who goes to New York—standing there, clearing her throat.

"Very good. Very good," she says, clapping. "I haven't seen a performance like that in . . . since ever. The after party is going to be in three hours at my apartment, so you all have time to wash up and do whatever else it is that you need to do. It starts at eight-thirty. I hope to see you all there. Additionally, I went ahead and posted the names of the dancers who will be moving on to New York. It was a tough selection, but after today's performance there were a few people who clearly stood out. So congratulations to you all. I was going to wait until tomorrow to post these, but Blue Illusion needs its talent to arrive and start practicing with the rest of the dancers yesterday. Meaning, you'll be asked to arrive there no later than Tuesday. Any questions?"

Lance and I make the same scrunched up face at each other. A few of the other dancers seem confused, too.

"Did you just say, Tuesday?" Lance asks, raising his hand.

"Did I stutter, Mr. Ridley?" she bites, raising an unamused eyebrow at him.

Everyone laughs.

Lance speaks again, his tone a little more biting this time. "I understand, it's just that you'll want us to leave tomorrow to be in New York on Tuesday? I mean, that's not a lot of time."

"Well, someone's assuming they made the cut." She winks. "I think you'll all realize that this is the chance of a lifetime, and when the big boss says you need to be in New York on a certain day, you do as they say and don't ask questions. Do we have any other non-stupid questions? No? Okay, wonderful. I'll see you at eight-thirty. Bring a bottle of wine if you want."

The group of forty of us rushes outside to look at the tiny list, forming a bottleneck.

My stomach does somersaults as I jackknife through the crowd to see if I made it.

I feel good—no, great about my performance today. But if there's one thing I've learned over years of performance, it's that high expectations and making assumptions equal major disappointment.

I hold my breath as I near the list. Lance grips the back of my shoulders tight. He's nervous too. Even though, based on his question about New York, he might be doing a little bit of assuming.

Finally, we get close enough to read the tiny names.

My heart skips a beat as I read through them.

Davina's name is at the top. Lance's is second.

I scroll through until I see my own name in print at the bottom, then let out a squeal to end all squeals. Lance spins me around and hugs me tight. "You did it, you sexy bitch!" he screams so loud that a few people give us weird looks.

A few of the girls start to cry, and I draw us away from the crowd.

"Maybe we shouldn't celebrate here," I whisper.

"Right. Don't want to rub it in everyone's faces. I'm just so excited for you. I know how hard you worked for this. So, congratulations."

As we walk back into the green room to grab our bags, I heave a deep sigh.

Lance narrows his eyes. "You okay?"

I swallow. "Yeah, fine," I say, not sounding the least bit convincing, even to myself.

We walk out of the green room and pause backstage.

Lance grabs my shoulder and stops me. "Wait. What the hell is the matter. You worked for eight weeks—no, your whole life—for a moment like this. And now you're all melancholy. What gives?"

I avert my eyes from his gaze, and he parts his lips.

"Oooh. Dear God. It's Carter, isn't it?"

I don't even nod, just make eye contact with him.

"Ho-ly balls of a Greek God. You fell for him and his sexiness."

I roll my eyes. "It's not about his sexiness. Well, not totally. We've been going through some stuff. About his father. And stuff."

I swallow, realizing I'm repeating nothing words, but I'm trying to stay purposefully vague. I don't think it's my place to let Lance in on the whole 'new brother' thing that Carter is dealing with right now, as well as questioning whether or not he wants to meet his father or just move on with his life. And I definitely don't want to open that can of worms when we're fifty feet from exiting the building and seeing my family.

Lance raises his eyebrows.

"Really? *More* daddy issues for Carter?"

I nod.

"Of course I'm pumped to go to New York," I say, trying to take the subject off daddy issues. "You're right. I've earned it. But I really like him, Lance," I say with tired eyes. "But I don't know if he feels the same way about me. He's been getting all weird about me leaving. Saying stuff like 'well it was inevitable anyway' and . . . I don't know."

A few people walk by, and Lance lowers his voice. "Sounds like we need another wine night to talk this through."

I shake my head. "We don't even have time. We have to be in New York by Tuesday! That means I have to leave tomorrow!"

"*We* have to leave tomorrow," he corrects. "And I'm still salty that Georgina dropped that one on us at the last minute. How are you getting there, anyway?"

"No idea. How much are flights?"

"You want to fly your entire life to New York?"

"I don't have much, really."

"I'm renting a car and driving. Just come with me."

"Really?! Oh my gosh, that's a life saver."

"And we can talk it out." He sighs. "I guess we'll do without the bottle of wine."

We make plans to meet up tomorrow and leave at ten A.M., a reasonable hour. Together, we head outside, taking the side entrance.

I see my family, Mrs. Flynn, and Carter mulling around just outside the entrance on the sidewalk, and I walk up to them.

"Oh my God!!!" my sister screams as she wraps her arms around me tightly. "You were so incredible. Great job."

My mom and Mrs. Flynn hug me, too. I turn to Carter.

Warmth floods me for a moment, and my heart speeds wondering what he thought of my performance. His face looks tense and pained.

He wraps his arms around me, and whispers quietly in my ear. "Good fucking job Laces. I'm proud of you. Have fun in New York."

I pull back with a slightly confused look on my face. "How'd you know?"

He shrugs. "Lucky guess. You crushed it out there."

He turns to everyone. "Look, I'm not feeling so hot. I'm going to head back to my apartment. Have a good dinner. I'll see you guys later."

My heart drops a little. "You're sick? You sure you don't want us to come back with you?"

Carter waves me off. "Stomach thing. I don't want to ruin the night you're having with the fam. I made a reservation for you all at The Big Lake Restaurant overlooking Lake Michigan. Go have fun."

Carter exits, and I'm left with a distinctly bad feeling in my gut, like a little gnome is doing yoga twists inside me.

AFTER DINNER, WE HEAD BACK TO THE APARTMENT. WE'RE all exhausted, and I notice Carter is sleeping on the couch, passed out. I cover him up with a blanket.

A litany of thoughts swirl in my mind, mostly about how Carter and I haven't had any sort of chat about our future.

Something Carter once said repeats itself in my mind. Don't let ghosts of the past kill dreams of the future. Sometimes, though, he's so closed off, I just have no idea what Carter's thinking. Has he even thought about us having a future, though? We've stayed away from anything remotely close to a relationship status chat. And now that I'm leaving tomorrow, everything feels so rushed.

Before I go to bed, I take one last glance at him sleeping on the couch. He appears to be in a deep sleep. I smile at him.

"I don't care what anyone says about you, Carter. You're actually not a bad guy."

Something tumbles in my stomach when I say those words, though.

I worry that maybe I'm giving my heart to a man who will always be too cold to reciprocate.

35

CARTER

My mom, Mrs. Benson, and Lacy's sister hit the road early Monday morning.

Lance and Joseph help Lacy move the rest of her stuff out of my apartment. I watch them load up their double-parked car as I blow out the smoke from a cigarette on the balcony.

I don't even smoke cigarettes. But I bought a pack this morning after my mom left. I just felt like trying to kill myself a little bit today.

As I watch the three of them load up Lance's car for the cross-country drive to New York, I wonder what it would be like to jump. Forty-four stories down. You'd probably be pretty euphoric at some point in that fall. Right before you hit the ground and smashed the soul right out of you.

I stare a little longer than a sane person should, and then my phone buzzes. I'm expecting a call, so I pick it up.

"Carter, this is Detective Gates," the man says on the phone. He's got a gritty south-side-of-Chicago accent and I remember why I liked the man so much when I hired him to verify that the man that Chandler had said—Jack Whitehead —is indeed my father.

"Mr. Gates. What do you have for me?" I say as I blow out a puff of smoke.

"Quite the interesting findings. I'm actually at your apartment right now. Mind if I come up?"

"Of course not," I say.

"Good."

The phone hangs up and I walk out into my living room and see Detective Gates standing in my living room in jeans and a polo.

"What the fuck? How'd you get in here?"

He shakes his head. "Wanted to test out the security of this building. It's shit, by the way. And you left your door open."

"They're moving," I say, pointing to the last bag of Lacy's sitting on the floor.

"RIght. Well, have a seat."

I join him at my dining room table.

"What was was so damn important that you couldn't just tell me on the phone?"

"I could have. But I've never seen something like this. And I didn't feel comfortable telling you over the phone in case it was tapped."

My heart hammers. "What do you mean?"

"Let me start at the beginning. I went down and checked out that guy. Jack Whitehead. I followed him around for a few days in Murphysboro."

"Yeah. That's where Chandler said he lived."

"So the guy is a total loser. Drinks more cans of light beer than anyone I've ever seen. Keeps to himself. Drifts from construction site to site doing odd jobs. Sometimes working on a farm. Something didn't add up."

I nod slowly as I process this information, thinking how

my mother had sworn the man she'd been with wasn't the man that Chandler had pinned down—Jack Whitehead.

"Since this guy was such a loser, I couldn't help but think. How could such a total degenerate seduce women and have not one, but *two* NBA star player sons? With that in mind, I did some digging. I found out both you and Chandler had perfect ACT and SAT scores."

I narrow my eyes. "How the fuck did you find that?"

A slight smile pulls at his lips. "I'm a fucking P.I. That's basic shit, Mr. Flynn. Anyway, I checked his scores. Let's just say Jack Whitehead didn't even get half that, sorry to say. Now I'm not saying your mothers couldn't have just done an incredible job raising you both—which they obviously fucking did. But in the old nature-versus-nurture debate, nature at least plays a part."

My thoughts run wild with the implications this could have. I lean in closer to him. "Go on."

So I took a DNA sample from the source, and had a friend of mine run it and compare you and Chandler. Turns out you don't share one iota of DNA with that man."

My blood runs cold. "But how is that possible? The test is nearly one-hundred percent accurate. And I verified the results with the company."

"Right. It's accurate. But only if you submit the DNA of the right person."

"I don't follow."

"Those tests are crowd sourced. So, somebody submitted their DNA under Jack Whitehead's name. They did this to throw everyone off who took the test."

"Ho-ly shit," I say, dropping my jaw.

I straighten my back and rake both hands through my hair.

"That means . . ."

"Whoever your real father is? He doesn't want anyone to be able to trace your identity to him."

My heart skips what feels like several beats. "Why would he care that much about throwing people off the trail?!"

He shrugs. "That's a great fucking question. And it's why I came here in person. I don't know why someone would go to that much trouble, but I'm guessing your father is someone else. Someone pretty damn smart. And he damn well doesn't want you to find out who he is."

I swallow nervously, blinking several times. "This is mind-blowing. What's the next step?"

"If you want to find out more, it's going to cost you. By the way, here's everything I found, documented."

I nod as I take the manilla file folder, my gaze unfocused.

He gets up. "I'm sure this is a lot to process, so I'll leave you to do that in private. You know where to find me if you wish to go further. Don't mention any of these details on our phone calls, please. You never know when the NSA is listening."

I nod, then reach for an envelope on my counter and hand it to him. "Your payment," I say.

"Thank you," he says, and shakes my hand.

Detective Gates leaves, and I feel like a brick has just been deposited inside me somehow.

A few months ago, I was fine not knowing any of this. Now—it's become an obsession. I need to know. Even with the high fees that Gates charges. But he's the best in the city.

My eyes drift to Lacy's last bag. It's got a few of her toiletries in it, and I can smell that fresh, fruity shampoo scent emanating from it.

It sends shockwaves straight to my heart.

I hear the elevator ding, and I recognize Lacy's steps padding on the floor toward my room before she even turns the corner.

That's how you know you love someone. When you recognize their steps.

I squash the silly thought as quickly as it appears in my mind.

I feel like I've learned every damn thing about Lacy in the last two months.

What she likes to eat.

What she doesn't like.

What turns her off.

The dirty things that make her toes curl for hours on end.

What sends shivers up her spine.

She turns the corner and stops abruptly when she sees me, staring at her.

I give her an up-and-down.

She's got on gym shoes, black short shorts, and a pink tank top that doesn't leave much to the imagination. Her black hair spills onto her shoulders.

"I came up to get my bag," she says evenly, eying her blue duffle. "Lance is waiting for me."

I nod, clenching my jaw as I just stare at her.

She purses her lips together and looks around the apartment, as if checking one more time if she's forgetting anything. Throwing the bag over her shoulder, she flits her eyes toward the door. "I guess this is goodbye then," she adds.

I clench my jaw and just stare at her. I don't know what the hell she wants from me. Another lie about how I can't wait to keep in touch when she heads to New York?

I don't say anything, and she huffs and takes a few steps toward the open door to leave. My chest tingles as I see her turn on her heel for the last time and stride toward the door.

The black shorts say 'pink dancer' on the back. It's a small detail, but it's something I've gotten used to poking fun at Lacy for over the past month.

In spite of our highs, I'm left with a sour taste in my mouth.

Before she reaches the door, she pauses and twists her head to the side, as if she's about to say something, but then keeps going, almost to the doorframe. Her hair swishes behind her with her little twirl, and I smell her shampoo for the last time.

"Stop," I grit out in a low voice, and she freezes just before she makes it to the door.

"I think it's best if I just go," she says weakly, trembling as she stands. Heaving a deep sigh, she starts toward the door again.

With fast, long strides, I close the space between me and the door, and slam it shut just as she gets to it. "We're not done yet," I growl, turning to face her and gripping her hip.

Beads of sweat have formed on her forehead, and I don't know if it's because it's hot outside, or because she has an inkling of what I'm about to do.

Locking my eyes on her, I grab hold of the duffle bag strap, and slip it off her shoulder.

"What are we not done with?" she swallows breathlessly.

I smirk. "You really don't know by now?"

Fisting up her hair into a ball, I smash my full lips into hers. She gasps, trembling in my grasp.

I pull my face back for a moment, tipping my chin up as I watch her.

She's got a hand on my arm and a leg wrapped around my waist already as I grind my cock against her through my shorts, pressing her into the wooden door.

She looks up at me with big doe eyes and runs her tongue along her lips.

"Carter," she begs. "I really don't think this is a good idea. We haven't even talked about our future yet."

"You're right," I say, as I slip off her shorts. "It's a horrible idea. Just like it was the first time. And the second time."

"And the third," she mouths into my ear as she wiggles her hips, helping me get her shorts off and over the curve of her ass.

The truth is, she's right. Hooking up again is a horrible idea.

But I can't watch her go without having her one more time. In spite of our differences, there's no one else I've connected with like I have her.

Even with our issues—or maybe because of them—we leave it all out on the table every time we go at it. And even with her on the cusp of being gone, I'll regret it if we don't do this one more time.

Despite her feeble protests, the way she's grinding her bare pussy against my shorts right now, I know how badly she wants this.

I slide my shorts off, my throbbing cock ecstatic to be out of its cage. Lacy reaches down and wraps her hand around my thick base, panting with need.

"This is the last time," I growl into her ear as she slips her shirt off.

She moans as I squat down and I run my tongue up her stomach and between her tits before I take her nipples between my teeth. She quivers as I hold onto her hips, working my mouth down to her sweet pussy for one more taste.

I hear her moan as I lick around her clit for the last time, grabbing her ass as I eat her like I'm starving.

Threading her hand through my hair, she calls out my name one more time. "Cartwheel," she says.

I flinch at my nickname, but it only serves to make me angry. I stand up, and wrapping my hands around her ass, I lift her up and walk her over to the kitchen counter, spread her legs, and run the tip of my hard dick over her hot pussy.

I press in inch by inch, savoring the tightness and the look in her hooded eyes as I take her over. I wrap my thumb and fingers around her neck, and she arches her head back as I pump and pound into her.

Reaching her fingers around my back, she runs her nails across my back.

"Carter," she whispers. "Oh God, Carter."

She opens her eyes to find me, her hips shaking as the pleasure takes her over. I feel her pussy clench as she comes and it's too much.

I pump once more before I pull out and come on her beautiful creamy tits.

She lays convulsing in pleasure on the kitchen counter, her hand still wrapping around my arm. "Carter," she says desperately, then brings her mouth to my ear. "Let's be a couple. Let's cut out all this bullshit and be us, on our own terms. We're better people together than apart."

My heart pounds at her suggestion, but my teeth stay clenched.

Her skin glistens with sweat as she looks up with me with pained eyes, her chest heaving.

"Carter? Did you hear me?" she whispers again.

I lower my eyes.

"I hear you."

"So what are you thinking? I can see the wheels turning. It's scaring me, a little."

"Laces."

Her eyes redden, and gloss over with tears.

My chest swells. I want to tell her that I'm ready for a relationship. That I'm prepared to love her forever and be with her until the day I die.

But the truth is, I'm not ready for all that.

As much as I want to be ready.

"This summer has blown my mind. I care about you very much. But we would never work long distance. You've got to follow your dream."

"So this is it?" There's pure sadness in her voice. "We're done?"

Gathering her clothes, she puts them on.

"I just found out I have a brother. You're moving away again. You've got to concentrate on your dancing."

"When did I say that I couldn't make a relationship with you a priority?"

I swallow. "You didn't."

"It sounds more like you're the one who's just not ready, and you're projecting that onto me."

I think I see her wipe away a tear, but I'm not sure.

I'm still standing there, naked, as she leaves without saying another word.

Wiping tears away from her bright pink face, she runs out. I hear her sniffle in the hallway as the elevator dings.

Then silence.

She's gone.

Without saying goodbye.

Underlying questions, left unresolved.

It's for the best, though.

Lingering, and drawing out what we both knew would never work--a long distance relationship--would have been more painful than what I'm feeling right now.

Although the lump in my throat isn't making this easy.

Love isn't the opposite of hate. Far from it.

I love Lacy.

And that's why I've got to let her go.

I throw on my shorts and walk to the window, then watch her get a little black sedan.

Fuck it.

My instinct takes over. I rush to the elevator without even locking my door, press the first floor button.

I call her phone. It goes right to voicemail, though. The elevator's a dead spot.

On the bottom floor, it dings, and I sprint out into the lobby, calling her phone again.

Straight to voicemail.

I rush through the revolving door, and onto the street, panting.

The car is gone, and a distinct feeling of nervousness comes over me.

A text comes in.

LACES: WELL IT WAS A FUN SUMMER CARTWHEEL. HAVE A *nice life*

I CALL ONE MORE TIME, BUT IT GOES STRAIGHT TO voicemail again.

And my text comes back unable to deliver.

She blocked me.

A bomb explodes in my chest. My senses heighten, and I look out at the cars on State Street, when I see a black sedan one block down.

Shirtless, and sprinting, I almost cause a crash as two cars have to slam on their breaks.

Sprinting up the next block, I see her stopped at a red light.

I bang on the rolled up window, but she looks at me like she doesn't know me.

The car pulls away, and cars honk at me until I get out of the road.

BACK UPSTAIRS IN MY APARTMENT, I NOTICE MY COPY OF *The Great Gatsby* sitting on a shelf.

Lacy left it.

I pop it open to the last page, and I feel a lot like The Great Jay Gatz himself.

Maybe I'm wrong for distancing myself from Lacy. But considering my track record of ruining women, I'm doing her a favor by getting out of her life.

My father was a monster.

Like father, like son.

Strolling out onto my balcony, though, I get the distinct feeling that the two of us are far from over.

Gripping the tattered book in my hand, I glimpse over the balcony railing, and get a rush as I stare down forty four stories.

I tear out the last page of the book, and let it go.

Because Unlike Jay Gatz, I'm not dead.

And I can write the end of my story any way I want.

F. Scott Fitzgerald was a good writer, but he didn't know everything.

I'll get my green light yet.

Chills roll through me.

Lacy has no idea what my end game is.

THE END...

Until The End Game, which is now live!

Get it here:
The End Game (Book 2 of The Game Duet)

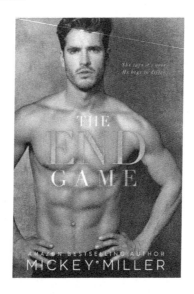

ABOUT MICKEY MILLER

Hi. I'm romance author Mickey Miller. I write light, hot, fast-paced romance that will make you smile and probably blush.

I've written top 100 Amazon Bestsellers, including my Amazon Top 25 Hit ***The Substitute*** which is now available in audio featuring narrator Sebastian York.

The easiest and best way to stay in touch with me for news and new releases is to sign up for my email list here:

https://mickeymillerauthor.com

You can also find me on Instagram @mickeymillerauthor. Reach out and let me know what you think about my books! I love hearing from readers, so don't be shy!

Lots of Love,

Mickey

THE SUBSTITUTE - New Standalone Contemporary Romance:

When the NFL goes on strike, Super Bowl champion Peyton O'Rourke ends up back in his hometown as a substitute teacher and high school football coach.

The one thing he didn't count on?

His best friend's ex being newly single.

Ballers Romance Series:

It was supposed to be just sex. But it became so much more.
(Chandler + Amy's Book!)

I've always been the good girl. Until one night in Tijuana. When a gorgeous stranger struck up a conversation with me. He was so damn cocky, I decided to play a trick on him. So I made up a fake name. It was innocent, even if he was sinfully sexy.

The Blackwell After Dark Series:

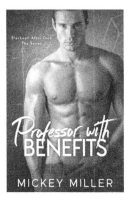

I'm studying to be a sex therapist, and I haven't even had sex yet. Which is why I decide that Professor Hanks is going to be the one to take my virginity.

How to find a wedding date at the last second: 1) Overheat your car on your cross country road trip 2) Make sure it's storming 3) Have a one night stand with the sexiest mechanic you've ever seen

Sebastian Blackwell isn't only the sexiest man I've ever met. He's also my boss.

My best friend's sister. A tiny white lie to get a loan. A fake fiance?

Standalones:

No sex for ten dates, which sounds easy. Despite the biceps
bulging through his shirt. Despite the tattoos I desperately want
to lick-- I mean, know more about. Despite the hunger in his eyes
when he looks at me. No, it won't be easy.

You'll get a free book here if you sign up for my mailing list:

https://dl.bookfunnel.com/mgr4nddhh2

Thank you for reading!

THE END GAME - SNEAK PREVIEW - CHAPTER 1

T hree Months Later

LACY

NEW YORK, NEW YORK

I LEFT CHICAGO FOUR MONTHS AGO.

These days, I'm happily finding out there's nothing quite like the buzz of New York City.

Like right now. The noises of the bar swirl around me. Loud music and voices hem together, and I flash a cordial smile at my date.

He's got brown hair, blue eyes, and a soft smile. To top it off, he's *nice*.

I haven't gotten a single asshole vibe from Brandon in the hour we've been on this date.

And that's exactly what I'm looking for right now.

He's opposite of the last man I "dated" last summer.

If you want to call it that.

I'm about to inch toward him a little more when his eyes light up at something on the flat screen TV behind the bar.

"New York is playing Chicago tonight," he blurts out. "And I fucking love this guy on the Wolverines."

"Which guy?" I ask.

The bartender turns up the volume on the television. When I follow Brandon's pointer finger and realize who he's referring to, my heart practically smashes through to my lungs.

The post game show is of Carter being interviewed.

Carter freaking Flynn.

I massage my forehead with my thumb and forefinger.

Just when I'm finally starting to feel like I'm actually over him, he appears again. It's like the universe won't let me let me move on.

I fix my eyes on the TV, watching as Carter leans back for his interview with a smug look, the dimples on his face coming out. His sunglasses are on even though he's inside.

I have to fight so that my body doesn't respond to the man with butterflies in my stomach.

"Carter, you scored more than half your team's points tonight. But toward the end of the game, you appeared to be trash talking Josh Evans pretty heavily," the reporter begins.

My heart thumps, seeing Carter on the flatscreen.

Carter smirks, and chills roll through me watching the muscles in his face move. "You know I'm just extremely grateful that our team is coming together this year. He was riding my bro Chandler all game. Chandler was going to let it go, but I decided not to."

The reporter seems confused. "You didn't answer my question. Do you have an apology for him?"

Carter takes off his sunglasses, squinting at the reporter.

"Apology? Look, Mr...whatever your name is, asking all the questions for the hot takes—you want a quote to print, is that it?"

Brandon seems as entranced by Carter's actions as I am.

The reporter shrugs. "Sure."

"I don't like it when people step on my laces, and Josh Evans deliberated did that. Anyways, I'm looking forward to lacing them up for the next game." He turns, looks right at the camera, and winks.

My cheeks flush, involuntarily, when Carter talks about this laces, and I hear his voice in my head without even trying.

Every second I see you, Laces, I want to rip your clothes off and do terrible, unspeakable things to you.

Lifting my head up, I force a smile that I can't quite seem to make reach my eyes, trying to stay engaged in our conversation. "What were we just talking about?" I ask him.

Brandon ignores my question, revved up by Carter's interview.

"That's funny how Carter Flynn was talking about his laces. And your name is Lacy. What a coincidence."

"Yes, weird." I echo, clearing my throat. I take a long pull of my beer.

I was a passing fancy for Carter, so I doubt he's still thinking about me. Not that I'd know if he was trying to contact me, since I've blocked his email and phone number.

Brandon smiles and rubs my shoulder. "I've had a great time tonight, Lacy. You're a cool chick. Be right back. I'm going to hit the bathroom real quick."

I nod. "Alright."

As he jumps down, he jiggles his jacket and something

falls out of his side pocket. He doesn't notice, and I pick it up and I'm about to call to him, but Brandon is already to the bathroom hallway.

It's a small black notepad, and when I pick it up I can't help but glance at the page it opens up to. Inside he's got a list of dates and names.

Curious, I read on. It seems to be a planner of some sort. I squint when I see today's date.

Tuesday, November 27th Dates

Laura - 8 pm — The Big Frog Bar - Fiorella - Blonde, 27, met off Christians in NY, not very cute. Seemed super uptight. I bailed and said my mom was sick so I needed to go be with my sick mom.

Lacy - 9 pm. - The Big Frog Bar - Lacy, 26, black hair. Met online - cute. Modern Dancer.

   Hot Dancer = good sex? (Hopefully find out tonight)

Scrolling through the other pages, I see the dates are filled with names of girls and notes on them. The bathroom door swings open, and I plant the little notepad back in Brandon's jacket pocket.

As he strides toward me, I catch the bartender's eye.

"Will you have another one, Laura?" she asks.

I sigh, trying not to glare. "It's Lacy."

Not her fault this guy is stacking dates by the hour at the same place.

"Oh," she says, her face turning a little red. "I must have confused you with someone else."

Damn right you do.

"Yes, I'll have another Yuengling," I say.

She flashes a faint smile and pours me another beer as Brandon sits down again.

"You know," he says, putting his hand on my forearm. "I've really enjoyed tonight. I haven't met someone special in the city lately. So many people. So many options. It's hard to find someone who sticks out."

My heart hammers as I come up with an impromptu plan in my head for how to deal with Brandon. Should I just come right out and tell him I read the list of girls in his notepad—and how I'm clearly just *hot dancer = good sex?* to him, and he doesn't have a shot in hell with me?

I secretly bunch my fist next to him as the bartender slides another beer in front of me, and flash Brandon a look I make sure is extra sexy, batting my eyes, a playful smirk tugging at my lips.

In spite of my rising desire to confront him, I decide to go another route. Why not play a little?

"I completely agree," I say, bubbly. "It's hard to find someone genuine. I haven't been on a good date in way too long. I'm just ready to open up. Have a good time. And let the good times roll."

He swallows a pull of his drink and nods. "Good times. That's exactly what I'm talking about. After we finish this drink, we could head back to my place and check out my fish tank."

"Your fish tank?"

He winks. "Yeah, my fish tank."

I take a little swig of my drink, and turn my body toward him, spreading my legs as I toss my hair.

Breathing heavily, I lower my voice to a whisper. "That sounds amazing. And we could explore other things, too. I mean Brandon, you *do* know what they say about dancers. Don't you?"

"I've heard a few things. But by all means, tell me more. Enlighten me."

"Well it's a known fact that dancers have very tight...Oh, hang on, text coming through."

Pulling out my cell phone, I shoot a quick text to Lance before turning back to Brandon.

"Sorry about that."

"You were saying?" Brandon's eyes are as wide as a kid at the candy store as he hangs on my every word.

I grin, putting my hand on his leg. Leaning forward, I brush my lips close to his ear and whisper. I use my throaty voice for maximum effect. "That we're really good at getting bent into those hard-to-form positions. Do you understand what I mean, Brandon?"

I linger close to his ear for a few breaths in his ear before I pull back. I can practically hear his heart beating harder than the music as he swallows. He puts his hand on my leg, and licks his lips. "I think I do."

The bar has a glass of pretzel rods on it. Grabbing one, I dip it into my mouth and let my bright red lipstick bleed onto it as I pull it out of my mouth slowly, keeping my eyes on Brandon.

I hand him the pretzel, which he takes with a confused look on his face. "Mmm," I whisper with a devilish grin.

"You want to get out of here?" he asks.

"Definitely. And I can't wait to—"

My phone buzzes on the bar.

Shaking my head, I pick it up.

"Hello...Mom?...No....She's where?...Oh my goodness, I'll be right there."

Hopping off of my bar stool, I throw on my jacket.

"Wait...who was that?"

"I'm so sorry Brandon. My mom's sick. I have to go. This was fun though."

He throws his palms open. "Are you fucking serious? You can't just...just....leave me like this?"

"It's a shame, I know." Without saying goodbye, I walk away from him, heels clicking on the ground. "I'm sure the bartender won't mind you paying my tab. See you soon. Have a good night."

"We could meet up later tonight?" he calls over my shoulder.

I turn and, I'm about to shout what I have to say, but I think better of it. Brandon might be a good guy. But I'm feeling devilish tonight.

Walking back to him. I put my lips to his ear again and whisper, no idea where the stream of consciousness comes from: "Actually, I'm meeting up with my ex tonight. Carter Flynn. Ever heard of him?"

His jaw drops and he recoils from me.

I don't know why I feel the need to name drop Carter.

I'm not meeting him again tonight – that's something I definitely won't allow myself to do. Seeing him on the flat screen stirred up a stew of feelings I've been trying my best not to acknowledge.

With a satisfied smirk, I speak again. "Maybe you could call Laura and see if she still wants to hang out." I wink. "Since you're too good for her."

Carter does have a talent for bringing out the forthright side of my personality. Turning again on my heel, I walk out of the bar and hail a cab to my place.

I don't feel bad about it.

———

Sign up to Mickey's Email Mail list for news, a free book, and more!

https://landing.mailerlite.com/webforms/landing/y8s9b0

———

Read THE END GAME here:

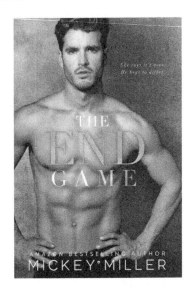

Made in the USA
Coppell, TX
12 June 2022

78763458R00173